MRS. JEFFRIES ON THE TRAIL

EMILY BRIGHTWELL

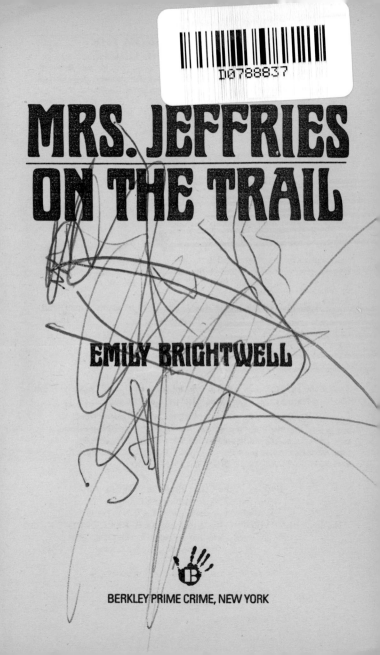

BERKLEY PRIME CRIME, NEW YORK

MRS. JEFFRIES ON THE TRAIL

A Berkley Prime Crime Book / published by arrangement with the author

PRINTING HISTORY
Berkley Prime Crime edition / April 1995

ISBN: 0-425-14691-X

Berkley Prime Crime Books are published by
The Berkley Publishing Group,
200 Madison Avenue, New York, NY 10016.
The name BERKLEY PRIME CRIME and the BERKLEY PRIME CRIME
design are trademarks belonging to Berkley Publishing
Corporation.

PRINTED IN THE UNITED STATES OF AMERICA

10 9 8 7 6 5 4 3

To Bob and Virginia Woods. Two wonderful people who never minded opening their hearts or their home to a horde of nieces and nephews. With love and thanks for golden afternoons of summers past and for letting a daydreaming little girl spend hours on your front-porch swing.

CHAPTER 1

"It's deader than a ruddy rat's arse tonight, ducks. You might as well pack it in and give yer feet a rest," Millie Groggins yelled to her friend on the other side of the Strand. She tossed the end of her thin, tatty scarf over her shoulder and sauntered towards the flower seller.

Annie Shields smiled wearily and glanced around the deserted street. Millie was right. It'd been over fifteen minutes since the last person had passed and that had been a copper. Suddenly she heard footsteps. She tensed and stared hard in the direction of the sound.

" 'Bout bleedin' time we 'ad some trade," Millie muttered, cocking her head to one side and plastering a warm smile on her bony face.

From out of the fog, a man dressed in a caped greatcoat and carrying an umbrella came towards them. Annie stared at him hopefully. He brushed past her without so much as a glance.

" 'Ello, love," Millie called. But the man ignored her too.

Disappointed, Annie sighed. There wasn't any point in hanging about any longer. They weren't coming. No one was coming. She gave the street one last, long look, but she couldn't see much of anything now. Even the bright lights of the theatres just ahead had been dimmed by the thick fog drifting in off the Thames. She shivered and shuffled her feet. It was bloody cold too.

The whole area was empty. Almost frightening. Annie shook herself and was glad that Millie hadn't left yet. She'd been stupid to come out tonight.

"I reckon you're right, Millie," she said as she reached for a basket of chrysanthemums and stacked it on her cart. "We both might as well pack it in. Neither of us'll 'ave any business tonight."

"You can say that again," Millie agreed, her tone disgusted. She gazed thoughtfully at the flower seller. "What you doin' out this late?"

Annie hesitated. "Just tryin' to pick up some extra business," she finally said. No sense in telling Millie everything.

"You picked a bad night for it," Millie muttered angrily. "Bleedin' riots." She glared in the direction of the theatres.

"What's the riots got to do with it?" Annie asked. She didn't really care all that much. But she was starting to feel fidgety and the sound of a familiar voice helped keep her nerves steady.

"They've got everything to do with it. Them riots today is what's kept our customers away. Everyone's afraid to go out what with them damned nationalists takin' to the streets. Bloody Irish! Always screamin' and fightin' about somethin'. And who pays fer it? We do! That's who." She snorted angrily. " 'Ow's a body to make a livin' when the bloomin' streets are empty? And 'ow am I gonna make me rent tonight? That's what I'd like to know?"

Annie gave her one quick, sympathetic glance and then looked away. Millie stood huddled under the gas lamp, blowing on her fingers to keep them warm. "Ruddy 'ell, it's cold tonight," she said in between puffs.

Annie knew desperation when she heard it, but she didn't look up. Millie Groggins wasn't her problem. It didn't do to go sticking your nose in other people's troubles. But then she heard the familiar clicking sound of chattering teeth. She couldn't stand it. She patted her coat pocket and bit her lip. Despite the lack of customers, she had money. Swallowing hard, she forced herself to look towards the dim circle of light where the other woman was vainly trying to keep warm.

Annie's heart sank. From the look of things, Millie was flat-out skint. With her threadbare coat, a scarf that was nothing more than a scrappy bit of thin yarn, and a tatty hat with droopy plumes, even in the poor light, Millie looked pathetic. Her expression was stark and fearful, her body thin from not having enough food, and her clothes were no protection at all against the damp cold of night.

Annie shivered. At least she had a roof over her head tonight, she thought. Poor Millie would be sleepin' in a doorway if she didn't help her. Besides, she reasoned, tomorrow *he'd* come and he was always good for a fiver. But what if he didn't come?

Millie suddenly ran her hands up and down her arms in another futile attempt to get warm. Annie made up her mind. Millie was her friend, and if she had to kip out tonight, she might get sick. It was too bloody cold.

Never mind that any coins she slipped to Millie would probably never be repaid. She'd had a bit of good fortune lately and it wouldn't hurt to share it with someone who was down on their luck.

Annie finished putting her few remaining flower baskets onto the cart. When she loaded the last one, she glanced at her friend again. Millie was still muttering curses on the heads of the Irish, the anarchists, the police and the cowardly toffs who were locked up safely in their houses. Her colorful curses made Annie smile.

Most of the other flower sellers wouldn't even speak to someone like Millie, but Annie liked her. She was good company and she felt sorry for her too. No one liked havin' to walk the streets at night and sell their bodies just to keep a bit of food in their bellies. Horrible, that was. But she could understand why some had to do it. She'd come close to having to do it herself.

Even if *he* didn't come, she had a bit tucked away for a rainy day. Annie reached into her coat pocket. Her gloved fingers were stiff with cold, so it took her a moment to get the coins in her hand. She strolled over to stand next to her friend. " 'Ere, take this," she ordered.

Millie stared at Annie's outstretched palm, her eyes widening at the sight of the florins and shillings. "What's all this, then?"

"What's it look like? It's money. A loan. It's too bleedin' cold out tonight to have to spend it on the streets. You can pay me back when business picks up."

"I don't like takin' it off you," Millie muttered, but she reached for it anyway. "I'll pay ya back tomorrow, just see if I don't." She laughed. "Trade'll be good, you'll see. There's lots of men that can't go more than a day or so without it. They'll be 'ere tomorrow night."

"Pay me back when ya can," Annie said. "I'd best be gettin' these flowers back to the market, then."

"Thanks, luv—fer the money, I mean," Millie called as she turned and darted towards the river.

Annie watched her disappear into the fog. The heavy, yellowish gray mist had thickened and now it covered the street like a cotton-woolly blanket. She could barely see her cart.

She stood for one more minute before moving, her head cocked and her ears straining for the sound of approaching footsteps. But she heard nothing. Grasping the handle, she turned and began to push the cart slowly forward.

The wheels squeaked and groaned as she crossed the road and eased the old contraption around the corner and up Southampton Street. It seemed as though the fog thickened with every step she took. The farther she got from the gas lamps of the Strand, the darker and colder it got too. She was suddenly jerked forward as the front wheels of the cart crashed off the curb. Blast, Annie thought, squinting down into the heavy mist. It's worse than walkin' through a cold bowl of soup, it were so bleedin' thick. She'd better slow down or this old contraption wouldn't make it back to the garden. Annie grimaced as she pushed the heavy cart across the road.

The wheels didn't squeak so loud now, but that was somehow worse. Made her realize how quiet the street was. Goose bumps rushed up her arms and she didn't know if it was from cold or fear. Because suddenly she was scared. Like someone had just walked over her grave. Nights like this wasn't natural, she thought, looking over her shoulder and seeing nothing but the gray fingers of fog. Too empty by half.

Sundays weren't usually real busy, but this was the first time she'd ever had to go back to the market without sellin' something. She frowned. Mr. Cobbins weren't goin' to be pleased, that was for sure. But it weren't her bloomin' fault there weren't no one out and about.

From behind her, she heard footsteps. Annie stopped. The footsteps stopped as well.

She opened her mouth to call out who she was, then just as quickly clamped it shut again. Every instinct she had was screaming at her to be quiet. To run. Annie glanced down at the heavy cart. Run? She couldn't do that. She was bein' silly, actin' like one of them fancy ladies she saw goin' in and out of those elegant shops on Regent Street where she had her regular flower stand. The cart might be old and rusty, but Mr. Cobbins would have her head and she'd be out of a job if she come back without it.

After a moment Annie took a deep breath and told herself the footsteps probably belonged to another flower seller or streetwalker. She grasped the handles tightly and moved forward.

So did the footsteps.

She stopped and whirled around. Staring into the fog, she tried to see if the person behind her was male or female. But the mist was too thick to see anything. She turned and started forward again. So did the footsteps.

Her heart slammed against her chest, her throat went dry, and the hair on the back of her neck stood up. "Who's there?" she called frantically, hoping against hope that it was a copper.

The only reply was the sound of the steps coming closer. They seemed to be moving faster as well.

"Bloody 'ell." Annie took a deep breath and tight-

ened her fingers around the wicker handle of the cart.
The sense of danger she'd had a few moments ago
was back, and this time she wasn't going to ignore the
warning.

With all her might, she shoved the cart hard and
charged up the street. The wheels screamed in protest,
but Annie didn't care.

The footsteps started to run.

Annie ran, too, pushing the cart with all her might
and flying towards the end of the street and the safety of
Covent Garden. Flowers flew off the cart in every direction, but she didn't care. A bundle of chrysanthemums
bounced to the ground, a nosegay of violets flew past
her arm, and a bunch of expensive roses landed in a pool
of mud, but she didn't slow. The footsteps were gaining
on her. She could hear them closing the gap behind
her.

Suddenly a wheel popped off and the cart careened
wildly, pulling out of Annie's hands and tumbling onto
its side. Annie tripped, tried to regain her balance and
fell over the end of it. The fall knocked the wind out
of her. Gasping, she struggled to sit up. Her instincts,
honed by working the city streets for the past year now,
were screaming for her to run. She was in trouble. Bad
trouble.

She opened her mouth to scream just as a cloaked
figure burst through the fog.

But the scream abruptly ended as the first blow landed
on the back of her head.

"It was appalling, Mrs. Jeffries," Inspector Gerald
Witherspoon said. "Utterly appalling." He took off
his regulation uniform hat and sat it down on the table
next to him. His clear blue-gray eyes were troubled, his

thinning brown hair mussed, and even his mustache drooped.

"The whole experience must have been dreadful for you, sir," Mrs. Jeffries agreed. As housekeeper to the inspector, she knew him very well. The poor man was upset. Unlike most policemen, until she'd come to work for him, Inspector Witherspoon had spent most of his career working in the records room. Today he, along with practically every other policeman in the whole city, had been called out for a show of force against a mass procession in Trafalgar Square. Handling unruly mobs was as foreign to the man as eating buffalo steaks for breakfast. Mrs. Jeffries gazed at him sympathetically. "Civil unrest is a terrible circumstance."

"I'm not so sure there would have been any civil unrest if Sir Charles had let them have their silly procession." Witherspoon shook his head and reached for his sherry.

Mrs. Jeffries couldn't believe her ears. Perhaps some of her "freethinking" ideas were actually making an impact on the inspector. "Whatever do you mean, sir?"

He brushed her question aside with a wave of his hand. "Forgive me, Mrs. Jeffries, I'm talking nonsense."

"You never talk nonsense, sir." She was curious about what he'd been thinking, though now she suspected he wasn't going to share it with her. Surprising really, the inspector generally shared everything with her, including the details of each and every one of his murder cases. Sometimes he startled her by hinting or almost revealing something quite extraordinary about how his mind worked. "Did you mean that you thought the police commissioner caused the riots by issuing the edict against the procession?"

"No, no," he said hastily. "Really, it's not for me to

question the wisdom of my superiors . . . yet I can't help but think that it might have been the police regulation posted on every lamppost in the city that got so many people there in the first place. After all, how many people are really interested in the Metropolitan Radical Federation?"

"The Metropolitan Radical Federation?" Mrs. Jeffries queried. "I thought the whole thing was about Mr. O'Brien. You know, that Irish MP that was arrested."

"Oh, it was," the inspector said. "But you know how these things happen. Some of the people there were no doubt truly disturbed by the problems in Ireland, but many of them were there to protest all kinds of what they call 'social ills.' Frankly, Mrs. Jeffries, if the Police Commission had just ignored the whole thing, most people wouldn't have bothered to turn up at all." He set his glass down. "I mean really, who wants to listen to the rantings of a bunch of politicians, socialists and anarchists?"

"There are many who seem to feel that people with such ideas are dangerous," she remarked. "Sir Charles Warren is obviously one of them."

"I mean no disrespect to the commissioner of the police," Witherspoon said, "but I do feel that the entire incident should have been handled differently. An unruly mob is certainly an impediment to public safety, but we don't know that they'd have been an unruly mob if they'd been allowed to have their march. Perhaps there would only have been a few speeches, a couple of banners waving about, a slogan or two painted on a wall. In which case, the only danger they'd pose is boring their audience to death."

Mrs. Jeffries laughed.

"Still," the inspector continued thoughtfully, "whether

allowing them to have their march was right or wrong isn't really for me to say. But I do know I was quite shocked by the way some of my fellow policemen behaved. There was some dreadfully uncalled-for roughness." He looked troubled. "Some of the constables were quite brutal."

Mrs. Jeffries gazed at his face. She knew the inspector was no coward. So his distress wasn't merely the result of fearing for his own safety. Since she'd come to work for him, he'd gone from being a records-room clerk to an outstanding Scotland Yard detective. Naturally, no one could understand this metamorphosis. No one, of course, except the household of Upper Edmonton Gardens.

If the inspector was upset by the brutality of what he'd seen at Trafalgar Square this afternoon, it must, indeed, have been a frightening spectacle. "Were any of the marchers equally brutal?" she asked gently.

"Oh yes." He sighed. "There was the requisite number of rocks and missiles thrown."

"Then perhaps the police were merely defending themselves," she ventured. She did hate seeing the inspector so despondent. Gracious, from the way he acted, you'd think he felt personally responsible for everything that had happened today. But she really ought not to be surprised. Inspector Gerald Witherspoon was one of nature's gentlemen. Save for his salary, he'd never had any money until the death several years ago of his aunt Euphemia. He'd inherited a modest fortune and this beautiful home. Yet he was still as kind and compassionate as he'd ever been.

"For the most part, you're right." He sighed again. "But there were one or two—" He broke off and shook his head.

"Well, sir," Mrs. Jeffries said briskly, "it's over and done with. Mrs. Goodge has fixed a lovely dinner for you."

Witherspoon got to his feet. "I'm sorry, Mrs. Jeffries. But I think I'll go right on up to bed. I don't have much of an appetite this evening."

Mrs. Jeffries watched him leave. Beneath his uniform jacket, which he'd had to wear today for the first time in a long while, his shoulders drooped as he trudged towards the door. Poor man, he hadn't liked having to do what he'd done today, and even worse, he certainly hadn't liked watching what some of his fellow police officers had gotten up to.

She turned and hurried down to the kitchen. There was no point in delaying the staff's evening meal. The inspector would bounce back in his own good time.

Half an hour later Mrs. Jeffries and the other servants sat down to their dinner.

"It's not like the inspector to be off his food," Betsy, the maid, said. Blond, blue-eyed and very pretty, she was also intelligent and perceptive beyond her twenty years. "Is he not feeling well?"

"He's a bit depressed, that's all," Mrs. Jeffries replied. "The riots in Trafalgar Square today upset him. I don't think he approved of the way some of his fellow officers dealt with the crowd."

"Too kindhearted, he is," Mrs. Goodge, the plump gray-haired cook, said bluntly. "They ought to have arrested the whole lot of them. That's what I say."

"Why should them people have been arrested?" Wiggins, the footman, asked. With his dark brown hair, pale skin and round apple cheeks, he looked much younger than his nineteen years. His youth, however, didn't

stop him from having an opinion on most subjects. He
wasn't particularly bothered about whether or not it was
an informed opinion. "This is a free country. They've
got as much right to 'ave a march and a meetin' as
anyone else."

"They don't have a right to throw rocks and go about
breakin' windows and upsettin' decent folk," the cook
shot back. Behind her spectacles, her eyes narrowed
angrily. "What do they want anyways? Some Irish MP
gets arrested and every Tom, Dick and Harry's got to
take to the street. Let the courts do it, that's what I
say."

"Sometimes," Smythe, the coachman, interjected,
"you've got to take matters into yer own hands." He
leaned back and crossed his muscular arms over his
broad chest. Dark-haired, tall and with heavy, almost
brutal features, he wasn't anyone's idea of male beauty.
But his warm brown eyes and cocky grin made more
than one pretty maid turn her head when he passed by.
"We do it often enough."

Mrs. Jeffries smiled at the coachman. Everyone knew
he was referring to the fact that all of them frequently
nosed about in their employer's murder cases. As a matter of fact, they did it every time Inspector Witherspoon
had a homicide. And, of course, that was one of the reasons they were all being so argumentative this evening.
They were bored.

Here it was November and they hadn't had a good
murder to work on since last June. If she were truly
honest, Mrs. Jeffries thought, she'd have to admit she
was as bored as the rest of them. Not that she condoned
murder, of course. However, human nature being what
it was, she didn't think the foul deed would stop just
because she personally found taking a human life abhor-

rent. If murders were going to happen, then wasn't it lucky that she and the rest of the staff were available to help bring the miscreants to justice?

Fred, their brown-and-black mongrel dog, who wasn't supposed to hang about the kitchen but did anyway, especially at mealtimes, suddenly jumped up from his spot beside Wiggins. Barking excitedly, he raced out and down the darkened hallway to the back door.

"What's Fred on about?" Mrs. Goodge complained as loud pounding sounded on the back door.

Wiggins started to get up, but Smythe put a restraining hand on his shoulder. "It'd dark, lad, best let me see to this."

They waited curiously to see who'd come visiting on a cold, foggy evening. There was the sound of the door opening and then muffled cries of greeting. "It's Luty Belle and Hatchet," Smythe called.

Luty Belle Crookshank, resplendent in a bright orange evening dress, matching feathers in her thin white hair and hanging on to a magnificent black walking stick, hobbled quickly into the kitchen. Hatchet, her tall, dignified, white-haired butler, was right behind her.

"Luty Belle and Hatchet," Mrs. Jeffries said, rising from her chair. "How very nice to see you."

"Evenin' everyone," Luty called gaily as she headed for an empty chair. "Hope you don't mind me and Hatchet droppin' by, but it's as quiet as a grave out tonight." Fred bounced joyously around the hem of Luty's skirt. She bent down and patted him on the head. "Howdy, nice feller. My, my, you're happy to see your friend Luty, ain't ya, boy?" Fred licked her hands, butted her knees with his head and generally made a fool of himself.

"If you and Fred have finished greeting one another," Hatchet said, "perhaps we can sit down."

"So where have you two been tonight?" Smythe asked, slipping into the chair next to Betsy.

Hatchet sniffed delicately.

Luty grinned. "Don't mind him," she said, an impish twinkle in her black eyes. "His nose is out of joint 'cause of my women's meetin'. Me and a few other ladies get together every once in a while and try to come up with ideas fer gettin' females the vote."

"Getting women the vote," Wiggins repeated in a puzzled voice. Suddenly his eyes widened. "You mean you want *women* to be able to vote?" He sounded absolutely flabbergasted at such an outrageous idea.

"That's what I said," Luty shot back. "What's wrong with women votin'? Or doin' anything else a man can do?"

Smythe laughed. "Get on with you," he said. "Gettin' the right to vote is one thing, but thinkin' they can do anythin' a man can is daft. Why, the next thing ya know, you'll be sayin' they can drive trains or carriages or sit in Parliament. I tell ya, it's daft."

"Daft, is it?" Betsy interrupted. "Hmmph. Seems to me that exceptin' for heavy labor, a woman could do anything a man could. Why shouldn't a woman have a few chances at life?"

"But a woman is supposed to get married, take care of her 'usband and her little ones," Wiggins said quickly. "If all the women was out workin' and votin' and drivin' trains and doin' typewritin', who'd take care of the children? That's what I want to know."

"What about women who don't have husbands?" Mrs. Jeffries said, warming to the subject. She'd long thought the division of labor in society utterly ridiculous. "What are they supposed to do? Live off their relatives? And what about the police? Do you honestly think a woman couldn't be as good at solving crimes as a man?"

That shut everyone up. Every one of them knew that it was Mrs. Jeffries who'd been responsible for solving virtually every one of the inspector's murders. The only person who wasn't privy to this knowledge was the inspector himself. They'd all agreed to keep him in the dark about their various investigations on his behalf.

Luty cackled. "That's tellin' 'em, Hepzibah."

"Really, madam." Hatchet gave her a quelling glance, which she completely ignored. "I hardly think that comparing Mrs. Jeffries's undoubted superior detection skills to the average woman outperforming a male is a true test."

"You don't, huh?" Luty said smugly. "Well, I danged well think it is."

"Obviously," Hatchet continued, "Mrs. Jeffries has a special gift. But that was one of nature's . . . well, shall we say, errors. In the true scheme of things, it should have been the inspector who was blessed with such a talent. However, nature does occasionally make a mistake. But that's hardly evidence for your contention that females are as capable as males. Let us be truly honest here, everyone knows how women are."

"And precisely how is that?" Mrs. Jeffries asked softly.

Hatchet, who didn't notice the gleam in the women's eyes, went blithely on. "Women are, of course, delightful creatures. But they are also weak-willed and emotional. They need the firm guidance of a man."

"Hatchet's right," Wiggins said smugly.

"Hatchet needs his head examined," Mrs. Goodge said tartly. "It'll be a cold day in the pits of hell before I'd let some man 'guide' me."

"Really, Mrs. Goodge," Hatchet said defensively.

"You misunderstand my meaning. All I'm saying is that if women begin trying to take over everything and forget their true place in the scheme of things, the entire fabric of society will come unraveled."

"Maybe it should be unraveled." Betsy snorted. "It's not like it's all that wonderful for everybody. There's only a few that have much of a decent life. For most people, life's hard. There's more that's poor than there is them that's rich. There's plenty of sufferin' and plenty of starvin' in lots of places in this city. So maybe it wouldn't be so bad if there was some changes made, some unravelin' done."

"You tell 'em, Betsy," Luty said encouragingly. "That's what I've been tryin' to get through his thick head, but like most men, he ain't got the brains to listen to a different point of view."

Hatchet swelled with outrage. "I'll have you know I'm exceedingly open-minded and liberal in my thinking."

"Cow patties," Luty shouted. "You're about as liberal as the kaiser and just as much of a stuffed shirt too!"

The argument raged in earnest then. For once, Mrs. Jeffries didn't try to intervene. She agreed with everything Luty and Betsy had said. Even Mrs. Goodge had surprised her.

"It's not enough for you to actually correspond with those females," Hatchet said heatedly to Luty. "But you're giving them money!"

"What females?" Wiggins asked curiously.

"The American Woman Suffrage Association," Luty said. "I've been writin' to 'em for over a year now." She turned to glare at Hatchet. "And you're doggone right I'm sendin' them money. I'd give the women on this side of the ocean some cash, too, if they wasn't such a bunch of twittering gits!"

"Why don't we have a contest?" Betsy yelled to make herself heard.

The room fell silent. They all turned to stare at her.

"What kind of contest did you 'ave in mind?" Smythe asked, giving the maid a cheeky grin. "Drinkin'? Sawin' logs? One of them bicycle races?"

"You can wipe that smirk off yer face, Smythe." Betsy crossed her arms over her chest. "I'm not talkin' about anything that would give you men a physical advantage over us. I'm talkin' about our brains. You know, that little thing that rattles around up in yer head when you try and think."

The women laughed. Smythe narrowed his eyes but managed to keep silent.

"Are you thinking what I think you're thinking?" Mrs. Jeffries asked. She couldn't quite hide a smile. The men *were* awfully arrogant.

"That's right," Betsy said. "I'm thinking that the next time we 'as us a murder to investigate, let's just see who's the smartest."

Witherspoon was far more cheerful the next morning. Mrs. Jeffries was glad to see him tuck into his breakfast with his usual gusto.

There was a hard knock on the front door. "Were you expecting someone this morning, Inspector?" she asked as she hurried out to the front hall.

"No, not that I remember," he called.

Mrs. Jeffries threw open the door to see Constable Barnes standing on the stoop. "Good morning, Constable. Dreadful day, isn't it?"

Behind him, she could see the thick yellow fog lying like a blanket of wool over the whole street.

"Not fit for man nor beast," Barnes agreed cheerfully.

"I'd like to see the inspector, if you don't mind. It's urgent, or I wouldn't be disturbin' his breakfast."

She ushered him into the dining room. "Would you like a cup of tea, Constable?"

"That'd be lovely, Mrs. Jeffries."

"Gracious, Barnes." Witherspoon frowned. "I thought I was meeting you at the station."

"You were, sir." He smiled gratefully at Mrs. Jeffries as he accepted a cup of hot, steaming tea. "But there's been a murder. Inspector Nivens is right upset, too, because he was due to get the next homicide and he got called out on an important jewel robbery late last night at the Duke of Hampton's residence. So you're gettin' this one."

"Oh dear." Witherspoon sighed. "Nivens always takes it so personally. I do hope he doesn't raise a fuss."

"Don't matter if he does," Barnes said. "Heard some gossip that you're gettin' this one because someone very important wants to make sure the investigation's handled right. Wants to see justice done."

Mrs. Jeffries tried to make herself invisible while she took in every word. She prayed that Barnes would keep talking. Anything, even a name and address, would be enough to get them started.

"Who's the victim?" Witherspoon reached for his teacup.

"A flower seller name of Annie Shields. Young woman. They found her late last night. A hansom driver on his way out come across her in the fog. It were so bloody thick over near the Strand that he practically run the body over. She'd been coshed on the head."

"Poor woman," Witherspoon murmured. "How old was she?"

"I haven't seen the body," Barnes replied. "They've

taken it to the mortuary. Potter's going to have a look at it this morning."

Witherspoon groaned. Dr. Potter was his least favorite surgeon. The man kept threatening to retire and go off to Bournemouth and grow roses, but he never did.

Barnes reached inside his pocket and whipped out a small brown notebook. "According to the uniformed lad that made the first report, Annie Shields was well-known in the area. The body was discovered on Southampton Street. The victim lodges over in Barston Street and worked for Harper's out of Covent Garden."

"You're certain she was a flower seller and not a, er . . ."—the inspector reassured himself that Mrs. Jeffries was still busy with the tea things—"prostitute?"

"She were layin' over a cart of flowers when she were found," Barnes replied.

"I suppose we'd better get to the mortuary." Witherspoon's lip curled. He really did hate this part of being a policeman. Corpses were not very pleasant. Especially when he had just had breakfast. But he knew his duty. "Er, Barnes, did you say the woman had been hit over the head?"

"Right, sir. And she were a bit mangled by the hansom cab." Barnes gulped the rest of his tea. "But it were just her limbs that was mangled, sir, or so the street copper said."

Witherspoon gulped but gamely forced himself to stand up. Head injuries were so nasty. Not quite as bad as bullet wounds or an ugly slashing, but not very nice nonetheless.

Mrs. Jeffries tried to contain her impatience as she fetched the inspector's hat and coat and generally got him out of the house. The moment the door closed behind him and Barnes, she flew down the hall to the backstairs. Pausing at the top, she listened for voices.

From below, she could hear Betsy and Mrs. Goodge chatting quietly. Satisfied, she hurried down the stairs and into the kitchen, taking care not to say a word until she made sure the men were gone.

"Are we alone, ladies?" she asked. Mrs. Goodge glanced up from the dough she was kneading. "Just us women, unless you count Fred. And like most males, he's sound asleep." The cook was still very irritated by the battle of the sexes they'd had last night. So were Mrs. Jeffries and Betsy.

"Smythe is over at Howard's and Wiggins is picking up the meat order from the butchers," Betsy added. "Why?"

Mrs. Jeffries, who would have sworn she didn't have a childish bone in her body, grinned. She certainly wasn't going to exclude the men of the household from the investigation. Oh no, that would never do. But the discussion they'd had last night had been most enlightening. She'd honestly been surprised to find that Smythe and Wiggins had such ridiculous notions about women.

"Because, ladies, we've much to discuss. Betsy, do you think you could pop over and get Luty here?"

Betsy wiped her hands on a towel. "Of course I could."

"Good, make sure you speak to Luty alone. I don't want Hatchet overhearing anything."

"What's this all about, then?" the cook asked curiously.

"We've got a murder," Mrs. Jeffries announced. "Isn't it a pity the men are all out and won't be able to start their own investigations until later?"

CHAPTER 2

"Oh dear," the inspector murmured as he stared down at the body on the table, "she's hardly more than a child. Who could do such a vile thing?"

Witherspoon didn't want to look directly at the hideous wounds on her temple. But he knew he should. Fighting nausea, he forced himself to gaze at her for several moments. Disturbing as the sight might be, he knew his duty. As his housekeeper had once pointed out, knowing precisely where the fatal wounds had been inflicted might come in handy during the questioning of a suspect. It was amazing what people gave away when they started talking.

"Sad, isn't it?" Barnes clucked his tongue. "She was a pretty young woman too." He cleared his throat. "As far as we can tell, the victim was killed sometime before eleven last night."

"That was when the hansom driver found her, I take it." He looked at Barnes. "Does Dr. Potter have any idea of the actual time of death? Had she been dead long before she was found?"

"Really, Inspector," a petulant voice said from behind them, "you know very well I don't like guessing games." Dr. Potter, portly and pompous as ever, came towards them. He was wearing a heavy apron and carrying a satchel. On his heels were two young porters pushing a gurney.

"I was merely hoping you'd be able to tell us something," Witherspoon said. He leapt out of the way as the porters pushed the gurney level with the table.

"Well, I can't give you any information yet," Potter snapped. "But as the victim was found on a public street, I suspect she couldn't have been there very long. Really, Inspector, I'd have thought even you'd have reasoned that out. You there, boy," he shouted at one of the porters, and pointed to the victim's head. "Mind you don't leave any skull fragments on that table when you shift the body. Take her down to number three. I'll be along in a minute or two to open her up."

Witherspoon's stomach turned over. If he hadn't suddenly felt like he was going to faint, he would have pointed out to Potter that though the victim was on the street, the streets had been so deserted the poor woman could have been lying dead for hours before that hansom came across her. "Er, we'll just get out of the way," he murmured, turning his head to avoid the sight of the porters starting to move the corpse. He decided to try one more time. Even Potter must have some notion of how long she'd been dead. "But surely you've some idea as to when the victim was killed? It's frightfully important that we have something to go on."

"Blast it, Inspector. I've only given the woman a cursory examination. The best I can say is that death probably didn't occur until fairly latish in the evening. But that is just a guess and you won't hear me saying it at the coroner's inquest." Potter glared at the two policemen. "At least that's my estimate from the temperature of the body. But don't go taking that as the gospel. You'll have to wait till a proper postmortem's been done before I'll say another word, and even then, you know as well as I do that estimating time of death is risky. There are far too many factors to ascertain with any degree of accuracy when someone actually died."

Witherspoon knew that was the best he was likely to get out of the doctor. He started to edge towards the door. "Thank you, Dr. Potter."

Barnes was gazing at the victim. "Was she interfered with?"

"Do you mean raped?"

One of the porters snickered.

The inspector glared at the man and his grin faded.

"That's what I'm askin', sir," Barnes clarified. "Was she raped?"

Potter sighed. "I've already told you, I've *not* done a proper examination yet. Besides"—his lips curled in a sneer—"with these street girls it's almost impossible to determine if they've been forcibly raped."

"She was a flower seller," Witherspoon snapped, suddenly incensed. He didn't like Dr. Potter's attitude. The victim, whatever her life had been, deserved to be treated with respect. "Not a prostitute."

Potter's eyes widened at Witherspoon's tone. He actually took a step back. "I'll let you know when I've finished the postmortem," he said frostily. "Until then, kindly leave me in peace to do my job."

"The local PC's outside," Barnes muttered in Witherspoon's ear. "We can talk to him while we're waiting for the victim's clothes and personal effects."

The inspector nodded.

The uniformed officer who'd been called to the scene waited outside in the reception hall. He was a tall, red-haired chap with a pale complexion and weary, bloodshot eyes. He sprang up to attention when he saw Barnes and Witherspoon coming towards him. "Good morning, sir," he said. "I'm PC Popper."

Witherspoon nodded. "Good morning. You look as though you're tired."

Popper smiled wearily. "Up all night, sir. As soon as we got this victim brought in, I had to go right back out on another call. Robbery down at the docks, sir."

"Well, then, I'll not waste any time. I expect you'd like to get home and get some sleep." Witherspoon glanced at Barnes and saw that the constable had whipped out his notebook. He turned back to Popper and asked, "What time were you called to the scene of the crime?"

"Just past eleven last night, sir. I was walking the Strand when I heard someone screaming for help," Popper explained. "It took a while for me to figure out where all the shoutin' was coming from, though; that fog was so thick you couldn't see two feet in front of your hand. Finally I figures it was comin' from a ways up Southampton Street. When I got there, I saw this hansom cabbie hanging on to his horses and screamin' his head off."

"Where, precisely, on Southampton Street?" Witherspoon was fairly certain this was a pertinent question. Sometimes he had the feeling that none of the questions he asked were appropriate.

Popper thought for a moment. "About halfway between the Strand and the flower market. I reckon she were on her way back to the market when she was killed."

"Is it possible the hansom ran her down?" the inspector asked.

"No, sir," Popper replied. "Even if he'd hit her, he wouldn't have done much damage to the poor woman. He was movin' too slow because of the fog. Besides, the horses make enough noise that if she'd been alive when he come near her, she'd have heard him comin' and gotten out of the way."

"Had the cab run completely over her?" Barnes asked.

Popper shook his head. "No. Matter of fact, I don't think the horses or the cab even touched the body. It was the cart they hit first."

"What did the hansom driver tell you?" Witherspoon asked.

"He said he were goin' down the street on his way in for the night when all of a sudden one of the horses stumbled and reared back. He pulled up then and jumped down to see what the problem was. Then he saw her. She was lying to one side of the cart, her head bashed in."

"Do you think he's telling the truth?" Witherspoon didn't think it impossible that the driver might be lying. If he'd accidentally run the flower seller down, he might not want to admit it. Then again, the story did make sense. It was dreadfully foggy last night. And the constable was probably correct. Unless the victim was as deaf as a post, she would have heard the approach of a cab. He made a mental note to ask Potter to check for deafness.

"Yes, sir," the police constable replied. "He's got no reason to lie. If he'd run her down and not want to be admittin' it, he wouldn't have been screamin' blue blazes for help. He'd have just left. There weren't no one on the streets last night to be seein' what he'd done."

Witherspoon nodded. "Were there any witnesses?"

"Not really, sir. But one of the other constables had passed by the corner where Annie Shields was sellin' flowers at around nine forty-five. She was alive then, of course. There was another woman there as well. A prostitute."

Witherspoon knew that was important information. It meant that Annie Shields had been alive at a quarter to ten. Her body had been discovered a little after eleven. "What's this constable's name?"

Popper told him. "Blackman, sir. Ronald Blackman."

Barnes scribbled the information in his notebook and then asked, "Any sign of a weapon?"

Popper shook his head. "None that we could find. Had a good look about the area, but couldn't find anything with blood on it. Of course, the fog's not helping any. But I did ask around about the victim early this morning when we was finished up at the dock."

"Excellent, Constable." Witherspoon beamed. This young man would go far. Showed initiative. "What did you find out?"

Popper smiled proudly. "Well, sir. She's quite well-known in the district. Annie Shields has worked as a flower seller for Harper's for about a year. Decent woman, worked the theatre area a couple of nights a week and the rest of the time she took her cart over to Regent Street. She's widowed and she has lodgings on Barston Road."

"Widowed," Witherspoon repeated. "Did she have any known enemies? Anyone who might have a reason for wanting her dead?"

Popper looked surprised by the question. "Well, sir, I didn't think to ask."

"Why not?" Witherspoon asked curiously. Surely that would be one of the first things one should ask.

"Because, sir, the victim was robbed," Popper said hesitantly. "I mean, sir. She didn't have any money on her when we found her."

Witherspoon smiled patiently. "That means nothing, Constable. The lack of money on her person could mean she hadn't sold any flowers. It doesn't necessarily mean she'd been robbed."

"I hadn't thought of that." Popper smiled sheepishly. "After that riot yesterday the streets was pretty empty last night. But that wasn't the only reason I thought she might 'ave been robbed. Her glove was off, you see."

"I'm sorry." The inspector frowned. "I don't quite understand."

"Well, sir," Popper explained, "it were a cold night. The cart had fallen over because it had lost a wheel. I reckon she were runnin' from whoever coshed her. But she had her gloves on—at least there was still a glove on her left hand when she was found. But the right hand glove was laying on the street, like someone had ripped it off to get at her rings."

"Rings?" Witherspoon mumbled. "What would a flower girl be doing wearing rings? Was her wedding ring gone?"

"No, sir, it were still on her finger."

"Exactly my point, Constable," Witherspoon said. "Why steal a ring from her right hand and then leave a perfectly good wedding ring on her left?"

Luty clapped her hands together. "Hatchet'll be madder than a wet hen when he finds out."

"Smythe and Wiggins'll have their noses out of joint too." Betsy giggled.

"Serves 'em right," said Mrs. Goodge.

"Now, ladies," Mrs. Jeffries cautioned, "we're not going to exclude them entirely. That wouldn't be fair. However, given their attitudes about our fair sex, I don't feel in the least guilty about getting the jump on them."

"So tell us what all you know," Luty ordered. "I'm rarin' to go."

"Uh . . ." Mrs. Jeffries hesitated. There really wasn't any polite way to mention this, and really, if she hadn't been so annoyed with those arrogant males, she'd have thought of it before she brought Luty over here. "Luty, uh . . ."

"Come on, Hepzibah," Luty said irritably. "Quit tryin' to think of a polite way to say it and just spit it out."

"How did you know that was what I was doing?"

" 'Cause yer cheeks always get pink when you're tryin' to come up with a nice way to ask me somethin' you don't want to ask."

"Yes, I suppose they do." She took a deep breath and plunged ahead. "Well, if we're not going to inform Hatchet about the murder, how on earth are you going to—"

"Get around without him?" Luty cackled and held up a beaded handbag. "Got me a purse full of coins here, Hepzibah. I reckon there's enough hansom drivers in this town to get me where I want to go." She patted the fur muff in her lap. "And don't worry none about someone botherin' me. I may be an old woman, but I've got my protection right in here."

Alarmed, Mrs. Jeffries stared at her. "Oh no, you don't have that horrible gun, do you?" On several of their other investigations Luty Belle had brought along her gun, a wicked-looking weapon popular in her native America, a Colt .45.

" 'Course I've got it." Luty looked at her incredulously. "Don't get yourself all het up, me and my Peacemaker won't have no trouble if'n people stay out of my way. You've got to admit, it's come in handy a time or two."

Unfortunately for Mrs. Jeffries's arguments, Luty was absolutely correct. Her gun had come in very handy indeed a time or two. "For goodness' sakes then, be careful with it."

"Is it loaded?" Betsy asked, staring wide-eyed at the muff.

"Yup." Luty patted the muff again. "Loaded and rarin' to go, just like I am. Now"—she grinned at Mrs. Jeffries—"what should we do first?"

Mrs. Jeffries drummed her fingers on the tabletop. "We don't have all that much to go on. The victim is a young flower seller named Annie Shields. From what I heard, she was probably killed sometime last night."

"A flower seller," Mrs. Goodge muttered. She frowned. "I won't have much luck learnin' anything about a common flower seller."

Mrs. Jeffries gazed thoughtfully at the cook. Mrs. Goodge looked very troubled. "Now, Mrs. Goodge, just because our victim isn't well-known in society doesn't mean you won't be able to learn as much as you always do."

When they were investigating one of the inspector's cases, Mrs. Goodge never left her kitchen. But she certainly did her fair share. She knew every morsel of gossip in London. A veritable army of people trooped through her kitchen and she pumped them ruthlessly. From the gasworks man to the rag-and-bone man to

the chimney sweep, Mrs. Goodge plied them with buns
and tea and wrung them dry. But as most of their other
cases had involved members of society, the poor woman
was worried no one would know anything about a mere
flower girl. Well, Mrs. Jeffries would have to convince
her otherwise. It was easier than trying to get her out of
this kitchen!

"But who'll know tuppence about a flower seller?"
Mrs. Goodge wailed.

"Very few, probably," Mrs. Jeffries said crisply. "But
once they've heard she was murdered, they'll all be
learning every scrap they can about the poor girl." She
smiled. "You, of course, will find out exactly what they
know. Besides, with your chain of connections I'm sure
you must know someone who works at Covent Garden."

Mrs. Goodge cocked her head to one side. "Come
to think of it, my cousin Ada's second boy delivers
for Pearson's. Maybe I'll have him round to see what
he knows. If this girl's been sellin' flowers from over
there, Augustine should know her."

"Augustine," Betsy repeated. "Your cousin named her
son Augustine?"

"Horrid, isn't it?" the cook agreed. "But Ada never
did have much sense. That and she was right fond of
saints."

"What should I do?" Luty asked.

"Constable Barnes said the victim was known in the
area where her body was found. She was found on
Southampton Street up from the Strand. A hansom driver
practically ran over her. Perhaps you can ask about and
see what you can find out from the people in the area.
For all we know, someone might have seen something
last night."

"Maybe you should let me do that," Betsy suggested.

"You think I'm afraid to ask a few questions?" Luty charged.

Betsy smiled and shook her head. "You're not afraid of anything! I only meant that if I ask about, I might run into someone I know." She looked helplessly at Mrs. Jeffries. "Oh, you know what I mean. . . ."

"Of course I do, Betsy," Mrs. Jeffries agreed. "And you're absolutely right." She turned to Luty. "Betsy has a number of acquaintances. Any one of them might be useful if she should run into them. They'd be more apt to answer her questions than yours."

"Then what in the blazes am I gonna do?" Luty snorted. "If'n you think I'm gonna sit around and do nothin', you've got another think comin'. This is the first chance I've had to show that stiff-necked old fool that works fer me that females is as smart as men and I ain't gonna miss it."

"Of course you're not going to miss your chance," Mrs. Jeffries said calmly. "I quite agree that Hatchet as well as the other men need to be shown up a bit. But I've got something entirely different in mind for you."

Luty leaned closer. "Now yer talkin'."

"Annie Shields had lodgings in Barston Road," Mrs. Jeffries explained. "I don't know the address, but if you go over there and ask about, you might be able to find where she lives. Talk to her landlady and anyone else who might have known the woman. Find out anything you can."

"Mrs. Jeffries," Betsy said slowly, "what if Annie Shields was killed by someone who didn't even know her? You know, like a robbery or even a . . . a . . ."

"Rape?"

Betsy blushed and nodded.

"I've thought of that. It could well be the case." Mrs. Jeffries pursed her lips. "But remember, the streets were deserted last night. Luty mentioned that when she dropped by. The riot in Trafalgar Square had sent everyone inside. Therefore, you have to ask yourself, if there was no one on the streets, why would a young woman bother going out and trying to sell flowers when there wasn't any foot traffic? Furthermore, why would a robber wait until the one night of the year when his victim hadn't made any money before he committed murder, a hanging offense? If I was going to take a risk like that, I'd at least wait until my victim had something worth stealing."

"You mean, the streets was empty, so the girl probably hadn't sold any flowers, so she couldn't have had any money?" Mrs. Goodge said. "That makes sense . . . I think. But what if she were just raped?"

"Then why kill her?" Mrs. Jeffries sighed. "Look, it could well be an incredibly stupid killer who hadn't even the intelligence to realize his victim didn't have anything worth taking. Or it could have been a rape by some maniac. We don't know. We won't know until the inspector gets home this evening. But do we want to miss this opportunity to learn what we can?"

" 'Course not," Luty declared.

"Reckon we can get a bit of a head start," Mrs. Goodge muttered. "If it turns out to be one of them stupid, senseless killin's that never get solved, well, it won't be because we sat on our backsides and didn't even try."

"Uh, Mrs. Jeffries," Betsy asked, "we are going to tell the men about the murder, aren't we?"

"Let 'em read about it in the papers," Mrs. Goodge said.

"Do the whole uppity bunch a world of good to be left out of this one," Luty agreed. "Teach 'em not to be so dang-blasted arrogant all the time. Especially that old fussbudget Hatchet."

"Now, really, ladies," Mrs. Jeffries said quickly. "We mustn't let our competitive instincts completely overrule our consciences." Though if she were to be honest, she was sorely tempted. "Of course we must tell them."

"All right," Mrs. Goodge said grudgingly.

"Do ya have to do it tonight?" Luty asked hopefully. "Couldn't you delay fer another day or two?"

"Delayin' tellin' them won't do us any good," Betsy said. "They're bound to hear somethin' from the inspector."

"Not necessarily," Mrs. Jeffries mused. She caught herself. Surely, she wasn't seriously considering Luty's suggestion. Surely, she wasn't that small and petty-minded. Oh, but she was. Last night her blood had boiled with some of the asinine statements Hatchet, Smythe and Wiggins had thrown about the table as if they were the gospel truth. "Actually, Smythe said he wouldn't be in until late tonight. He's taking the carriage out for a run."

"What's he doin' that for?" Betsy demanded.

"He claims the horses need the exercise. Come to think of it, Bow and Arrow did look a bit pudgy the last time Smythe brought the carriage round."

"I can send Wiggins out this evenin'," Mrs. Goodge announced. "I've been meanin' to get that ruddy sausage-makin' contraption fixed. I'll send the lad over to the ironmonger, as slow as old man Craxter is, Wiggins'll be there half the night."

"And Hatchet's way behind in Jon's lessons," Luty mused. "Maybe it's time fer me to remind the two of them about our agreement."

"How's the boy doin'?" Betsy asked. "It's hard to imagine Hatchet havin' much patience with a mouthy little beggar like Jon."

On their last case, which Luty had missed because she'd gone to America to avoid the Queen's Jubilee, Hatchet had ended up bringing a homeless lad, one of the principals in their investigation, into Luty's household.

"Jon's doin' just fine," Luty replied. "Squawks about doin' his lessons, but he's a sharp one. Hatchet and I are already squabblin' on where we're goin' to send him to college." She rose to her feet. "Much as I've enjoyed chattin', ladies, I expect I'd best be off. Do you want me to pop back round here this evenin'?"

Mrs. Jeffries nodded. "Come after eight. The inspector should have finished his dinner by then. He always retires early when he's on a case."

Betsy got up too. "Hang on a minute, Luty, while I get my coat. I'll walk out with you."

"I'd best get crackin' too," Mrs. Goodge said, glancing at the clock as the two women made their way to the back door. She heaved herself to her feet and walked over to the china cupboard. Opening the glass door, she took out a brown glass bottle with a cork stopper.

"Is your rheumatism bothering you?" Mrs. Jeffries asked sympathetically.

"Just a bit," she replied, unstopping the bottle and rubbing some of the strong-smelling clear liquid into her hands. "But this here liniment helps." She smiled wryly. "I used to only put it on when my fingers got really achy. You know what I mean. It's bloomin' expensive, this stuff. But since some good soul around here's taken it into their heads to make sure there's always a full bottle, I use it whenever I need it. Got to keep me fingers limber. The grocer's boy comes round about four and I want to have a bit of bakin' done. As well as I remember, Albert's right fond of my currant scones."

"Odd, isn't it?" Mrs. Jeffries said thoughtfully, her gaze on the brown bottle. "We've all become so adept at solving mysteries, but we can't solve the one that affects us every day of our lives."

She referred to the fact that objects kept appearing out of nowhere. Not only did some mysterious benefactor ensure that Mrs. Goodge always had a full bottle of her expensive medicine, but this same person also kept Wiggins supplied with notepaper so he could write his poems and love letters, bought Betsy several useful and expensive items of clothes and slipped the latest edition of Mr. Walt Whitman's poems into Mrs. Jeffries's bookcase.

"Reckon we're not tryin' to solve that one all that hard," the cook said dryly. Mrs. Jeffries knew just what she meant. Whoever their benefactor was, he or she was a member of the household and that person obviously wished to keep their identity secret. Of course, Mrs. Jeffries knew perfectly well who this person was. But naturally, she wouldn't say a word.

Inspector Witherspoon looked around the shabby but clean room which had belonged to Annie Shields. He and Barnes stood just inside the door of what was a combination bedroom and sitting room. On one wall, a lumpy bed with a faded dark green covering stood next to a small cot covered with heavy layers of gray blankets and quilts. A rickety table with two chairs, one of which had a spool missing at the top, stood near the only window. Pale gray light pierced the limp rose-and-green curtains, bathing the room in a depressing light. On the other side of that was a small nook containing a wooden cupboard with crockery stacked on top. A wardrobe, one of its knobs missing and its mirror cracked, stood next to a dented trunk.

"Who's goin' to pay the rent, that's what I want to know," the querulous voice of Mrs. Basset, the landlady, sliced through the chill air.

"Was Annie Shields behind in her rent?" the inspector asked. He turned to face the landlady.

She stared at him through angry, slitted hazel eyes as a dull red flush crept slowly up her fleshy cheeks. "Not yet," Mrs. Basset replied, lifting her three chins just a fraction. "She were paid up to the first of next week. But she's had this room fer a long time. It's downright inconvenient tryin' to find a new tenant without proper notice."

"I don't expect she thought she'd be murdered," Barnes said softly. "How long had she lived here?"

"Four years," Mrs. Basset said. "Moved in right after her and David got married."

"And when did Mr. Shields die?" Witherspoon felt that knowing as much as possible about the victim was a very good thing. One never knew. It certainly wasn't unheard of for someone from the past to pop up with a motive for murder.

"A bit over a year ago." Mrs. Basset pursed her lips. "He were killed in an accident down at the brewery. Annie had to go out and work then, what with David not havin' anythin' to leave her."

"How very dreadful," the inspector murmured. Poor girl. Life hadn't been very kind to her.

"Did Annie Shields always go out to work at night?" Barnes put in.

Mrs. Basset shrugged. "Not really. Sometimes when she were a bit short she'd go out. Never more than a couple of nights a week, though. Mostly she worked days. Had a patch over near Regent Street that did right well."

"What time did she leave last night?" Witherspoon asked.

"Right after it got dark," she replied. "Annie liked to get the supper trade if she was goin' to bother workin'."

"Do you know of any particular reason Mrs. Shields needed money last night?"

"Everyone needs money." Mrs. Basset stared at him incredulously.

"But last night wasn't a very good night to be going out to work, was it? There were riots yesterday afternoon and the streets were deserted." Really, Witherspoon thought, did he have to explain every little thing?

"Oh, I see what ya mean. Well, I guess she must have been in a bad way if she went out, mustn't she?"

"Was she ever late paying her rent?" Barnes asked.

"No. Always paid right on time. First of every week—" She broke off and frowned thoughtfully. "Come to think of it, it were odd her goin' out last night."

The inspector's spirits lifted. Now they were getting somewhere. He noticed Barnes staring uneasily around the small room. "Why?"

" 'Cause she ain't been short of money lately," Mrs. Basset said bluntly.

Witherspoon was surprised. Before he could ask another question, though, they heard the front door slam.

"That's that bleedin' Maples feller." The landlady spun around and ran toward the hall. "He owes me a week's rent."

"But, Mrs. Basset," the inspector called, "we've more questions for you."

"You'll have to ask 'em later," she yelled as she charged down the stairs. "Maples," she screamed. "It's no good hidin' in yer rooms. I want me bloomin' rent."

"Honestly," Witherspoon murmured. "One would think her precious rent money was more important than finding a murderer."

"Should we search the room now, sir?" Barnes asked. He scratched his chin.

"As we're already here, we might as well." He noticed that Barnes was shaking his head and looking puzzled. "I say, Constable, is something wrong?"

"Well, sir, since you ask, there is something that's botherin' me." He gestured around the shabby room. "This place, sir, it's much too grand for a flower seller."

"Really?" Witherspoon was genuinely surprised.

"Yes, sir," Barnes continued. "You don't know how poor most of the people over in this end o' town is. . . ."

"Come now, Constable. I realize the East End isn't by any means affluent. But this isn't the East End, is it?"

"No, sir, it ain't and that's one of the things I'm wonderin' about." Barnes shook his head vigorously. "Annie Shields was a flower seller. How could she afford to live here? She'd be lucky to make a farthin' or a couple a tuppence on any bunches she sold. And a room like this, in a clean house and with this much furnishin', would cost a good deal more than she could bring in."

Witherspoon thought about it. Dash it all, Barnes was right. There was something decidedly odd about Annie Shields living in a room all on her own. Most poor people lived crowded in horrid tenements or doss houses. Yet this room, for all its shabbiness, was clean and warm. "Good observation, Barnes. Where did she earn the money for this room?" He thought of something. "Perhaps she did more for her customers than just sell them flowers."

Barnes laughed. "Even if she were a prostitute, sir, she'd still not be able to afford this place. Most girls earn just enough to pay for a bed in a doss house and buy a pint of gin and a bit of tea. There's too much competition for any of 'em to make much money at the game. According to last month's report, there's over twelve hundred prostitutes in Whitechapel alone."

The inspector felt a flush creep up his cheeks. He knew he was a bit naive about some things. "Er, then, if she wasn't supplementing her income, how on earth did she earn enough money to pay her rent? Perhaps her husband left her something her landlady didn't know about."

"Maybe." Barnes shrugged. "I don't know, sir. But knowin' you, I expect we'll find out. Expect we should get crackin' on the search. Are we lookin' for anythin' in particular?"

"Not really." Witherspoon wished they were looking for something specific. He suddenly remembered that Barnes had told him someone important was pressing for an investigation into this poor woman's murder.

For the first time he wondered who that person could be and, more to the point, what their interest was in a young flower seller. A flower seller who apparently lived beyond her means.

He glanced around the room, again noting the limp curtains, the threadbare carpet. How sad, he thought, a room this shabby was all the woman had to call home, and he, by virtue of being a policeman, thought it more than someone of her station could ever hope to aspire to. Witherspoon wasn't sure what it was he felt. Yet he was decidedly uncomfortable. There was something very wrong with a system which kept people like himself in the lap of luxury while others lived in such abject poverty.

"Barnes," he said quietly, "do you know the name of the person who pressed for an investigation in this case?"

The constable hesitated. "Well, sir, officially, the chief inspector isn't admittin' anyone pressured him to put you on the case."

"But unofficially." Witherspoon laughed. "Come now, Constable. You know you've more sources at Scotland Yard than the East End has pickpockets. Who is it?"

"It was a solicitor, sir. Important one, too. Man named Harlan Bladestone." Barnes raised his finger and pointed. "Should I start with that wardrobe?"

"Right, I'll take the trunk."

They searched the victim's room. Under the bed, the inspector found a wooden box. Opening the lid, he found a small, empty drawstring pouch, a lock of blond hair, some buttons and a slim bundle of papers. The papers were empty envelopes. David Shields's old pay packets with the name of the brewery written on the front and some plain white envelopes as well. "It appears Mrs. Shields was frugal. She saved old envelopes to be reused."

In the wardrobe, Barnes found a few dresses, a set of woolen underwear, a worn shawl and a pair of scuffed shoes. Oddly enough, he also found a bundle of baby clothes. On the floor of the wardrobe, he found a wooden rattle.

Further examination turned up nothing interesting, certainly nothing that indicated where Annie Shields had obtained her rent money. "We might as well go," the inspector said when they'd finished. "We've found precious little here."

"Where are we going next, sir?" Barnes brushed the dust off his hands.

"Let's pay a call on her employer," Witherspoon said. "Perhaps he can be of some help. First, though, I'd like to have another word with the landlady."

Mrs. Basset was standing in the front hall, her arms folded across her chest. "Bleedin' Maples, if'n he don't have my rent by tomorrow, out he goes," she declared as the two policemen came down the stairs.

"Did Mrs. Shields have a family?" the inspector asked quickly. Really, he thought, he should have asked that question straightaway. If there were relatives, they had to be notified.

"Annie were an orphan," Mrs. Basset snapped, glaring at the closed door of the impoverished Maples. Her tone implied that it was Annie's fault she had no parents. "David never mentioned his family. Certainly none of them turned up 'ere offerin' to take Annie and the girl in."

"Girl?" Witherspoon's eyebrows shot up. "What girl?"

"Emma. Annie's daughter."

CHAPTER 3

"Well, dang and blast," Luty Belle muttered to herself as she spotted Inspector Witherspoon and Barnes coming down the steps of a shabby house at the end of the street. Quickly, she looked around for a place to hide. Spotting a cart pulled up waiting to unload barrels, she scurried behind it just as the two policemen turned and headed her way. Luckily, they were on the other side of the road, but Luty wasn't going to take any chances.

"You lookin' fer somethin'?" a voice asked.

Luty glanced up. A young man with dark curly hair and the brightest blue eyes she'd ever seen grinned down at her. "No," she replied tartly. "If I was looking for something, I'da said so."

"Really, now." His smile widened. "Then whatcha hidin' behind me cart for?"

Luty rolled her eyes. "Why do ya think? I'm tryin' to not be seen."

He lifted his chin and gazed across the road. "Ah, I see. You're not wantin' them coppers to spot you, eh?"

"That's right." Luty saw Witherspoon glance towards the cart. She ducked her head.

"You an American?" he asked, looking down at her.

"Yup." Luty was completely crouched behind the row of barrels right behind him. If the silly fool kept turnin' his head and blatherin' at her, the inspector might see him. Luty didn't relish the thought of trying to explain why she was hiding behind a cartful of barrels. "Listen, if'n you don't mind, would you kinda look the other way, least until they gets past?"

He chuckled but turned towards his horses. "Now, ain't this something? Here I finally meets me a Yank and she's hidin' from the law. You'll be fine in just a second, luv. They're almost gone." He paused. "There. They've rounded the corner. You can get up now."

She groaned as she rose from her crouch. Her knees creaked and her ankles felt like they were on fire. Gettin' old was hell, she thought. Maybe she should have brought her cane along. "Thanks fer not givin' me away," she told him.

He stared at her, his expression frankly curious as he took in her fancy peacock-blue dress, elegant feathered hat and fur muff. Not to mention her white hair. "If you don't mind me askin', what'd you do to have the coppers lookin' fer ya?"

Luty was tempted to make up some wild tale involving shoot-outs, radical politics and six-guns, but as she actually had a Colt .45 in her possession, she thought better of it. The young man appeared to be sympathetic, but you never knew. "They ain't actually looking for me," she admitted. "But I thought it best if they didn't see me, that's all."

"Last I heard it was a free country," he retorted. "You've a right to go where you like. You've made me right curious. What's a woman like you doin' hidin' from the law?"

Dang, Luty thought, a feller with nose trouble. He was goin' to keep at her until she told him something. She could tell by the way his chin jutted. Stubborn cuss. 'Course she really couldn't fault him for being curious. She was of a curious nature herself. "Let's just say I'm doin' a bit of private inquiring round here. I don't think the police would take kindly to my activities."

"So they know who you are, then?"

"What makes you say that?" Dang, Luty thought, a smart feller with nose trouble.

"Because if at least one of them coppers didn't know who you was, you wouldn'ta bothered to be hidin' behind my barrels, would you? Even coppers don't go about aggravatin' well-dressed ladies unless they've got a reason. So I figures, they know ya."

"All right, so they know me." She started to walk away.

"Hey, just a minute, luv," he called. Luty stopped and turned to face him.

"Whatcha inquiring about?" he asked seriously. "I live around these parts, maybe I could help ya some."

Luty thought about it for a moment. "Young woman who lived over there"—she pointed to the house at the end of the row—"got murdered last night. I aim to find the one that did it."

He gaped at her. "You mean Annie Shields?"

"You knew her?" Dang, Luty thought, she should have been spending her time askin' him questions, not wittering on about why she was hiding.

His face tightened and all the amusement vanished from his eyes. "Everyone round here knew her. Liked her too. Poor Annie, I hope they hang the one that did it."

"Sounds like you feel pretty bad about what happened to her."

"She were real nice. Loaned me a bob or two when I was short." His expression became wary. "Why is Annie your business? What was she to you?"

"I can't really tell ya," Luty said honestly. "But like I said, I'm tryin' to help find who killed her, if that's any comfort to ya. What's yer name?"

"Harry Grafton. What's yours?" He still looked a bit frosty, but Luty could tell he was starting to thaw.

"Luty Belle Crookshank." She walked back to the wagon and stuck up her hand. He gazed at her for a brief moment and then reached down and grasped her fingers in a firm handshake. "I reckon you knew Annie pretty well, didn't ya?" she continued.

He nodded. "Her and her husband. Me and David worked together. He was a driver too. We both worked for the brewery. It were right sad when he got killed. Poor sod was crushed by a load of barrels." He shook his head in disgust. "And now Annie gettin' coshed on the head by some bloody thief so's they could steal the only decent thing the woman owned. It makes me sick, it does, right sick to my stomach."

Luty stared at him sharply. "You sure know a lot."

Harry shrugged. "News travels fast round these parts."

"What makes you so sure it was a robbery?"

"Why else would anyone kill her? She didn't have any enemies. Worked hard, minded her own business and tried to do right by others, too, when she could. It's bloody obvious, is'n it? Someone murdered Annie for a bleedin' ring. Kitty—that's me wife—was always sayin' that opals was unlucky. Looks like she were right. Annie had that damned ring on last night and some bloody bastard saw her wearin' it and killed her for it."

"How do you know she had the ring on?"

Harry pulled off his flat workingman's cap and scratched his head. "I saw it, didn't I? Annie come over to see the wife last night. We was all down at the Cock o' the Walk havin' a bit of a drink. She had the ring on when she come in. Kitty told her she shouldn't be wearin' it. But Annie said she had to. Said she needed to show it to someone. Daft it was, wearin' that bloody ring just so she could show off a bit."

"The Cock o' the Walk?" Luty repeated. "Where's that?"

"Just round the corner there," he said, pointing up the street.

"Did Annie often go in there for a drink?" Luty was trying to decide if she should go there next or to Annie's house. She wanted to get as much information as fast as possible.

He laughed. "Nah, Annie didn't hardly drink. She come in lookin' for Florrie Maxwell. Needed Florrie to look after her girl 'cause she were goin' out that night."

"Girl? What girl?" Luty asked.

"Her daughter, Emma. Sweet little mite, she is. Smart as a button too. Well, Annie don't like leavin' Emma at night, unless'n she can leave her with Florrie. 'Course I can understand her feelin's. Emma's hardly more than a baby. She's only three."

"How on earth can that woman be so callous," Witherspoon exclaimed. Barnes grunted in assent. "She as good as admitted Emma Shields had lived in her house since the day she was born, yet she's no idea of her where-abouts!"

Barnes cleared his throat. "Now, sir, all Mrs. Basset said was she didn't know who took care of the lass while Annie worked."

"That doesn't do us any good," the inspector moaned. "Somewhere out there"—he gestured expansively with his hand as they hurried down the road—"is a poor orphan and no one seems to care in the least about her. Certainly not that landlady!"

"I expect we can find out by askin' about the neighborhood," Barnes said soothingly. "Do you want me to get onto it?"

Witherspoon hesitated. He hated the thought of that poor child being all alone out in the world, but if he personally took time to look for her, he'd delay find-ing her mother's murderer. "No." He sighed. "We'll have some of the uniformed lads start inquiring. The local coppers can probably find the girl faster than you and I. We still need to get over to Covent Garden and speak with her employer and we also must interview this Harlan Bladestone."

"That shouldn't be difficult, sir," Barnes said, whip-ping out his notebook. "I looked up his address before I left the Yard this morning."

"Constable." Witherspoon came to a full stop. "This won't create difficulties for you?"

"You mean because I wasn't supposed to know who'd been on the chief?" Barnes laughed. "Don't worry about it, sir. I may have me sources at the Yard, but Bladestone's comin' in and raisin' a ruckus weren't no secret. It was all over the canteen by eight o'clock this morning."

"Excellent." Witherspoon stopped again and looked around. "Now, let's see. Where are we exactly? Ah,

yes." He waved towards the busy crossroads just ahead.
"There's a constable just past the hotel. We'll have him
nip round to the local police station and find some lads
to start inquiring about Emma Shields."

It took only a few minutes to give the constable his
instructions. Witherspoon hailed a passing hansom and
he and Barnes were on their way to see Mr. Harlan
Bladestone.

"What are your ideas, Barnes?" Witherspoon asked.

"Reckon she was killed durin' a robbery," the constable replied thoughtfully. "Least that's what it looks
like. I don't know, though, sir. After seein' her room,
somethin' don't seem right."

Witherspoon frowned. Much as he hated to admit
it, the constable had a valid point. There was something decidedly odd about the victim living in such
circumstances. Furthermore, he didn't altogether trust
that landlady. He couldn't put his finger on what it was
that bothered him, but he'd learned to trust his feelings.
Why, just a few months ago, Mrs. Jeffries had told him
he was gifted with a strong, "inner force." The inspector
wasn't precisely sure what she meant, but he no longer
worried about that either. Whatever this force was, it had
helped him solve a number of homicides. It was going
to help him solve this one too. "Apparently, there's more
to Annie Shields than meets the eye. For one, she was
living in quarters far more extravagant than an average
flower seller could afford."

"She might have had a settlement or some kind of
income from her husband's people," Barnes replied.

"That's possible."

"But you think it's doubtful?"

"I do," Witherspoon explained. "From what Mrs. Basset said, it certainly didn't sound like the husband's

family was all that keen to help the woman. And there was something about that landlady I didn't quite trust."

"What do you mean, sir?" Barnes asked curiously.

Witherspoon hesitated. It was difficult to put his feelings into words. "She didn't seem to know enough," he explained. "Oh, I can't quite say what I mean, but Annie Shields had lived at that house for four years, and in all that time, the landlady didn't know how she got the money to pay her rent, who took care of the child while she went out to work or if either Annie or her husband had any relations." He shook his head. "I'm sorry. But my experience has been that landladies as a whole make it their business to learn as much as they can about their tenants. Mrs. Basset didn't seem to know anything."

"Or she wasn't tellin'," Barnes muttered darkly.

"That's a possibility too," the inspector agreed. "It's amazing how many people there are in this city who have no sense of duty. But there's something that bothers me a great deal more than what Mrs. Basset does or doesn't know."

"What's that, sir?"

"Why is a prominent solicitor putting pressure on Scotland Yard to solve this murder? More importantly, how did Harlan Bladestone know about the murder?"

"Couldn't have read about it in the papers," Barnes said. "For me to hear about it in the canteen, he must have been onto the chief before the mornin' papers come out. Well, sir, however he found out, we shall soon know."

The offices of Harlan Bladestone were located in chambers near the Temple Bar. An unsmiling clerk dressed in a stiff collar and black frock coat led them down a dark hallway and into a quiet room where two other clerks were hunched over their desks busily scribbling.

"Please wait here, Inspector," the clerk said, pointing to a single high-backed chair. "I'll tell Mr. Bladestone you're here."

A few moments later a tall, smiling man with dark brown hair, an enormous mustache and a florid complexion barreled into the room. "Inspector Witherspoon." He extended his hand. "I'm so glad you've come. I'm Harlan Bladestone. I've been waiting to talk to you. I told your chief I particularly wanted you to investigate this dreadful business." He smiled at Barnes.

"How do you do, sir," Witherspoon said, getting up and taking the proffered hand. He was surprised by the warmth of the man's greeting. "This is Constable Barnes."

"Good, good, please"—Bladestone turned abruptly and started back the way he'd come—"do come into my chambers."

They followed him down another dark hallway and into a room with floor-to-ceiling shelves of books on all the walls. Pale light from the overcast day filtered in through two narrow windows behind a massive desk.

Bladestone gestured at two well-worn leather chairs and the constable and Witherspoon sat down.

"I expect you're here to find out why I'm so interested in Annie Shields's murder," he said bluntly.

"Yes, sir." Witherspoon was rather taken aback. Gracious, another surprise. Not only did the man greet him like he was a long-lost friend, but he was actually going to get to the point. How very peculiar. It had been his experience that most legal men wittered on for hours without saying anything. Especially as this was a murder investigation. Why, most people became positively tongue-tied when you tried getting any useful information out of them. "We've several questions to ask you,

Mr. Bladestone. The first one, of course, is what your interest in this poor unfortunate woman was."

"Don't you want to know how I found out about the murder so quickly?" Bladestone asked.

"Er, yes, of course we do. How did you know?"

"Actually, I sent my footman along to Covent Garden this morning with a message for Annie. Well, of course, by the time he arrived at the flower market, the news had already spread that she'd been murdered. As soon as I heard that, I went straight to your chief." He smiled wryly. "He's an old friend."

"And your interest in Annie Shields?" Witherspoon was getting more curious by the minute.

"Ah." Bladestone sat back in his chair and steepled his fingers. "This may take a while in the telling, sir."

"We've plenty of time, Mr. Bladestone."

"I suppose I must begin at the beginning." The solicitor's eyes took on a wistful, faraway expression as he stared over the inspector's shoulder at a spot on the far wall. "You see, I've known Annie for over a year now. Ever since her husband died. But my meeting Annie isn't where it all began."

"Where what all began?" Witherspoon asked, getting more confused by the moment.

"The murder, or at least the circumstances leading up to it." The lawyer smiled apologetically. "Do forgive me, sir. But this is most difficult. You see, I may be completely wrong. It could well be that Annie was murdered by some vicious animal who wanted to steal what little she had. The events of twenty years ago may have had absolutely nothing to do with her death."

Betsy glared at the young, dirty ruffian blocking her way. Keeping her gaze locked to his, she lifted her hand and shoved hard against his shoulder. "Get out of my bleedin' way," she ordered in a harsh voice.

" 'Ere now, I was only tryin' to be friendly like." The oafish lad stumbled backwards, his filthy porkpie hat sliding off his greasy blond hair in the process. "No call fer you to be so pushy." His small, piglike eyes narrowed as he stared at her.

Betsy knew he was taking in every detail of her neat, oxford-cloth blue dress, her shiny black shoes and the fact that the cape she wore wasn't patched with holes. Her fingers tightened on her purse. He was either a pick-pocket or an out-and-out thief. He'd been following her for ten minutes now and she was fairly certain it wasn't because he'd fallen in love with her face. Whatever he wanted, she knew how to deal with the likes of him. She glanced to her left and saw that the constable was still there, walking his patrol. She'd picked her time careful-ly, waiting until she was in full view of the policeman and on a busy public street. This stupid lout hadn't even noticed the copper. "I'll be plenty pushy if'n you don't stay out of me way," she said, deliberately roughening her tone of voice even further and reverting back to the speech patterns of her childhood. "I'm not some doxy streetwoman you can manhandle any way ya like." She jerked her chin towards the constable. "So keep yer bloody distance or I'll call that copper."

Surprised, he gaped at her as she stepped past him. Betsy forced herself not to look over her shoulder as she hurried towards the flower market.

A sigh of relief escaped her when she didn't hear any footsteps coming from behind her. Besides having to put up with that stupid oaf, she'd had a miserable day. She'd learned nothing on Southampton Street, so rather than go back empty handed, she'd decided to try her luck here.

After all, Covent Garden was where Annie Shields got her flowers. But so far, everyone she'd talked to hadn't told her a blooming thing. The best she'd gotten was that Annie Shields had usually set up her cart over near the arcade on Regent Street.

Maybe I'll go there next if I don't have any luck here, she thought. Betsy slowed as she came near a flower seller humping a load of flowers into a wheeled cart. "Excuse me," she said politely, "but I'm wonderin' if you could help me."

"You wantin' to buy somethin'?" the girl asked. She was short, thin to the point of emaciation, dark-eyed and pale-skinned, with reddish hair bundled under a cotton head scarf.

Betsy hesitated. She had plenty of coins. Thanks to their unknown benefactor back at Upper Edmonton Gardens, she hadn't had to spend any of her wages to buy the new shoes she was wearing. Truth was, she hadn't had to spend any of her own money on anything lately. Their benefactor kept her well supplied.

"I'll take a nosegay, please," she said, digging out her coin purse.

The girl handed her the flowers. "That'll be sixpence, please," she said. "They's a bit more than usual 'cause during the fall and winter they's grown in the green-house."

Betsy wondered if the girl told all her customers this. She handed her a shilling. "Keep the change." She smiled warmly. "I'm wonderin' if you could help me with some information? I'm lookin' for a woman named Annie Shields."

"What you want with Annie?" She eyed Betsy warily.

Betsy decided to try a bit of subterfuge. Honesty hadn't gotten her any information today. "Oh, we used

to live on the same street back when I was a girl. I heard
she was workin' round these parts as a flower seller and
I thought I'd look her up."

"You're a bit late." The girl's smile was both cynical
and sad. She picked up another bundle of flowers and put
them on the cart. "Annie got herself done in last night.
She were murdered."

Betsy tried to look suitably shocked. "Oh no. Poor
Annie. What happened?"

"They say she got coshed over the head and robbed.
But I don't believe a word of it." She dusted off her
hands and grasped the handle of the cart.

"Why don't ya believe it?" Betsy said quickly, lest the
girl get away. "I mean, from what I remember of Annie,
no one would want to hurt her. She weren't the kind
to be makin' enemies." She fervently prayed this was
true. As she'd found out very little about the victim, she
could only hope that Annie Shields hadn't been a right
old harridan from hell.

The girl studied her for a moment. " 'Cause like you
said, Annie weren't the kind to make enemies. She
weren't no fool either. She knew 'ow to take care of
'erself when she was workin' nights. There's only one
person I know of that'd want to 'urt her. That bloody
Bill Calloway."

"Who's he?" Betsy stepped directly in front of the
cart. She didn't want her source leaving before she was
through asking her questions.

"He's a mean bastard, that's who 'e is. 'E's been
sniffin' around Annie since the day she buried her Davey.
And if'n 'e's the one that killed 'er, I hope they catch 'im
and hang him." Her eyes narrowed in anger. "You sure
you were a friend of Annie's? You don't talk much like
she did."

Betsy was ready for that question. "Oh, I went into service over near Holland Park. The housekeeper's been 'elpin' me to learn to talk proper. About this Calloway feller, why do you think he killed 'er?"

She laughed harshly. " 'Cause she told 'im to sod off. Billy didn't take kindly to that. No, sir, not the way Annie did it. Stood right where you are and told 'im to leave her the 'ell alone." She stopped abruptly, her gaze growing even more suspicious. "You're asking an awful lot of questions. You sure you're not a friend of Bill's? Be just like 'im to send out one of his fancy pieces to find out the lay of the land."

"I don't know this Bill Calloway," Betsy retorted, stung by the words *fancy piece*, "and I'm askin' questions 'cause I'm curious."

"Don't pay to be curious around these parts."

Betsy ignored this. "Listen, did Annie have any special friends round 'ere? Someone I could talk to? I'd some nice things to give her, and if'n she's dead, I might as well try and find someone else to give 'em to. By the way, what's yer name?"

"Me name's Muriel. Muriel Goodall." She licked her lips. "Uh, what kind of things you got? Come to that, I was as good a friend to Annie as anyone round 'ere."

"I've got a cloak and a pair of good boots—oh, and a nice woolen sweater and a pair of gloves." Betsy smiled widely. "Why don't we go have a cup of tea somewhere and you can tell me all about Annie. I would so like to hear what my friend's been up to these last few years."

Muriel glanced over her shoulder towards the flower market. A big, burly fellow with a fierce frown and a stained apron over his fat belly glared in their direction. "That's Mr. Cobbins. I work for 'im. So did Annie. Tell you what, I'm supposed to do Annie's shift over at the arcade on Regent Street. Why don't you meet me there in an hour or so?"

Luty cocked her head and plastered what she hoped was a grandmotherly smile on her face. She lifted a gloved hand and knocked on the door of the small row house. A moment later the door opened and a short, heavy woman wearing an old-fashioned mobcap and a huge apron over her starched brown dress opened the door.

"Yes?" the woman said cautiously.

"Good day, ma'am," Luty began in her politest voice. "Are you Florrie Maxwell?"

"I am. Who might you be?"

"My name is Luty Belle Crookshank." She smiled, pulling a pristine white, elegantly printed calling card from her muff. "My card. I'm wonderin' if you'd be so kind as to spare me a few moments of your time."

Impressed by the calling card, Florrie Maxwell held the door open and motioned her inside. "Uh, please, come in."

A few moments later Luty was sitting smack in the parlour. From upstairs, she could hear the sounds of children playing. "I'm sure you're very curious as to why I'm here," Luty began. "Actually, it's, well . . ." Ye Gods, what if this poor woman didn't know Annie Shields was dead?

"Is it about Annie?" Florrie asked quietly.

Luty nodded. Florrie's eyes filled with tears. She swiped at one that rolled down her plump cheeks. "I don't know who I expected to come claim Emma, but you look like a kind lady. Are you a relative of David's? He had some family that went to America."

For the first time in many years Luty was stumped. But that only lasted a second or two. "Does Emma know her mama's gone?" she asked softly.

Florrie nodded. "But she doesn't really understand what it means. She's just a baby. I'm so glad you've come. Much as I hated the idea, I was goin' to have to take the child to the orphanage. Not that I wouldn't love to keep her myself, but I can't afford another mouth to feed around here, not with my Arnold down sick and Edgar bein' out of work. Fact is, we're goin' to be goin' to Leicester today. Edgar's mother says one of the shoe factories is hirin'. We might not be back."

"I'm sure you'da been right good to the girl," Luty said sympathetically, "but it's best she be with her relations. Uh, where is she?"

"She's upstairs taking a nap."

Luty's mind raced frantically. Was taking an orphan child the same as kidnapping? Oh hell, what did she care anyway? She had a big empty house, dozens of staff and an army of lawyers. Surely, one of them ought to be smart enough to keep her out of jail. Taking the girl in for a few days would be better than lettin' the poor little thing go to one of them orphanages or, even worse, a workhouse. "Good, then we'll let her sleep. Why don't you and I talk a spell while we wait for Emma to wake up. Tell me, do you have any idea why anyone would want to hurt Annie?"

Florrie swiped at another tear. "Gracious, no. Annie worked hard and minded her own business. She was a good mother too. She always brought Emma round here when she was workin', not like some that just leaves 'em on the streets all day."

"I know it was right hard for Annie to get by," Luty said cautiously. "I reckon she had to work day and night sellin' flowers to afford to keep a roof over her head and food on the table. I'm real sorry Annie didn't let me know how bad things was. I'da liked to help her."

"Oh, but aren't you the one that's been sendin' her—" Florrie broke off in confusion.

"Sendin' her what?"

"Money," Florrie replied. "Haven't you been sendin' Annie money every week? Or is it someone else in the family that's been doin' it? She couldn't have afforded her own room or to pay me if someone hadn't been helpin' her. I just thought it were someone from David's family. The money started right after he were killed."

Luty shrugged nonchalantly. "It was probably my cousin Herbert," she lied. "Tell me, how'd Annie get the money? Did she get a paper she had to take to the bank every week?"

"You mean a bank draft or a check?" Florrie's tone grew a mite frosty.

"Sorry, didn't mean no offense." Luty grinned. "Just back where I come from half the folks wouldn't know what a check or a bank draft was, that's all."

"It's all right." Florrie smiled. "Half the people round here wouldn't know either. The money come in cash. First of every week. That's usually how Annie paid me. As soon as the boy brought the envelope, she'd come round here and pay me in advance for watchin' over Emma. Then she'd pay her landlady."

"A boy brought her the money?" Luty frowned. "Huh, musta been one of the other relatives," she muttered, getting into the spirit of her fib. "That don't sound like Herbert. He'da brought the money himself and made Annie sign a receipt. I expect it was Eugene that was sendin' the cash. He's a right trustin' sort. When did the boy come? I mean, what day of the week was it?"

"Every Monday morning. Annie'd be round here by ten to pay me."

"So he come to her rooms?"

Florrie nodded. "Annie didn't tell me anything else about him. Why? Does it matter?"

"Not really, exceptin' that if it was Eugene sendin' the money, I'd like to know." She leaned forward. "There's been a bit of bad feelin' between Eugene and Herbert ever since David died. You know what I mean, family trouble."

"I know just what you mean," Florrie said, bobbing her head again. "My aunt Geraldine went twenty years not speakin' to her sister, Lydia."

Satisfied that the mythical Herbert and Eugene and their alleged feud had quenched Florrie's curiosity, Luty tried to think of another plausible reason to keep asking questions. Florrie was sympathetic but not stupid. "I expect it was good that Annie found you to take care of Emma. Especially as she was workin' evenin's."

"I was pleased to do it. But Annie didn't work all that often. Only a couple of times a week." Florrie chewed on her lip. "Fact of the matter is, she hadn't planned on workin' last night at all. It come up sudden like." Florrie glanced down at her hands. "She still owes me for last night."

Luty reached for her muff and drew out a wad of notes. She peeled two off the top. "I'll settle up fer her. After all," she lied, "she was family."

"Gracious." Florrie stared at the notes like they were fixing to bite her. "This is way too much!"

"Seein' as how you've been so good to Annie and Emma, why don't you just keep it?"

Flustered, Florrie hesitated.

"Go on now," Luty urged.

A towheaded lad about eight came running into the parlour. "Here now," Florrie scolded. "You're not to run in the house. Haven't you got eyes in your head, boy. We've a lady visitin'."

"Sorry, Mama," the boy said. He stared at Luty.

"This here is Mrs. Crookshank," Florrie said.

"Pleased to meet you." Luty smiled.

The boy's eyes widened at her accent. "You sure do talk funny."

"Hush, Harvey." Florrie turned to Luty. "I'm so sorry."

Luty laughed. "That's all right. I don't mind the boy's honesty."

There was a loud thump and then a distinct wail from the room over their head. Florrie got to her feet. "That's probably Emma. I'll go up and get her."

Harvey continued to stare at her. "You one of Emma's relations?"

"Yup," Luty lied. "You one of Emma's friends?"

"Nah, she's just a baby."

"So you don't play with her none."

"What can a baby do?" Harvey shrugged. "But I do keep me eye on her when we goes outside. Sometimes Mam makes me take her out to get the fresh air."

"I bet you take good care of her too," Luty said.

"Sure do. I kept that woman from botherin' her, didn't I?" Harvey's thin chest swelled with pride. "She were probably one of them baby stealers or one of them god-awful heathens. But I run her off good, didn't I?"

"What woman?"

"That veiled lady. The one who was hangin' about and watchin' the house every time Annie brung Emma over here."

*   *   *

"Now be real quiet, Wiggins," Smythe commanded as he eased open the back door. "Slip up the hallway, make sure the kitchen's clear, and then nip up the back steps right to the top."

Wiggins gripped the three bunches of flowers closer to his chest. "Who gets what?" he hissed.

"Roses go to Mrs. Jeffries, carnations to Mrs. Goodge and the mixed bunch are fer Betsy." He glanced back at the carriage. "Now hurry up, before someone spots us."

"I still don't see why we've got to give 'em flowers," Wiggins whispered. "Besides, I'm supposed to be gettin' the meat order. What if Mrs. Goodge asks where it is?"

"Tell her the butcher's deliverin' it later today," the coachman replied impatiently. "You know Mrs. Goodge, she loves havin' goods delivered. And we don't *have* to give them flowers. But seein' as how we probably offended all three of 'em last night, I'm thinkin if we ever want a decent meal or kind word from any of 'em again, we'd best mend some fences."

"These musta cost a bloomin' fortune. Where'd you get that kinda money?" Wiggins eyed the coachman suspiciously.

"I hit a winner at the races last week," Smythe lied smoothly. "A long shot and I got these on the cheap, so they didn't cost us 'ardly anythin'. Now go on, get movin'."

"Do we have to take Luty Belle flowers too?" Wiggins asked. "We was just as rude to 'er."

"We wasn't rude, boy." Smythe resisted the impulse to grab the ruddy flowers and take them upstairs himself. He would have, but he didn't want to leave the footman in charge of his beloved horses. "And Luty Belle is Hatchet's problem, not ours. Now 'urry up. I don't want Mrs. Goodge gettin a spot of nose trouble and comin' out to see what we're up to. These flowers is supposed to be a surprise."

"Still don't see why we're givin' them flowers," Wiggins muttered as he started down the hall. As he neared the kitchen he heard voices, so he quieted his steps.

"So you don't know Annie Shields?" he heard Mrs. Goodge say.

"Never heard of the girl until this morning," a squeaky but decidedly male voice replied. " 'Course, once we heard she'd been murdered, everyone was talkin' about her. Poor woman. Mind you, Henrietta Tavers said she wasn't in the least surprised that Annie had been killed. And she didn't think it were no robbery neither."

Murder? Wiggins's mouth gaped open. He sidled up to the edge of the door so he could hear more.

"Really," Mrs. Goodge said, "why's that? Do have another bun, Augustine. They're awfully nourishing."

"Thank you, I don't mind if I do. It was ever so nice of you to invite me round today. I was ever so surprised to get your message this afternoon. Mum will be right pleased."

Message? This afternoon? Wiggins didn't need to hear more. He knew instantly what those females were up to. They were trying to get the jump on a murder case. Both he and Smythe had come in for lunch. Mrs. Goodge had looked surprised to see them, but she hadn't said one word. Not a bloomin' word. Now he knew why she'd looked so guilty when he'd asked where Betsy and Mrs. Jeffries were. They was out investigating.

He stared down at the flowers in his arms.

"Hmmph," he snorted as he turned on his heel and marched towards the back door, not caring how much noise he made. "Flowers, indeed!"

Once he told Smythe that those females were investigating a murder without them, the coachman wouldn't want to give them flowers either. And he'd bet his next month's wages that Luty Belle Crookshank was in on it too!

Just wait until Hatchet found out about that.

CHAPTER 4

———◦◦◦◦———

"Then again, in good conscience I must tell you everything." Harlan Bladestone sighed dramatically. "Inspector, as I said, there is a real possibility that what happened twenty years ago could have a direct bearing on Annie's murder. It's a rather complex narrative, so please bear with me."

"You have my full attention, Mr. Bladestone," Witherspoon said. Really, he did wish the man would make up his mind.

"Twenty years ago one of my clients, someone who, for the moment, really must remain nameless, fell in love with a charming young woman. Unfortunately, he wasn't able to marry her." Bladestone smiled wryly. "Due to financial circumstances, my client married another woman."

"Financial circumstances?" Witherspoon wondered if Bladestone meant his client had married for money. Well, there was nothing particularly mysterious about *that*. From what he'd observed, more couples came together for gain rather than for love. Though, to be honest, Witherspoon thought it rather sad.

"Financial in the sense that the man was very poor, but very talented at his occupation." Bladestone shifted uncomfortably. "He was, at that time, a carpenter. I suppose it would be more accurate to say he married not for love, but for a, well, a business opportunity."

"Yes, I suppose I understand."

"To make a long story short," Bladestone continued, "my client married the wrong woman. He prospered financially, but at great cost to his personal happiness. As a matter of fact, he's now quite rich. But as is often the case in these matters, 'fate,' as they say, 'is stronger than anything I have known.' " He paused dramatically. "Euripides," he murmured, when the two policemen stared at him.

"Er, yes. I suppose some do think fate is quite strong," the inspector retorted.

Bladestone gave him a world-weary smile, then cleared his throat. "My client"—he jabbed his hands in the air for emphasis—"and I daresay, my friend, was miserable in his marriage despite his prosperity."

Gracious, Witherspoon thought, this man has missed his calling. He should have been an actor. "Yes, sir, you've already mentioned that."

The solicitor blinked, seemed to catch hold of himself and gave them a self-deprecating smile. "So I did, sir. Forgive me. Sometimes I do get carried away. But back to my narrative. As chance would have it, my client's wife died several years ago. Not that that fact has any direct bearing on this matter, of course. However, what does matter is that my client was now a widower. Rich, successful and suddenly unencumbered. For the first time in his life he had the time and leisure to take stock of his life, and what he found did not please him. More importantly, the young woman my client left behind so many years ago was with child."

Witherspoon drew in a quick breath and Barnes glanced up from his notebook.

Bladestone raised his hand. "Please don't think harshly of the man. In his defense, my friend did not know about the child. He would never have abandoned the woman had he known."

Well, I should hope not, the inspector thought, but he did manage to keep the sentiment to himself. Despite Mr. Bladestone's defense of this man, he didn't much care for him. He sounded like a selfish cad. "I take it this child or this woman you speak of has something to do with Annie Shields's murder?"

Bladestone nodded. "I think it might have everything to do with this foul crime." He smiled sadly. "The sins of the father . . ."

Honestly, Witherspoon thought, a poetic lawyer. He did wish the fellow would get on with it. Beside him, Barnes shifted restlessly.

Suddenly the door burst open. A tall man with dark hair liberally sprinkled with gray at the temples charged inside. On his heels was the stiff-faced clerk.

"Have you heard the horrible news, Harlan," the man cried. "She's dead. Oh God, how can I bear it? She's been foully murdered."

"I tried to stop him, sir," the clerk sputtered, wringing his hands.

Harlan Bladestone paled and leapt to his feet. "Henry, for God's sake, get a hold of yourself." He gestured at Witherspoon and Barnes. "These men are from the police. This is Inspector Witherspoon and Constable Barnes."

"The police? Oh, thank God." He hurried towards them. "You can help me, then. You can find the savage animal that took my darling from me."

"And who would you be, sir?" the constable asked in his soft, calm voice.

"Henry Albritton."

"And are you referring to Mrs. Annie Shields, sir?" Barnes continued.

"Well, of course I am." Henry's eyes filled with tears, but he bravely blinked them back.

"You knew the victim, sir?" the inspector managed to ask. He did so hope the man would get hold of himself. Egads, what if he started to cry?

"Knew her!" Henry swallowed heavily. "How could I not know—"

"Henry," Bladestone interrupted. "Before you say another word, I'd like to speak to you in private."

Henry ignored him. He turned beseeching eyes to the two policemen. "How could I not know her? She was my darling, my angel. My future. Inspector, you must find the fiend that took her from me."

"Were you planning to marry her?" The inspector blurted out the question without thinking.

"Marry her?" Henry repeated, his tone incredulous. He shook himself slightly as though he couldn't quite believe what he'd heard. "Good God, no. Why would you suggest such a vile thing!"

"Excuse me, Inspector," Bladestone interrupted again, "but you don't quite understand. We've reason to believe that Annie Shields was Henry's daughter."

"And then, Mrs. Jeffries, this Henry Albritton practically insisted I come along home with him and arrest all his relations." Witherspoon picked up his glass of sherry and

took a gulp. "The poor man was at his wit's end, I tell
you. He's got a whole passel of relatives, none of whom
he likes, and Albritton, of course, can't decide which
one of them actually murdered Annie Shields. At one
point during the conversation he seemed to think they'd
all done it." He sighed wearily. "I don't see why this
couldn't have been a simple case of robbery. Just my
luck, isn't it? I get stuck with what looks like a very
nice, easy crime, and before you can snap your fingers
we're up to our elbows in complications, melodramat-
ic lawyers, greedy relations and a host of other loose
ends."

Mrs. Jeffries smiled sympathetically. Poor Witherspoon, he was in an awful state. For that matter, so
was the rest of the household. "Not to worry, sir. I'm
sure all the pieces will soon fall into place. They always
do. Now, sir. What else did you learn today?"

She listened carefully as he told her everything, beginning with his arrival at the morgue to his meeting with
Harlan Bladestone and Henry Albritton. Mrs. Jeffries
occasionally interjected with a question, but for the most
part, she listened carefully, filing away every little detail
in the back of her mind.

"So Henry Albritton is convinced that Annie Shields
was his illegitimate daughter?" she finally said.

"Virtually. Unfortunately, he'd only met the girl a
couple of weeks ago." He broke off and glanced at the
clock on the mantelpiece. "So he hadn't really established a relationship with her. I say, what time is dinner?"

Mrs. Jeffries curbed her impatience. "In about ten
minutes, sir. But from what you just told me, it seems
that Harlan Bladestone had suspected that Annie Shields
was Mr. Albritton's daughter for over a year. Why did
he take so long to tell him?"

"Because Bladestone wasn't sure." Witherspoon took off his spectacles and rubbed his eyes. "You see, he met Mrs. Shields last year when her husband was killed in an accident. Mrs. Shields had come to his office to see if she had a case of negligence against the brewery, but she didn't. The moment she entered the office, Bladestone noticed how much she resembled Dora Borden—that's the young woman Henry Albritton was in love with before he married Frances Strutts. Er, a, she's the one he married for money."

Confused, Mrs. Jeffries said, "But I thought you said that Mr. Albritton's wife had died. If Bladestone thought Annie looked like the woman Henry was once passionately in love with, why didn't he mention it to him?"

"Bladestone didn't want to upset Albritton. Furthermore, he wasn't sure that Annie Shields had had any connection at all with Dora Borden. He wasn't going to say anything to Albritton until he knew for certain if Annie was Dora's daughter."

"Why didn't he ask Annie when she came to his office?"

"He did," Witherspoon replied. "But Annie had no idea. Her mother died when she was a baby and she had been raised in an orphanage."

"Surely the orphanage kept records," Mrs. Jeffries persisted.

"It burned down five years ago." The inspector took another sip. "And all the records went up in flames as well. The truth was, the only thing Annie had known about her past was that she was illegitimate and that her mother was dead. She'd no idea who her father was."

"So let me see if I have this right," Mrs. Jeffries said slowly. "Bladestone notices the resemblance between

Annie Shields and the woman his client had loved and
abandoned twenty years ago, is that correct?"

"Yes."

"And he immediately sets about inquiring as to who
Annie's parents were, correct?"

"Correct." Witherspoon's stomach growled and he
took another quick peek at the clock.

"Then can we assume that Bladestone knew that Dora
Borden had been expecting a child? Otherwise why would
he begin the inquiries at all? I mean, if you meet someone
who looks like someone else, you don't immediately
assume there's a family relationship."

"I wondered the very same thing," Witherspoon
replied. Actually, it had been Barnes who'd raised
this issue with the solicitor. "Bladestone assured me
he hadn't known about Dora's condition at the time she
was expecting the child. But several years later he'd run
into a mutual acquaintance who'd mentioned that Dora
Borden had died during childbirth. When he asked *when*
she'd died, he'd realized there was a real possibility the
child might be Henry Albritton's."

"Did he tell Mr. Albritton?"

"No, at that time Albritton's wife was still alive and he
didn't think it would be wise to say anything. However,
Bladestone made some inquiries to try to find the child,
but he wasn't successful."

"I still don't understand. Bladestone thought Annie
Shields was Henry's daughter for over a year. Yet he
said nothing. Why? Albritton's wife is now safely dead,
so it's not as if she would be hurt by the knowledge."

"I gather Albritton's had a few problems with melancholy and, well, depression the past couple of years.
Bladestone didn't want the man to be upset or disappointed in case it turned out Annie's resemblance to

Dora Borden was merely a coincidence. So the upshot of it was, Bladestone said nothing until two weeks ago."

"What happened then?"

"It seems Albritton finally told Bladestone he was so miserable with his life, he was going to sell off his boatyards and move away." Witherspoon's eyebrows rose. "Bladestone was rather alarmed. I gather Albritton had gotten involved with radical politics. He thought that if Henry saw the girl and perhaps made some inquiries as to who she was, well, perhaps that would give him a new perspective about his life."

"Oh dear, how sad." Mrs. Jeffries wasn't sure she followed precisely what the inspector was saying, but she was sure she could sort it out later. "So he did actually meet Annie Shields?"

"Oh my, yes." Witherspoon smiled. "He's been buying enormous bunches of flowers from her every day for the past two weeks. And tipping her generously. I think it was his way of giving her money. Thank goodness he *was* tipping the girl; her employer at Covent Garden certainly wasn't wasting any of his time mourning the poor woman. I can't imagine what he must have been like to work for!"

"Did you learn anything useful there?" Mrs. Jeffries asked.

"Not really." The inspector sighed. "Dreadful, how hard some of these poor girls have to work to make a living. Absolutely dreadful. Oh, before I forget, we may be interrupted this evening. I left instructions at the police station that I was to be informed immediately when Emma Shields was located. So don't be alarmed if you hear someone knocking on the door in the middle of the night."

"Thank you for telling me, sir." Mrs. Jeffries got up.

"I do hope they find the little girl before too long."

"So do I, Mrs. Jeffries, so do I."

Hatchet was outraged. Eyes blazing and chest puffed up like a bullfrog's, he gazed resolutely at his fellow sufferers. "This is war, you know."

"War! Crimminey, all they did was get the jump on us with this murder," Wiggins protested. He'd calmed down some now that he'd had a few minutes to think about it.

"Don't be naive." The butler began pacing the length of his elegantly appointed rooms. Rooms that now contained three vases of fresh flowers. "Those women deliberately kept us in the dark. They're out to prove a point. They're out to prove they're superior to men." He stopped and straightened his spine. "And they'll stop at nothing to achieve their ends."

"Don't you think you're bein' a bit dramatic, Hatchet," Smythe said. He propped his feet up on a footstool and watched the agitated butler start pacing again. Cor blimey, if he weren't careful, he was goin' to walk a hole in that fine Belgian rug.

"I most certainly am not." Hatchet flung out his arms. "Are you two blind? Don't you understand what this means? If we let them get away with this, before you know it they'll want to run for Parliament, they'll demand to be let on the police force, they'll take over the banks, the schools, the hospitals. Soon no place will be safe for man nor beast."

"What do ya suggest we do?" Smythe rather enjoyed the butler's outrage. Made a change from listenin' to Wiggins's awful poetry.

Hatchet's expression grew thoughtful. Finally he said, "I think we must teach them a lesson."

Smythe snorted and Wiggins giggled.

Hatchet glared at both of them. "I fail to see what's so amusing."

"And how we goin' to be teachin' this lesson?" the coachman asked. "Don't matter much what we say, the truth is, they's a pretty sharp lot."

"Sometimes"—Hatchet smiled slightly—"it takes more than intelligence to achieve one's end. Sometimes, one has to be as sly as a fox and as merciless as a banker."

" 'Old on now." Smythe sat up. "What're you suggestin'?"

"If you'll give me a moment to explain. I wasn't suggesting anything untoward or improper. I was merely thinking that with this new murder, we've the perfect opportunity to show those heartless women exactly how much they need us."

"How we goin' to do that?" Wiggins asked.

"It's very simple, my boy." Hatchet gave them a wide smile. "With this case, we'll just have to make sure that we solve it first."

"But Mrs. Jeffries is usually the one that comes up with the answer," Wiggins protested. If the truth were known, Wiggins wasn't all that sure they could solve the case on their own. Mrs. Jeffries had somethin'. Somethin' special.

"Admittedly, that's the way it's been in the past," Hatchet said. "But that's no reason to think we're not as capable as she is of finding a killer."

"Bloomin' Ada," Smythe exclaimed, "we don't even know for sure the women was deliberately tryin' to keep this one to themselves! Wiggins only heard part of a conversation. For all we know, they might have 'eard about the murder after we left the 'ouse today."

"Oh no," Wiggins put in, "that's not so. We was both in ta lunch. Besides, I 'eard what that feller said to Mrs. Goodge. He said he'd got her message this afternoon. That means she musta sent it sometime this mornin'. Remember how funny she acted when we asked where everybody was."

"Of course they knew about the murder. Probaby fairly early this morning too. And as I recall, Madam slunk out of here like a thief in the night right after breakfast." Hatchet shook his head, his expression stubborn. "She was up to something, all right."

"Look"—the coachman gave up trying to reason with the other two—"you might be right. Maybe the women is tryin' to get the jump on us. We'll know tonight. If they say nuthin' about the murder, then we'll know they's tryin' to keep it to themselves."

"Indeed we will," Hatchet muttered. "If Luty Belle Crookshank thinks she can investigate a murder without me, well, she's got another think coming."

As soon as the inspector had retired for the evening, Mrs. Jeffries hurried down to the kitchen. She was eager to hear what the others had found out.

Betsy and Mrs. Goodge were waiting for her at the kitchen table. "Luty's not back yet," the cook said as Mrs. Jeffries took her usual seat, "and it's gettin' a mite late. I'm afraid the men's going to show up before she gets here."

"The men's already showed up."

They turned and saw Smythe and Wiggins, who had entered the house with unnatural quiet, standing just inside the kitchen near the entrance to the back hallway.

"Good." Mrs. Jeffries gave them a bright smile. "I'm so glad you're back. There's been a murder."

Some of the suspicion left Smythe's eyes and Wiggins visibly relaxed. "Well, looks like we come home just in time, then." Smythe strolled towards the table. "Good thing I cut Bow and Arrow's run short, or I'da missed this." He pulled out a chair and gave them a cocky grin. "Who's been murdered, then?"

Mrs. Jeffries, knowing darned good and well that neither man was surprised to learn of the homicide, decided to plunge straight in. After all, the women were already ahead of them. In good conscience, she couldn't exclude them further. "A young flower seller by the name of Annie Shields. She was bludgeoned late last night."

"Ah . . . Mrs. Jeffries," Wiggins said nervously, darting a quick glance at the coachman. "Maybe you'd better wait a minute to start. I think Hatchet might be on his way over."

"Really? How very convenient," Mrs. Jeffries replied. "We're waiting for Luty Belle too. Isn't it a remarkable coincidence that all of us should end up here when none of you even knew a murder had taken place?"

Smythe sighed. Irritated as he was with the women, it wasn't in his nature to play coy. "We knew there was a murder, Mrs. J," he said bluntly. "Wiggins overheard Mrs. Goodge pumpin' someone earlier today when he nipped back 'ere."

"Why didn't you come into the kitchen and get that ruddy sausage machine?" Mrs. Goodge asked, frowning at the footman.

"I, uh, didn't 'ave time."

Smythe ignored them and ploughed straight ahead. He wanted to clear the air. "And fer a while today, we was afraid you ladies was tempted to keep this one fer yerselves."

"We'd never do that," Betsy exclaimed.

He raised one eyebrow as he looked at her. "Then why didn't you mention the murder when Wiggins was 'ere earlier? Then we coulda all gotten started."

"How could I tell Wiggins anythin' if he was tip-toeing about eavesdropping," Mrs. Goodge snapped. Of course, it was an out-an-out prevarication. She'd seen the footman several times since learning of the murder and she'd seen both of them at lunch.

"I weren't tiptoein' about tryin' to listen to people," Wiggins shot back. "I come back for that bloomin' contraption and 'eard you goin' off behind our backs investigatin' a murder."

"Why shouldn't we try to get a bit ahead of you," Betsy said angrily. "After all them nasty things you men was sayin' about us. It's only natural we'd look for an advantage. It's not like *I* can go out pub-crawlin' at night lookin' for clues." It had long been a sore point for the maid that Smythe's activities weren't restricted to the daylight hours as hers were.

"We wasn't sayin' nasty things," Smythe protested. He was truly astounded that she'd taken such deep offense at what he'd thought was merely a spirited exchange of views. Blimey, maybe he shoulda made Hatchet give 'em back the flowers. He'd known her nose was out of joint, but he hadn't thought she'd still be steamin' over it. On the other hand, perhaps he shouldn't have made that comment about females being weak-minded and overly emotional during the full of the moon. Come to think of it, it had been a fairly stupid thing to say.

"Now, now," Mrs. Jeffries interrupted, "please calm down. This is getting us nowhere. We've already discussed our various opinions about the rights of women and I don't think any of us are going to change our views. But in case you've forgotten, we do have a murder to investigate here."

"What about Luty Belle and Hatchet?" Mrs. Goodge asked.

Mrs. Jeffries paused and then flicked a quick look at the clock. "We'll give them another few minutes and then we'll start. In the meantime I think we could all do with a spot of tea."

By the time Betsy was putting the pot on the table, they heard the back door open. Fred, who'd snuck down to the kitchen in hopes of cadging a treat off Wiggins, shot out from under the chair and scampered down the hall, barking joyously.

"Splendid, splendid," Hatchet's strong voice rang out. "Good dog, that's right, always guard your castle." He and the animal, who was now bouncing so hard at his feet that poor Hatchet practically had to skip and hop his way into the kitchen, took their spots at the table.

"Good evening, Hatchet," Mrs. Jeffries said.

He swept off his black top hat and pulled out a chair. "Good evening, everyone," he said, his tone formal and frosty.

Betsy and Mrs. Goodge exchanged a quick grin and even Mrs. Jeffries hid a smile. As Luty Belle would say, Hatchet had a bee in his bonnet about something and Mrs. Jeffries was fairly certain she knew exactly what it was.

"I'm so glad you're here," she said, "we've been waiting for you."

"Waiting for me?" he asked archly. He sniffed delicately. "Whatever for? I only decided to come round to see if Madam was here." He gave them a cool smile. "She's been gone all day on some mysterious errand of her own. An errand that she refused to talk about. You ladies wouldn't, by any chance, happen to know where she might be?"

"They knows, Hatchet," Wiggins said. "We've already 'ad a right old to-do about it and they claims they was only tryin' to get a bit of a jump on us, not keep us out completely."

"Really?" Hatchet stared straight at Mrs. Jeffries.

She couldn't stop herself, she laughed. "Really, Hatchet. Did you honestly think we'd try and investigate a murder without the valuable services of the male of the species?"

His features eased, the ghost of a smile softening his stiff mouth. "Well . . ." he said doubtfully. Then he laughed. "Of course not, though I will admit Wiggins and Smythe and I had rather a good time today imagining the worst and doing some plotting of our own."

Mrs. Jeffries sagged in relief as she saw the tight faces around the table relax. Like the steam off the teapot, the tension seemed to evaporate into thin air. No doubt they'd all enjoyed their dramatics, but none of them really wanted to damage the sense of camaraderie working on a case always gave each and every one of them. Well, not too much, she thought, noticing the determined lift of Betsy's chin and the sheer brightness of Smythe's brown eyes. "Good. I'm so glad you enjoyed yourselves. Now, should we wait for Luty or should I go ahead and start?"

"Why don't you go ahead and start," Hatchet said smoothly. "I can always tell Madam everything she's missed on the drive home."

Several other voices murmured agreement, so Mrs. Jeffries cleared her throat and started. She told them everything the inspector had told her earlier.

"Did the inspector give you the names of these relations this Mr. Albritton wanted arrested?" Smythe asked.

"I got them from him over dinner," she replied. She whipped a piece of paper out of the pocket of her stiff brown skirt. "There were so many of them, I wrote them down . . . let me see, well, first of all, there's Henry Albritton himself. He could have had his own reasons for murdering Annie Shields."

"Why would he do that and then raise such a fuss with the police?" Wiggins asked.

She shrugged. "I don't know, I'm merely saying that we mustn't take him or anyone else connected with this case at face value."

Betsy asked, "How many relations has he got? I mean, how many suspects have we got?"

"Several." Mrs. Jeffries frowned at her handwriting. She'd scribbled the names in such haste, she could barely make them out. "There's Albritton's sister-in-law, Lydia Franklin. She's lived in the household for years. Then there's Gordon Strutts and his wife, Hortense. Strutts is also one of Albritton's late wife's relations . . . let's see. I think that's the only ones actually living in the Albritton house."

"What about the solicitor, this Harlan Bladestone?" Smythe reached for his mug. "Seems to me he might be a suspect too."

"Why do you think so?" Mrs. Jeffries asked curiously. The coachman was very intelligent and perceptive. She had a lot of respect for his opinion.

He took a long, slow sip before answering. "Well, by 'is own admission, 'e's known Annie Shields for a long time. She come to 'im askin' for legal advice when her husband were killed. From what we've 'eard, Annie might 'ave been a comely lass. A widow. Maybe the victim and the solicitor knew each other a bit better than 'e let on."

"Annie wasn't like that," Betsy protested.

"How do you know?" Hatchet asked.

" 'Cause I learned a lot about her today," she replied. "And since David Shields was killed, she's not looked at another man."

"You do seem to have heard quite a bit," Mrs. Jeffries said encouragingly. "Do go on, I've finished with what I had to say."

Betsy smiled smugly. "All right, if you're sure you're finished. I spoke to one of Annie's friends today. A girl named Muriel. She said Annie kept to herself and worked hard. There's been several men who were interested, one more persistent than the others, but she didn't want nuthin' to do with any of 'em."

"Who was the persistent feller?" Smythe asked.

"A man named Bill Calloway." Betsy frowned. "I think we should definitely put him on our suspect list. Accordin' to what Muriel told me, he'd been hangin' about Annie Shields for ages. On the day of the murder, she'd gotten fed up with him and told him to leave her alone. Said she never wanted to see him again. Did it publicly too. Muriel said that Calloway looked angry enough to wring Annie's neck, only there were a police constable on the street, so he didn't quite dare lay a finger on her."

"But if he were in love with Annie," Wiggins said innocently, "surely he wouldn't hurt her."

They all stared at him incredulously.

"Who said he were in love with 'er?" Smythe retorted. "And even if 'e were, that don't mean he didn't do it. More women's been murdered in the name of love than for any other reason. Least that's what the man always says."

"Disgusting," Betsy interjected. "But true. I remember

when I was a little girl, the man living in the rooms next to ours almost killed his wife just because he'd seen her talking to another man." Her eyes grew troubled and distant as she recalled the ugly memory. "He half beat the poor woman to death and no one did anything at all about it. It was horrible. All that screamin' and cryin'. My sisters and I were so scared, we clung to each other and hid under the blanket till it stopped. That was even worse. There was just this awful silence."

They all stared at her. She looked down at the table.

"Sisters," Wiggins muttered.

Smythe motioned for him to be quiet. "Betsy, lass," he said softly. His voice seemed to draw her back into the room and she gazed around, blushing as she saw everyone watching her. "That must have been really 'orrible for you."

She nodded slowly. "It was." She laughed nervously. "But that was life in the East End. Always someone screamin' and cryin' and carryin' on about something." She picked up her cup of tea and quickly took a drink.

Wiggins opened his mouth to ask the question they were all thinking, but Mrs. Jeffries quickly said, "What else did you find out about Calloway?"

"He don't seem to have a position, but he's always got coins in his pocket, if you know what I mean." Betsy cleared her throat and then continued, her voice slightly off pitch. "Annie didn't trust him. She told Muriel she thought Calloway might be part of a ring of thieves. Calloway hangs about at a tavern on Pinchin Street down at the docks."

"What's the name of this tavern?" Smythe asked.

"The Sail and Anchor," she replied. "Why? You thinkin' of goin' over there?"

"Don't you think that'd be a good idea? You just said yerself that he might be a suspect."

"Well, yes," she admitted slowly, a suspicious frown creasing her forehead. "But I was kinda hopin' to nip over that way myself tomorrow."

"Don't be daft, girl," Mrs. Goodge exclaimed.

"You can't go into a place like that all on your own," Wiggins said.

"Absolutely out of the question." Hatchet sniffed.

"You'll go over my dead body," Smythe muttered, but he mumbled the words so softly only Betsy heard them.

"Betsy, for once I'm forced to agree with the others," Mrs. Jeffries said.

Betsy shot Smythe a puzzled glance and then turned towards the housekeeper. "But why? I've gone to the East End on me own before."

"You weren't quite alone, Miss Betsy," Hatchet said smoothly. "If you'll recall, I went along as well." He'd gone when they were searching for a missing woman on one of their other cases. Because of Betsy's familiarity with the district, it had only been logical that she should go and find the person they were seeking. But as a precaution, Hatchet had trotted along for protection. Irritated as he was with the ladies about some of their recent radical ideas and featherbrained thinking, he certainly wasn't going to let one of them put herself in danger.

"But you didn't go marchin' in and out of sailors' taverns on the last trip," Smythe shot back. "It's too bloomin' dangerous, you silly woman."

"Silly woman!" Betsy yelped.

"You don't need to be screamin' like a banshee now." He leaned towards her, his face set in a fierce frown. "There's nuthin' wrong with my 'earin.'"

"But there's somethin' wrong with your brain," she argued.

Wiggins, Hatchet and Mrs. Goodge jumped into the discussion. The conversation became so heated that none of them heard the back door open or the heavy footsteps.

"Where should I put her?" The voice was loud and unfamiliar.

They all turned and looked. A man holding a huge blanket-wrapped bundle cradled against his chest stood in the doorway next to Luty Belle.

"Well, madam," Hatchet said pompously as he rose to his feet. "It's about time you got here."

"Evenin', everybody," Luty said cheerfully. She jabbed her parasol in the direction of the butler. "Give her to that feller there," she ordered. Hatchet pushed back his chair and started across the room.

The driver, for that's what he was, a hansom driver, gave his bundle to the puzzled-looking Hatchet, tipped his hat, pocketed Luty's fare money and generous tip and took off out the way he'd come.

Hatchet stared at the bundle in his arms. "Madam," he said, "precisely what is it you've thrust upon me?"

From inside the bundle came a loud wail. Startled, Hatchet lifted his hand and threw back the top of the blanket.

A teary-faced child with brown curly hair and big blue eyes stared back at him.

"Well, I never."

The little girl gazed at Hatchet through her tears for a moment and then broke into a huge grin.

"Luty," Mrs. Jeffries said slowly. She couldn't take her eyes off the child and the stiff-necked butler who was now smiling so broadly it was a wonder his cheeks didn't burst. "Is that who I think it is?"

Luty sighed heavily. "Now, before you all go gettin' all het, I brung her here 'cause I didn't have no choice."

The child giggled, poked her hands out of the blanket and yanked at Hatchet's stiff collar.

"This here's Emma," Luty continued. "Annie's daughter."

CHAPTER 5

There was a moment of stunned silence as they each understood the exact implications of what Luty had done. Even Fred, who'd been sniffing the bottom of the blankets in Hatchet's arms, stopped wagging his tail and stared at the elderly American.

Then they all started talking at once.

"Good heavens, madam," Hatchet exclaimed, "what have you gotten us into now?" Emma squirmed and he obligingly tossed the blankets off and lowered her gently to the floor.

"We're really in the soup now," Mrs. Goodge added.

"Crimminey, the inspector'll 'ear about this for sure," Wiggins moaned.

"Luty, have you lost your mind? Bringin' the girl back here?" Betsy stood up. "That's all we need!"

"Now, before all of you decide I've gone loco," Luty began, "just hear me out. Like I said, I had to bring Emma here; otherwise, she'd have been put in an orphanage."

"Better that than the inspector sussin' out what we've been up to," Wiggins muttered.

"Oh, come now, madam," Hatchet snapped. "Surely there must have been another way."

"What we goin' to tell 'im when he finds out Luty took Emma?" Betsy wrung her hands. "And he's bound to find out. Mrs. Jeffries says he got coppers combin' the area lookin' for the girl. They'll find out she was taken by an American and then, sure as the sun follows the stars, they'll find out you brought her here. The first thing he'll want to know was why you was snoopin' about in one of his cases! And he ain't daft. He'll soon find out we've all been snoopin'."

"I really think everyone ought to watch what they're sayin'," Smythe said softly, his gaze directed at the child. He nodded in Emma's direction and gave her a gentle smile. "We wouldn't want her to think she was unwelcome."

But no one listened to him.

Hatchet continued berating his employer, Betsy and Mrs. Goodge were loudly lamenting the death of their detective days, and Wiggins was adding his tuppence worth as Luty vigorously defended her actions. Mrs. Jeffries said nothing. She was too busy thinking.

Fred, sniffing the discarded blankets, got excited by the raised voices. He woofed in confusion and bounced up and down. Emma, who'd been staring at the adults with a bewildered expression on her little face, whirled around. She saw the prancing dog and started to wail. Turning frantically, she spotted Smythe sitting calmly at the table and smiling at her. Emma took off for him at a dead run.

Fred dashed after her. Emma screamed as she heard his paws pounding on her heels. The big coachman opened his arms, scooped her into his lap and chucked her under the chin.

"Now, now, lass," he soothed. "There's nothing to be scared of. Fred's just a big friendly dog, that's all." He reached down and calmed the dog with a quiet word. Fred plopped down on his rump and nudged his head against Smythe's knees.

Emma stopped crying and watched as he slowly stroked Fred's head. She stuck out her hand, hesitated for a brief moment and then reached down and imitated his motions. She giggled as the animal licked her fingers.

Emma's outburst shut them all up.

"You've got a right nice way with younguns," Luty said.

"Cor blimey." Wiggins grinned. "You've sure charmed the little un."

"Thank goodness you kept your head," Hatchet agreed. "We really must watch raising our voices. No wonder the poor child was frightened."

"You ought to have a couple of your own," Mrs. Goodge said sagely. "Looks to me like you'd make a good father."

"Indeed," Mrs. Jeffries agreed. "Smythe does seem to have the knack. He did know how best to handle what is a very unusual situation."

The only one who didn't say anything, Smythe noticed, was Betsy. She simply stared at him and the child on his lap with one of those odd, female expressions where you hadn't a ruddy clue as to what was going on in her head. He would have given a lot to be able to read minds at that moment. Especially Betsy's.

Mrs. Goodge stood up. "Let me get the girl a bun to chew on," she said, hurrying towards the dry larder down the hallway. "Never seen a little one yet that didn't like sweet buns."

"Is she hungry, then?" Wiggins asked.

Luty shook her head. "No, Florrie fed her right afore we left."

"Who's that?" Betsy asked.

"The woman who was mindin' her for her . . ." Her voice trailed off. "You know, her *m-o-t-h-e-r*." She spelled the word out and gazed anxiously at the child. But Emma was too busy patting Fred to notice anything going on around her.

"Listen now," Luty continued. "I knows I was takin' a risk bringing the youngun with me. But I had to do something. Florrie Maxwell and her family was leavin' tonight and she was fixin' to take the child to the orphanage or the foundlin' hospital afore she went. She ain't goin' to be back fer a while, so they's no way the police can find out I took the girl. Who's gonna tell 'em?"

"I should think a whole host of informants could tell them," Hatchet said. "The neighbours, local tradespeople, shopkeepers—"

"Don't worry about it, Luty," Mrs. Jeffries interrupted the butler's morose litany. "What's done is done. I daresay, I, for one, think you did just the right thing. We'll think of something. Even if the inspector does discover you were the one who took Emma, he won't necessarily connect that act with all of us helping him solve his cases. Let's not go anticipating the worst."

Hatchet snorted in disbelief.

Luty shot him a glare. "You can stop acting so high-and-mighty, Hatchet. Seems to me this is a bit like the pot calling the kettle black. Who was it that come draggin' Jon home a few months ago?"

"That's hardly the same thing, madam," he protested. "Jon didn't have anywhere to go . . ." His voice trailed off as he realized that Luty had neatly trapped him.

"Just what I said," she said smugly, "and that poor little gal didn't have no place to go neither."

"Give it up, Hatchet," Smythe said softly. "Sometimes the ladies are right. Lettin' this child go to one of them orphanages wouldna been right."

"Here you are, ducks." Mrs. Goodge bustled up to the table and put a plate of buns in front of Emma. The child immediately ceased petting Fred and snatched up her treat. Wiggins reached for one as well, but the cook swatted his hand back.

"Ow," the footman yelped.

"You let that child eat her fill before you start stuffin' in yer mouth," she warned.

"We really must get on," Mrs. Jeffries said. She glanced at Hatchet. "Can you tell Luty everything on the drive home?" He nodded. "Good. Now, Luty, did you learn anything useful other than Emma's whereabouts?"

"Sure did." Luty told them about her meeting with Harry Grafton. "So, you see, Annie was wearin' the ring when she was ki . . ." She faltered and glanced at the child. But Emma, her mouth caked with bread crumbs, had fallen asleep against Smythe's massively broad chest. "You know."

"So it could have been nothin' more than a robbery." Betsy frowned thoughtfully. "If she was showin' that opal off in the pub, there's lots that could of seen her. But that don't sound right either. Accordin' to what Muriel said, Annie Shields knew how to take care of herself and she were careful."

"Perhaps this one time she wasn't careful," Mrs. Jeffries said.

"And she was wearin' that ring to show it off," Luty added. "That's what Harry told me. He and his wife had been onto her about wearin' it out at night. Annie had told him she had to, that she was goin' to show it to someone."

"The truth is, we have no idea whether or not she was killed for the ring or for some other reason," Mrs. Jeffries said firmly. "We don't have enough evidence to make any assumptions. Furthermore, the inspector's information has definitely been interesting. If Harlan Bladestone and Henry Albritton are correct, there are several other suspects with a motive for murder."

"Who's that? What other suspects?" Luty demanded.

Hatchet gave her an evil grin. "I'm afraid you'll have to rely on me to tell you, madam. You mustn't expect everyone to repeat themselves. It's getting too late."

"Hmmph." Luty's eyes narrowed. "Well, then, maybe I won't be so eager to tell ya what else I learned today."

"Oh now, Luty." Mrs. Jeffries determined it was time to intervene. They had enough troubles now with Luty having spirited Emma right into their midst. Whatever rivalries were brewing would just have to wait until the next case. "Please go on. We've really got enough on our plates to worry about at the moment without everyone getting secretive."

"All right," Luty agreed reluctantly. "I found out that someone's been sendin' Annie"—another quick glance towards the coachman to make sure Emma was still sleeping—"money."

"How often?" Smythe asked softly.

"Every week. Come in cash and was delivered to her lodgin' house by a young man."

"Who was sendin' it?" Wiggins asked.

"Florrie didn't know." Luty shrugged. "Annie was real closemouthed when it come to money."

Smythe shifted the sleeping child slightly. "What day did it come on?"

Luty smiled. "Every Monday mornin', like clockwork."

"Interesting," Mrs. Jeffries murmured. "Very interesting." The more she learned about Annie Shields, the more she was convinced that this was no simple robbery gone awry. "When did the payments start?"

"Right after Annie's husband was killed," Luty replied. "That's why Florrie was pretty sure that someone in David's family was the one sendin' the cash. She thought it was just his relations helpin' the widow out some."

"Maybe it was a settlement for her husband's death," Mrs. Goodge suggested.

"Oh no," Mrs. Jeffries assured everyone. "That's not true. Inspector Witherspoon told me specifically that the brewery had no liability in the accident that killed David Shields. Annie Shields had gone to the solicitor Bladestone for that very reason. That was how he'd met her in the first place. Bladestone also told her she had no case."

Luty tossed another disgruntled frown at Hatchet. "I hope you remember who everyone is," she told him. " 'Cause I ain't got a clue who you're all talkin' about."

Mrs. Jeffries smiled. "Did you find out anything else?"

"Not really," Luty admitted. "Harvey Maxwell, that's Florrie's boy, told me he'd seen some veiled lady hangin' around Emma. But I don't set much store by it."

"Why not?" Wiggins asked.

" 'Cause when I questioned him about it, he couldn't remember when he'd seen this woman, or how many times he'd seen her, or whether she was tall, short, fat, thin or walked bowlegged." Luty grinned. "Besides, his ma brought Emma in just as Harvey was tellin' me all this and Florrie told me not to pay him any mind. Said Harvey's got a history of tellin' some pretty tall tales."

Emma whimpered in her sleep. Smythe soothed her with a gentle pat on her back. "The little one's tired. She needs to get to bed."

Hatchet started to get up. "I'll take her."

"Before you go," Mrs. Jeffries said quickly, "we really must decide who is going to do what tomorrow."

The butler nodded and sat back down.

"I've got to try and find a woman named Millie Groggins," Betsy said. She shot Smythe a quick, impatient frown. "Seein' as Smythe has decided I'm not fit to set foot in a tavern . . ."

"I told ya," he shot back in a loud whisper, "it's too ruddy dangerous."

The maid ignored him. "I'd best see if Millie can tell me anything. Accordin' to Muriel, Millie was on the Strand that night, the same as Annie." Betsy deliberately didn't tell them that Millie's occupation was decidedly not a flower seller. She really didn't need Smythe or Wiggins, or for that matter even Mrs. Jeffries or the cook, trying to tell her not to be seen talking to a prostitute. She could take care of herself.

"Who's Millie?" Wiggins asked interestedly.

"She, uh, worked with Annie," Betsy replied.

"I'll pop round the Sail and Anchor," Smythe offered. "Even if Calloway's not about, maybe one of 'is mates will know where I can find 'im."

"See what you can learn about Henry Albritton as well," Mrs. Jeffries said.

"Albritton?" Smythe looked puzzled. "Now, why would he be killin' his own flesh and blood?"

"Flesh and blood!" Luty yelped. "Now, this is gettin' plum loco. Who the dickens is this Albritton?"

"I'll tell you later, madam," Hatchet said impatiently. "We can't sit here all night explaining every little detail."

"Annie Shields was probably Henry Albritton's illegitimate daughter," Mrs. Jeffries said quickly, reaching over and patting Luty's hand. "Hatchet will tell you all about it. Do you think you can find out about a woman named Lydia Franklin? She's part of Albritton's household. His sister-in-law, as a matter of fact."

Somewhat mollified, Luty nodded. "Where do they all live?"

"On Linley Close. That's just off the Edgeware Road." Mrs. Jeffries turned to Wiggins. "And could you nip over there tomorrow morning and see what you can find out about Hortense Strutts."

"What about 'er 'usband?" the footman queried.

"Of course," the housekeeper replied, "but I was also going to ask Hatchet to see what he can find out about Mr. Gordon Strutts." She gave the butler an encouraging smile. "You have so many different sources of information, I was rather hoping you'd see what you could learn about all the gentlemen involved in this case."

Hatchet smiled slightly, but he was pleased as punch. "That would be Albritton, Gordon Strutts and the solicitor Harlan Bladestone."

"Nell's bells," Luty exploded. "I'm a few minutes late and you've got more suspects than there are fleas on a dog."

They all ignored her outburst. Hatchet did have truly remarkable information sources. He easily knew someone in every gentleman's club in London. He also knew butlers, footmen, cabbies and a host of odd and rather colorful individuals.

"Exactly, Hatchet," Mrs. Jeffries replied. "Learn what you can about all of them. It would be most helpful to see if you can determine their whereabouts last night."

"In other words," Hatchet said cheerfully, "determine if they have alibis."

"I expect you want me to do my usual?" Mrs. Goodge asked.

"Of course," Mrs. Jeffries said. She rose to her feet and they all followed suit.

"Good, now that we've got a name to work with, so to speak," Mrs. Goodge muttered, "we'll see what we can find out." A name to her meant someone who moved in society. "My poor cousin's boy did the best he could," she explained. "But he really didn't know much about the victim. Claimed some around there weren't surprised about the killin' and most seemed to think it weren't robbery. But when I questioned Augustine a bit further, it turned out he was only repeatin' what he'd heard. He didn't know a bloomin' thing and he didn't have the ruddy sense to ask. But not to worry, I sent him back with a flea in his ear, and when he comes round on Thursday, I expect he'll know a few facts. Considerin' where he works, he should have learned somethin' by then."

"Here"—Hatchet reached for the sleeping child—"I'll carry her out to the carriage."

"Leave her ta me," Smythe said softly as he cradled the child tenderly against his chest. "I don't want us jostlin' her and wakin' her up. She might get scared seein' as we're all strangers to 'er."

"All right." Hatchet turned to Luty. "Are you ready to leave, madam?"

"Might as well." Luty rose to her feet. "I expect you'll jaw my ears off once we get home, might as well git it over with."

"Don't worry," Mrs. Jeffries said cheerfully, "we'll think of something to tell Inspector Witherspoon should he find out you took Emma."

"Poor little thing." Mrs. Goodge gazed sympathetically at the bundle in Smythe's arms. Then she looked at Luty. "What *are* you going to do with her?"

Luty shrugged. "Keep her fer a few days, I reckon. Maybe by then we'll know what kinda man this Albritton feller is. If'n he's decent and he turns out to be Emma's flesh and blood, maybe we'll take her round to him. But I sure as shootin' wasn't going to let her git dumped in some orphanage like she was a sack of flour."

As they said their good-nights Mrs. Jeffries noticed that Betsy watched Smythe carrying the sleeping child down the hall. Admiration and respect shone in her eyes. Considering how the maid and the coachman were frequently sparring with one another, Mrs. Jeffries thought Betsy's attitude rather telling. Goodness, she thought with an inward smile, the girl's staring at him like she expects him to sprout a halo and wings.

The Albritton house was located in one of the more fashionable areas off the Edgeware Road. The huge four-story Georgian structure of pale beige brick and white-trimmed windows stood at the end of the street, surrounded by its own garden and backing up against the grounds of St. Phillips Church.

Witherspoon gazed mournfully at his reflection in the ornate hall mirror as he and Barnes waited for the butler to return with his master. "Still no word on little Emma?" he asked.

"PC Popper reported they've located the house where the child was stayin', but it looks like the woman that was takin' care of Emma has gone to visit relations somewhere up in Leicestershire."

"Was the child with her?" Witherspoon asked hopefully.

"The neighbours didn't know," Barnes said. "But from everything Popper heard about Florrie Maxwell, she sounds like a decent woman. Not the kind to just abandon the girl."

"Do we know *where* in Leicestershire this Florrie Maxwell went?"

Barnes shook his head. "Not really, sir. One of the neighbours seemed to think it was some village outside Leicester, but another neighbour insists the Maxwells aren't in Leicestershire but at Nottingham. We're still trying to get it all sorted out, sir."

"Drat."

"Inspector Witherspoon," Henry Albritton exclaimed as he dashed into the hall. "A good morning to you, sir, and to you as well, Constable. Do please come into the drawing room. I'm sure you've an enormous number of questions you need to ask me. I do apologize for being in such a state yesterday. I daresay I was still in a state of shock. Do come this way, please."

Albritton swept them into the drawing room. The walls were covered with emerald-green-and-white-striped wallpaper. Emerald-green velvet curtains tied back with elaborate tassels surrounded three large windows which overlooked a good-sized garden. The floors were highly polished dark wood that gleamed brightly even in the pale autumn light. The other end of the room contained a huge marble fireplace adorned with silver candlesticks, exquisite porcelain pieces and large Oriental vases. Each vase

contained an enormous bunch of flowers. A multitude of
wing chairs, curved two-seater settees and tables covered
with fringed shawls completed the room. On every sur-
face were small objets d'art and more flowers. Exquisite
landscapes and seaside paintings adorned the walls.

"Exactly how many people are there in your household?" the inspector asked.

Albritton motioned them towards a settee by the fireplace. "If you include the servants, almost a dozen. But
I expect you're not including the staff, are you?" He
smiled cynically. "Servants aren't generally considered
people, are they?"

Offended by the comment, Witherspoon stared at him
for a long moment. "On the contrary," he replied honestly, "I consider every human being on the face of the
earth a person."

Albritton flushed slightly. "Forgive me, Inspector, that
remark was uncalled for. As you can understand, I'm
rather not myself today. Annie's death has caused me
great grief."

Witherspoon's annoyance evaporated in a wave of
sympathy. "I quite understand." The inspector gazed
at him for a moment and then straightened his spine.
Questions had to be asked, even painful ones. This was
a murder investigation.

"Mr. Albritton, do you know for certain that Annie
was your daughter?" The inspector needed to get this
point perfectly clear in his own mind. He wasn't quite
sure, but he felt it might be very pertinent to this case.
Perhaps, even, the very heart of the motive itself.

"For certain?" He smiled sadly. "Yes. In my own
mind, I'm absolutely satisfied that Annie was my daughter. Do I have proof?" He waved his hands dismissively.
"Not the sort that would satisfy a court or a policeman.

But I took one look at her face and I knew. She was the spitting image of my Dora."

"Excuse me, sir," Barnes said. "But did you ever say anything to Annie about this resemblance?"

Albritton hesitated. "Well, yes. As a matter of fact, I did. Last Friday, as a matter of fact. I asked her if she knew anything about her mother. Naturally, she didn't. After all, she was hardly more than a baby when she was taken to the orphanage."

"So she'd no idea that she had any connection with you," the inspector said.

"I don't think that's quite true," Albritton said hastily. "You see, Annie was very intelligent. I think she was beginning to suspect something. I asked her if she had any keepsakes from her mother. I was hoping she had a trinket or a letter or something which would help to identify the woman."

"And had she anything?" Witherspoon asked curiously.

"The only thing she had from her mother was a ring. An opal." He smiled shyly. "I can't tell you how I felt when Annie told me about the ring. You see, I know where Dora got that ring. I gave it to her over twenty years ago."

"Was it a betrothal ring?" Witherspoon asked.

"Oh yes, I'd given it to Dora when I asked her to marry me. I know they're supposed to be unlucky. But I was very poor and it was all I could afford at the time. Dora was thrilled when she saw it. She hadn't expected it, you see."

"And she didn't give it back when the engagement ended?"

Albritton gazed down at the floor. "She tried to. But I refused to take it. I felt so horrible about not marrying her that I wouldn't let her. You see, it was a few days after I proposed to Dora that the man who became my father-in-law, William Strutts, came to me and offered me the opportunity of a lifetime if I'd marry Francis." He looked up and the cold, empty expression in his eyes sent a chill down Witherspoon's spine. "I was young and greedy, Inspector," Albritton continued bitterly. "And I sold myself for the sake of a business opportunity. By doing so, I ruined the life of one I held dear and condemned my own flesh and blood to a lifetime of poverty and misery."

Witherspoon didn't know what to say. He could hardly agree with Mr. Albritton. The poor man was already dreadfully upset and morose. "Now, now, sir. You mustn't be so hard on yourself. I'm sure you didn't think things would turn out so badly."

Albritton appeared not to have heard him. He stared straight ahead, his gaze unfocused and his face set in misery.

The inspector cleared his throat. "Right, well, we must get on with this. Let me see if I have this straight. Mrs. Shields told you about the ring on Friday, correct?"

"That's right. She was going to bring it on Monday and let me have a look at it. I made it a point to stop at her stall on Regent Street."

"Why didn't she bring it on Saturday?" Barnes asked.

"I had a meeting with my partner, Sherwin August, on Saturday morning."

"But she was murdered on Sunday night," Witherspoon said. He glanced at his constable. Barnes nodded slightly. They were both thinking the same thing. There had been no ring on Annie's finger when her body was found, nor had there been a ring in her room.

"Yes," Albritton murmured. "She was murdered."

"And what would you have done when you saw this ring?" Barnes asked.

"Done?" He stared at them incredulously. "Why, I'd have done what I should have done years ago. Sold everything including my half of the boatyards and packed Annie and myself off to a new life in San Francisco. I'm quite a wealthy man, Inspector. Not that my money has ever brought me any real happiness, but I'd have enough to buy a good life for my only child." He stopped and stared at the painting of a sailing ship over the mantelpiece. "You see, I've known for a long time I ought to leave. Once I had real proof, proof that I could convince Annie with, I'd have taken her away. Taken her someplace where her lack of education, her lack of social graces wouldn't have made a difference. I'm not a fool. I wouldn't have brought her into this house and expected people to accept her. I know the only way she could have had the kind of life and happiness she deserved was if we went away."

"What do you mean, proof that would have convinced Annie?" Witherspoon thought that a rather odd statement. He'd learned long ago—well, actually, just since he'd begun investigating homicides—that one ought never to ignore an odd statement.

"Annie didn't know me, Inspector." He took a deep breath. "Because of the great wrong that I did her mother, my own flesh and blood was raised in poverty, ignorance and misery. To say the least, she was a bit cynical about the motives of a middle-aged man who'd started buying flowers from her every day. Annie was a good girl. She wouldn't have gone off anywhere with me unless she knew for certain I was her father. The ring would have proved it. The opal has a small flaw on one side of it, one that you wouldn't notice unless you knew exactly where to look."

"Was the ring your only evidence?" Barnes asked.

"No." He flushed slightly. "Annie's age was another factor. She was nineteen. Her birthday is in March. Well, let's just say that would put her conception at precisely the right time. And I know Dora wasn't involved with other men all those years ago. She loved me." He broke off and laughed harshly. "She loved me and I deserted her. But as God is my witness, I wouldn't have married Frances if I'd known Dora was carrying my child."

"I'm sure you wouldn't, sir," Witherspoon replied. Really, what else could one say to such a statement? He could hardly call the man a liar. "Did any of the other members of your family know about Mrs. Shields being your daughter?"

"I think they suspected something had changed in my life"—he glanced at a vase of chrysanthemums on the table—"but I never told any of them. Frankly, it wasn't any of their business."

"Then why, sir, do you think that one of them might have been responsible for Mrs. Shields's murder?" Witherspoon asked.

Albritton's expression grew cold. "Because each and every one of them is more than capable of murder, and even though I said nothing about Annie's existence, they could easily have found out. I'm not good at hiding my feelings. Meeting Annie made me happy. So happy that I'm afraid I got careless. I'd already started making plans, you see. I left some correspondence on my desk. An inquiry to my bank—I wanted them to

contact a bank in San Francisco and begin searching
for an adequate house for Annie and me. I suspect
that several members of my household saw that correspondence. That alone would be enough to rouse their
suspicions."

"Do you know for certain that anyone actually saw it,
or are you guessing?"

"Well, I wouldn't bet my life on it," Albritton retorted.
"But I could see that someone had gone through those
papers. I'm a most meticulous man, Inspector. I can tell
when someone's gone through my desk."

The inspector was beginning to think the man wasn't
thinking clearly. Really, he'd nothing more than suspicions about his relations. He hadn't actually seen any
of his family searching his desk, and he'd admitted he'd
told none of them about Annie Shields. But Witherspoon
realized that pointing this out would do no good. Henry
Albritton needed to focus his pain on someone. Grief
could do that to a person. However, he'd be remiss in
his duty if he didn't investigate the situation thoroughly.
"Yes, sir, I quite understand. Now, we'd like to speak to
the various members of your family."

It wasn't the food that attracted anyone to the Sail and
Anchor, Smythe mused as he looked at the man next
to him hacking at the crust of a pork pie. Unable to
stand watching any more of the fellow's futile attempts
to saw off a bit of crust, he turned and gazed at his
surroundings.

The tavern was crowded with dockworkers, day labour-
ers who'd earned the price of a pint, costermen, whores
and old sailors. A gang of toughs took over one corner of
the room, talking in hushed whispers and glaring at any-

one who dared come too close. Several thin, bedraggled women huddled in front of the small, mean fire sputtering in the hearth and vainly tried to warm their hands at the meager heat. The rest of the patrons sat at the rickety benches of the long, scarred oak tables or leaned against the bar. The few pathetic chairs scattered about the room were taken by gaunt, elderly men who looked like they'd been sitting there since the last coronation.

The tavern was an ugly place, not just in appearance but in what it was. A place without much hope. The room was crowded, yet strangely silent. Smythe fought back a wave of melancholy. Bloomin' Ada, this place'd depress a saint. He took a swallow of beer and grimaced. Stuff tasted worse than one of Luty Belle Crookshank's home remedies. 'Course, that was only to be expected. The only reason anyone would walk into this place was the beer. It was bleedin' cheap.

Smythe frowned as one of the toughs in the corner cuffed his companion on the side of the head. No one else even noticed. Blimey, what a miserable place. Thank God everyone had helped him talk Betsy out of trackin' down Calloway to this den of sin. Silly girl. Place like this would eat the lass alive and no one would lift a finger to help her. He squinted as the front door opened and a skinny male frame stood silhouetted against the light.

"That's 'im." The barkeep touched Smythe lightly on the elbow and pointed to the man standing in the doorway. "That's Fairclough. He's a mate of Calloway's."

Smythe slipped the publican a half crown. Information round these parts was expensive, but he didn't mind paying. He'd do anything to keep Betsy from nosing into a pit like this and he wouldn't mind getting ahead of the women on this case. It wasn't like he had much else to spend his money on, he mused as he watched Fairclough make his way towards the group sitting in the corner. Smythe frowned. Money. He'd made a ruddy ton of it, but because of a situation not of his own making, he was stuck living a lie.

Fairclough tugged at the sleeve of a heavyset bearded man. The man stared at him, shook his head negatively and brushed Fairclough's hand away. Smythe watched him appeal to the other men at the table, but the reaction was always the same. Whatever he wanted, they weren't going to give it to him. Shrugging, Fairclough wandered over to the bar. "Give us a pint," he called to the publican.

"Let me see yer coin first."

"Come on now, I've never cheated ya yet," Fairclough whined.

"Only because I ain't let ya," the barman replied. He swiped at the top of the bar with a greasy gray cloth.

"I'll stand ya a drink, mate," Smythe said amicably.

Fairclough's thin face grew wary, his pale, watery hazel eyes narrowed in suspicion. But his thirst for liquor overcame his mistrust. "That's right nice of ya, thanks." He jerked his chin at the barman. "Give us a pint, then."

Smythe waited till Fairclough had his beer and had taken several long, thirsty swallows. "You skint, then?" he asked.

Fairclough nodded. "Who isn't? Ain't had no work in weeks now. Used to make a bit cartin' coal or lumber, but me back's gone, so I can't do that no more."

Smythe nodded sympathetically. In this part of London, there was fierce competition for even the lowest of employment. "Ruddy 'ard to find a decent job. But maybe I can 'elp you some."

Fairclough put his tankard down. "You 'iring?"

"No, but I've a mind to buy some information."

"Information? What kind?" Fairclough asked slowly. He glanced at the corner, but the men there were intent on their own conversation and ignored him.

"You know a man named Calloway?"

Fairclough wiped his nose with the back of his hand and looked pointedly at his empty tankard. "Maybe."

Smythe got the hint. "Barman," he called, nodding towards Fairclough's empty tankard. "Another round 'ere."

They didn't speak until the tankard was full again and the barman had gone back to swatting the flies off the meat pies at the other end of the bar.

"Yeah, I know 'im," Fairclough said, with a sly smile.

"You know where I can find 'im?"

" 'Ow much you payin'?" Fairclough asked. He turned and looked Smythe up and down, taking in the well-fitting but simple clothes, the clean hands and the good boots. "Sometimes it ain't wise to go runnin' off at the mouth about people, if you know what I mean."

"I'm payin' enough. More than you'd be seein' in a day's honest work, that's for sure." Smythe wasn't about to flash his money in this place. He could handle himself as well as the next man—well, better than most if the truth were told. But he wasn't a fool. He didn't want to get his throat slit over a few quid. "Finish up yer beer and let's go for a walk."

Fairclough hesitated.

"I'll make it worth your while," Smythe promised as he lifted his tankard to his mouth. " 'Ow does five pounds sound?"

"Five quid?" Fairclough whispered, his eyes bulging. He picked up his drink and drained it in seconds. "Let's go, then, mate. For that kinda money, I'll tell ya everythin' I know about 'im. Believe me, it'll be worth every penny of it too. 'Cause I know plenty."

CHAPTER 6

Witherspoon took a deep breath. He sat down in a high-backed chair as he waited in the foyer for the butler to announce him to Albritton's nephew and his wife. Constable Barnes was busy looking at the row of paintings lining the wall of the staircase, so the inspector decided to use these free moments to get his thoughts in order.

Albritton was utterly convinced one of his relations was guilty of murder. But so far, he'd certainly not produced any real evidence. Then, of course, there were other aspects he must consider. Now that he knew for certain that Annie Shields was wearing an opal ring, he couldn't ignore the possibility that she'd been the victim of a robbery gone awry. Especially as he knew the ring was a keepsake. Annie might have been accosted, refused to give up the last link she had to her dead mother and tried to fight her assailant. Or at least tried to outrun him. But if it was a robbery, why did the thief leave Annie's wedding ring?

Witherspoon sighed inwardly. This case was not at all clear. Despite what his dear housekeeper had told him this morning over breakfast, he wasn't in the least confident of his abilities to bring this murderer to justice. His frown deepened. Mrs. Jeffries had also brought up a number of other matters. Now, what had she said? Something about widows? He remembered they'd been talking about his friend Lady Cannonberry, and Mrs. Jeffries had commented that she thought it nice that Lady Cannonberry had the opportunity to go visiting her friends in Devon. Actually, Witherspoon thought wistfully, he rather missed Lady Cannonberry. He did so hope she'd soon come home. But what exactly was it that Mrs. Jeffries had said after that? He wished he could remember. At the time he'd thought it might be a good idea to . . . to . . . Suddenly his eyes widened as he recalled everything his housekeeper had said. "Poor Mrs. Shields," Mrs. Jeffries had murmured sympathetically. "First she loses her husband, then probably has to put up with all sorts of revolting behaviour from other men—" At this point he'd interrupted and asked what she'd meant. She'd explained that it was quite common for young widows to be the targets of unwanted attentions after their husbands died. He'd been shocked, of course. What decent man wouldn't be? But then Mrs. Jeffries asked him if he had spoken to any of Annie's female friends at Covent Garden. She'd said that perhaps there had been a man in Annie's life. Someone who perhaps resented her for refusing his attentions. When he reminded his housekeeper that they had indeed questioned Annie's employer, she laughed and said that kind of information wasn't the sort of thing an employer, especially a man, would take any notice of. The inspector smiled slightly. Sometimes it was so good to have a woman to talk with. They had such a different perspective on life. In this case, a perspective which might be wise to pursue.

"Barnes," he said suddenly. "Have someone go back to the flower market and talk to some of the other flower sellers. Have them find the victim's friends, especially the women, and question them."

"Anything in particular you want them to be askin' about?" the constable wanted to know.

"We need to find out if there have been any men bothering the victim. You know, unwanted suitors, that sort of thing."

"Good idea, sir," Barnes said. He looked down the still-empty hall and saw no sign of the returning housemaid. "I'll just nip out to the constable on the corner and give him his new instructions. Anything else you want me to tell him?"

"Yes, have him find out if *anyone*, anyone at all, has been seen hanging around the victim."

Gordon and Hortense Strutts were not amused by the presence of the police. Perched stiffly on a green flowered settee at the end of the room, they stared at Witherspoon and Barnes with almost identical expressions of distaste.

Hortense Strutts, a chubby, brown-haired woman with a pale, moon-shaped face, a short pugnacious nose and lips that looked frozen in a perpetual pout, was the first to speak. "I've no idea why Uncle Henry chose to involve us in this ridiculously sordid affair," she declared. She smoothed one of the ruffles on the overskirt of her elegant lavender day gown. "He must have taken leave of his senses."

"It's positively absurd," her husband added.

Young Mr. Strutts was a handsome man with dark brown hair, green eyes, high, rather prominent cheekbones and lips that were so well shaped, they looked almost feminine. He was dressed just as elegantly as his wife.

"Why on earth would either of us know anything about this person?" He sneered, bringing a pristine white handkerchief to his lips and coughing delicately.

"Mrs. Shields was a flower seller," the inspector said. "That's all she was, you know. A decent, hardworking young woman who happened to sell flowers for a living. As to why your uncle thinks you may know something about her murder, well, you'll have to take that issue up with him."

"You can rest assured that we will," Hortense replied tartly. "Now, I've an appointment with my dressmaker in a few minutes, so please do get on with your business."

"Really, Hortense," her husband soothed. He flicked a speck of lint off the sleeve of his coat. "There's no reason to be so rude. I've an appointment as well, but I can at least be civil."

"Where were you last night?" the inspector asked. He wasn't going to mention Annie's possible relationship with Henry Albritton unless he had to. In domestic matters, he frequently felt that the less said, the better.

"I was here, of course," she replied.

"Really?" Witherspoon said. "Your uncle seems to be under the impression that you were out."

"Uncle Henry was mistaken," Hortense replied. "We'd planned on going to the theatre last night. However, with all those hooligans in Trafalgar Square, we changed our minds and stayed home."

Witherspoon smiled politely. "Are you quite sure, Mrs. Strutts? Mr. Albritton has already told us he heard the carriage pull up in front. He's quite positive you left. He didn't see you and he was here all evening."

"He didn't see us because we went to our rooms," she said. She glanced at her husband. "Gordon and I changed our plans at the last moment, that's why Uncle Henry heard the carriage. We sent it away, though, we didn't go out."

"I thought you'd changed them because of the riots in Trafalgar?"

"That was only one of the reasons we decided to stay home. Actually, after dinner I developed a headache. I went straight up to lie down, and Gordon, of course, stayed with me. Uncle Henry seemed most preoccupied. He shut himself up in his study the minute he finished eating. We didn't wish to disturb him, so when we decided not to go out, we went directly upstairs."

"Is that correct, Mr. Strutts?" the inspector asked.

"Yes."

"Did your maid or any of the other servants see you after dinner?" Barnes asked softly.

"Just the butler." It was Gordon who replied. "And he only saw me when I told him we wouldn't be needing the carriage. As my wife said, she had a headache. We've a suite of rooms upstairs—I helped her up to bed, turned off the lights and then went into the little sitting room to read. As I didn't see fit to tell the servants my plans had changed, there was no reason for them to come into my rooms. My wife and I aren't in the habit of having the staff wait up for us when we go out in the evening."

"So after dinner," the inspector prodded, "no one saw either of you?"

"That's correct." Gordon smiled and rose to his feet, clearly dismissing them. "Now, if that's all you wanted to know, I've a busy day planned and my wife must get to the dressmaker's."

Witherspoon got up and Barnes followed suit. "What were you reading?"

Gordon blinked in surprise. "Reading? Oh, I was—"

"You were reading Mr. Pryce's novel. I believe it's titled *An Evil Spirit*," Hortense interjected quickly. "You remember, you mentioned it to me the next morning."

"That's right." Gordon smiled at the two policemen. "As you can see, my wife has a much better memory than I do."

"You enjoy novels, do you, sir?" Barnes asked.

"Oh, not all that much," Gordon replied. "Actually, the book belongs to Hortense. Novels of that sort are much more suited to ladies than gentlemen. The book was amusing, but hardly the sort of literature one should take seriously. But I'd nothing else to read and I wasn't tired enough to sleep."

The inspector wondered what to ask next. If neither Mr. nor Mrs. Strutts had gone out, then they couldn't have had anything to do with the murder. He would, of course, check with the butler to make sure the carriage had been sent away and not used by one of the Strutts. "I see. Well, that takes care of that."

In a gesture of dismissal, Hortense rose to her feet. "If that's all you wanted, then I really must be going."

"Thank you, Mrs. Strutts, Mr. Strutts," Witherspoon said politely. He must remember to speak with the servants as well. Mrs. Jeffries was always telling him it was his ability to make people feel at ease and get them to talk to him that gave him his really useful clues. Perhaps it would be best to find someone who could confirm the Struttses' story. Surely someone in a household this size must have known they hadn't gone out. On the other

hand, even if no on had seen hide nor hair of them all
evening, it wouldn't prove they'd left the house. Drat.
Why did everything have to be so dreadfully difficult?
"If you would be so good as to ring for your butler, we'll
speak with Mrs. Franklin next."

The butler appeared as soon as the Struttses left. The
inspector asked him about the carriage. "They sent it
away, sir," the man replied.

"Are you sure, Mister . . . er a . . ."

"Nestor, sir. Simon Nestor. Yes, I'm quite sure they
sent it away." The butler sniffed.

"Thank you, Nestor. Would you please fetch Mrs.
Franklin for us?"

"Very good, sir."

"So it looks like the Struttses was tellin' the truth,"
Barnes said as soon as the double doors slid closed
behind the servant.

"At least about sending the carriage away," the inspector muttered. "But we'll need to interview the servants.
I'd like someone else to confirm their story."

"They claimed no one saw them," Barnes said, raising
his eyebrows and grinning. "But I'll warrant in a household this size, the servants knew exactly who was where
and what they were doin'."

"My thoughts exactly, Constable."

The doors slid open. A thin middle-aged woman
dressed in a drab but well-cut brown-and-gold-striped
dress with a high neckline and long, tight sleeves stepped
inside. "I believe you wanted to see me? I'm Lydia
Franklin."

Tall and blond, she swept past them and sat down
on the settee like a judge taking his seat on the bench.
She stared at them out of a plain, angular face, lifting
her chin slightly and watching them down her long,

sharp nose. The expression in her deep-set hazel eyes was mildly contemptuous and her lips were pursed in distaste. "I'd like to make it perfectly clear that the only reason I'm bothering even to speak to you is because Henry insisted."

"Thank you, Mrs. Franklin," Witherspoon replied. "We do appreciate your cooperation. I'm Inspector Witherspoon and this is Constable Barnes. Did Mr. Albritton explain the nature of our inquiry?"

She smiled coolly. "He said it was something to do with a murder. A flower seller, I believe. Though what that can have to do with me is certainly beyond my comprehension."

Witherspoon wondered if he ought to tell her and then quickly decided he shouldn't. He hadn't mentioned Albritton's relationship to the victim to the Struttses. Perhaps it was best to say nothing for the time being. One could always bring it up later. "May I ask what you were doing on last Sunday evening?"

"The same as I do every Sunday evening. I was at church."

"Evensong service?" Witherspoon suggested.

"That is correct."

"Which church did you attend?"

"St. John's. It's just across the way." She gestured vaguely to her left, fluttering her hand. The inspector noted she wore no rings.

"And what time did you leave St. John's?"

"As soon as the service was finished." She yawned.

"What time would that be, ma'am?" Barnes interjected.

"About eight o'clock," she replied. "No, wait a moment, that's not quite true. I stayed after the service and spoke to the vicar about some church matters."

"How long did you talk to him?" Witherspoon asked. He wished she'd ask him to sit down. Asking questions while standing was getting tiresome. He was beginning to feel like he was visiting a bank.

"I spoke with him for fifteen minutes or so. I don't recall exactly." Again she smiled coolly. "Then Mrs. Spreckles and I left the church. We walked most of the way home together. The Spreckleses live just down the street."

"What time was it when you arrived back?" Barnes asked as he glanced up from his notebook.

"I've really no idea."

"What's your best guess?" Witherspoon asked.

"Eight-fifteen or eight-thirty. But I can't say for certain. I simply wasn't paying any attention to the time. There was no reason to, was there?"

"What did you do when you arrived home?"

"I went straight up to my room."

"Did anyone in the household see you?" Witherspoon prodded.

"No."

"Isn't that odd?" The inspector was beginning to think that everyone living in this house must be invisible. "Surely in a household this large some of the servants must be in attendance when a member of the family comes home?"

She smiled again, but the smile didn't reach her eyes. "One would think so. But Henry, unfortunately, has come under some rather untoward influences recently. Out of the clear blue, he took it into his head to give the entire staff the evening off. He claimed we oughtn't to exploit people. He wouldn't even listen to me when I tried to point out that he was already exceedingly generous with the servants. They already had a reasonable amount of time free." Her voice rose slightly. "Now they were to have Sunday evenings as well. It's disgraceful. Utterly disgraceful. But Henry won't even discuss the subject calmly. It's all those books he's been reading. All those awful, radical, disgusting books that shouldn't be allowed to be published."

Witherspoon stared at the woman in alarm. Lydia Franklin's cheeks were flushed with rage and her hands were balled into fists. He really didn't think a discussion of Henry Albritton's changed social views was pertinent to Annie Shields's murder, so he quickly cast about for another, less controversial question to ask.

"Er, did you happen to speak to Mr. or Mrs. Strutts at all on Sunday evening?" He wondered why neither of the Struttses had mentioned Mr. Albritton giving the staff the evening off. For that matter, neither the butler nor Albritton had said anything either.

Lydia got a hold of herself and took a long, deep breath before answering. "No, I didn't. As far as I know, they went to the theatre."

"But they weren't at the theatre," the inspector corrected. "Both of them claim they changed their minds and stayed in."

She gave him another cold, mirthless smile. "If that's what Gordon and Hortense said, then I'm sure it must be true."

Betsy slipped behind a lamppost and stared at the young woman with the sad eyes and frizzy blond hair. Knowing she had to be careful, she waited until her quarry had wandered into a pub. Betsy took off after her. The best way to get someone like her to talk was to buy her a gin.

The pub was loud, dirty and filled with the kind of people Betsy had grown up with. The working poor.

Hungry, cynical and scared, most of them had such miserable existences they lived only for the moment. Tomorrow was bound to be worse, so you might as well have a few laughs today. Betsy wasn't sure they were all that wrong, either. If she hadn't been lucky enough to end up working at the inspector's, she was fairly certain her fate would have been much like Millie Groggins's.

She waited till Millie sidled up to the bar. Betsy stepped inside the pub. To her left, a fat, beefy man with a bright red face leered at her. " 'Ello, me lovely, new girl on the street?"

"Sod off," she snapped at him, and cringed as the fellow next to the fat man belched loudly. Quickly, she hurried up to the bar.

Millie didn't look up from her gin.

Betsy cleared her throat. "Can I buy you a drink?"

"You talkin' to me?" Millie slowly raised red-rimmed puffy eyes. It was impossible to tell if the woman was drunk or weeping.

"I said, can I buy you a gin?" Betsy ignored the interested stares of the men leaning against the bar.

"Bugger off," Millie growled. "I only does men." She turned her head away. The publican snickered.

"I ain't one of your bleedin' customers," Betsy snapped. "I only want to talk to you a bit. And I'll pay for what I need to know."

Millie turned her head and squinted, trying hard to focus her eyes. "You'll pay."

"Yes." Crimminey, Betsy thought, between givin' away some of her things and offerin' money for information, it was a good thing someone at Upper Edmonton Gardens was keepin' her supplied. But she really wasn't concerned. God knows, these people needed them a sight worse than she did. "I'll pay ya. You tell me what you know about Annie Shields and I'll give you five shillin's."

Millie jerked her head towards the back of the pub. "Get me another gin and we'll talk."

The prostitute chased a drunk away from a small table in the shadowed corner. Betsy carefully set the gin in front of Millie and then sat down.

"Ta." Millie picked up the drink and took a long swig. "So what do ya want to know?"

Betsy knew she'd get a load of rubbish if she wasn't careful. Millie might take her money and tell her nothing. She'd have to gain the woman's trust. "First of all," she began, "I used to live round these parts."

"Lucky you." Millie took another swallow.

"Nah, it weren't lucky. It was bloody awful. I got out 'cause a decent man took pity on me when I collapsed on his doorstep. But one of me little sisters weren't so lucky. She died." The memory sent a sharp stab of pain through Betsy. Pain she thought she'd buried years ago. "And me other sister went off with a feller years ago and we never heard from her again." More pain, but she ignored it. "So I'm tellin' ya I'll know if you're havin' me on. You tell me the truth about Annie and I'll be straight about payin' ya."

"Whatcha wanta know about Annie for?" Millie said. She looked curious and amused by Betsy's speech. "She's dead."

"And I aim to help hang the one that killed her," Betsy declared.

Millie eyed her shrewdly for a moment. "All right, ask me whatever you like. Maybe I'll even tell you the truth."

"I understand you and Annie was friends."

"Not really friends," Millie admitted. "Some of them sellers thinks they's too good to even speak to the likes of us, but Annie weren't like that. She were nice to me. Always treated me like I was someone, you know?"

"Did you see her on Sunday night?"

Millie nodded her head. "Yeah, we was both workin' the Strand." She broke off and laughed. " 'Course Annie was only tryin' to sell a few flowers. But there weren't no business at all. Streets were deader than a rat's arse and twice as mean."

"What do you mean?"

"It was bloody cold. There was a right horrid fog driftin' in and not a drop of business for either of us." Millie quickly tossed back another swallow. "I was bloody worried. If I didn't make a few bits, I knew I was goin' to end up kippin' on the streets."

Betsy looked down at her own gloved hands. She knew exactly what Millie was talking about. If you couldn't pay, you spent the night out on the streets. She'd done it herself a time or two. She'd die before she ever did it again. "Was Annie worried about money?"

"Annie was always worried about money," Millie replied. "Who isn't? She had the little one to take care of. But she weren't skint, if that's what yer askin'. Her business was off, too, but she still lent me a bit of coin so I wouldn't have to sleep in the street. But somethin' was botherin' her. The whole time we was out, she was always lookin' over her shoulder. Every time we 'eard footsteps she got all quiet and stiff like."

"You mean she knew someone meant to harm her?"

Millie's expression grew thoughtful. "No, more like she was expectin' someone. You know what I mean? We'd hear footsteps, but 'course it was so bloody foggy you couldn't see anyone till they was right on top of you.

Every time someone passed by, she'd sort of sag, you know, like she was disappointed."

"Did she actually say she was expecting someone?"

"No. But she must've been, mustn't she?"

"What makes you think that?"

Millie shrugged one shoulder nonchalantly. " 'Cause she never worked late. Annie always worked the crowds *before* they went inside theatres, never stayed to work 'em comin' out. Nah, she was waitin' for someone that night."

"Maybe she needed extra money?" Betsy suggested.

Millie shook her head stubbornly. "If she'd been short she wouldn't have lent me any, would she?"

Betsy thought that was probably true. No matter how kindhearted a body was, if your own survival was at stake, you wouldn't be handing out money to Millie Groggins. "What time did you last see her?"

"Ten o'clock," Millie said. "I heard the chimes at St. Matthew's ring the hour just as I was leavin'. Annie was fixin' to leave then too. She'd already packed her cart."

Wiggins smiled at the homely kitchen maid. "Let me help you," he said, nodding towards the basket of vegetables the girl struggled to hold on to while she futilely tried to relatch the back gate.

The girl gave him a wary glance, almost dropped the basket and finally nodded. "Ta," she said as Wiggins neatly slipped the bolt closed. "This thing's so heavy I'd never have gotten that gate latched."

"Can I carry it for you?" Wiggins asked politely. He concentrated on speaking properly. Sometimes young girls were a bit frightened of men, but if they thought you were a gentleman, they'd be a bit easier in their own minds.

"It's too much bother," the girl said, lifting the heavy basket onto her hip and turning towards the street at the end of the mews. "Really, I can manage."

"Oh please, miss, I'm walkin' the same way you are, I'd be pleased to help. That's an awfully big basket for a dainty little person like yourself."

"Well . . ." She smiled suddenly. "Thanks, awfully." She handed him the basket. "I'm takin' it back to Rutger's, the greengrocers on the Edgeware Road. Cook says half these vegetables is old and not fit to eat."

They started walking and Wiggins chatted amicably. By the time they reached the Edgeware Road, Abigail, for that was the kitchen maid's name, was talking freely.

"Sounds like your mistress has bloomin' high standards," he said casually, looking down at the basket.

"We ain't got no mistress, she died a few years back. We've a master." Abigail shrugged. "But he don't half notice what he eats. It's the rest of 'em that raise a ruckus if the food's not good."

"Hard to work for, are they?"

"Mr. Albritton's a right nice master," she said. "But he's got a pack of his dead wife's relations livin' there and none of them is very nice."

"That's too bad. But if they're his wife's relations, maybe they'll leave one of these days."

Abigail snorted. "It'd take a case of pox to get 'em out of there. They's all living off Mr. Albritton. 'Course I can see why he lets his sister-in-law stay on. I mean, Mrs. Franklin did help take care of his wife when she was so ill. But he's got his wife's nephew and wife there too."

"Uh, what's their names?"

"The Struttses." Abigail made a face. This was obviously a subject she relished talking about. "Hortense and Gordon. What a pair."

"Does Mr. Strutts, uh, take liberties?"

Abigail laughed. "Nah, he's too scared of his wife to say boo to a goose in a barnyard. Don't know why either. He's a right handsome fellow and she's as plain as a pikestaff. Not that she's built like one. She's gettin' big as a bloomin' house, she is."

"Doesn't sound like she's easy to work for," he murmured. He deliberately slowed his steps as they came closer to a row of shops.

"And the worst part is, poor Mr. Strutts spends every last pence of his allowance on her. He's always buyin' her gowns and jewelry and expensive chocolates." Abigail shook her head in disgust. "God knows why. She's never grateful for anything. Why, he even bought her one of them fancy bicycles last year and all she did with it was ride it once and then toss it in the back shed."

"I've never heard of a woman ridin' a bicycle," Wiggins said seriously. He'd always wanted a bicycle.

"Don't be daft," Abigail said, tossing her head. "Lots of women rides 'em. Even that stiff-necked Mrs. Franklin's done it a time or two. Mrs. Franklin's the sister-in-law." She snorted. "Not that it helps her be the lady of the manor. Mr. Albritton might be grateful to her, but he don't let her put on airs. Least ways not with the servants. Do you know she tried to talk 'im out of givin' us the evenin' off last Sunday. Stupid cow. Wonder how she'd like to spend every wakin' moment peelin' vegetables and scrubbin' pots."

Wiggins wanted to get Abigail back on the subject of the Struttses. "Maybe Mr. Strutts is madly in love with Mrs. Strutts," he suggested. "Maybe that's why

"Strange couple," Wiggins said slowly. He racked his brain to think of more questions. He had to keep her talking. Blimey, now he was stuck going out with her day after tomorrow.

"In more ways than one," Abigail said. "She's the really odd duck, though."

"In what way?"

"She listens at keyholes. Just two weeks ago I was goin' up to the butler's pantry to get the brewer's yeast for cleanin' the coppers? Well, them jugs was heavy, so I nipped down the front stairs instead of the back like I was supposed to, and there she was, Mrs. Strutts—her ear was pressed to the keyhole of Mr. Albritton's study. Mr. Albritton was in there talkin' to his solicitor too."

"Of course I know who Henry Albritton is," Miss Myrtle Buxton exclaimed. "Really, Luty, I know everyone in London."

Luty had no doubt this was true. That was precisely why she'd sashayed across the road from her own Knightsbridge home to call on Myrtle. The room alone, with its pale pink walls, matching pink settees and chairs, dozens of draped tables loaded with knicknacks and silver, Oriental carpets, flowery drapes and footstools so thick on the floor you had to be careful where you stepped, was enough to make her eyes water. The place gave her a headache. But the woman was very useful to know. Besides, Luty sort of felt sorry for her. For all her gadding about, Myrtle didn't really have many friends.

Myrtle Buxton, rich, silver-haired and still single, devoted every waking moment of her life to socializing. She knew everything about anyone of wealth in the entire city. Luty wasn't sure but that she didn't know about the rest of the country as well. Yet for all this, Luty had noticed that not many people came to call.

"He's not a real gentleman," Myrtle continued. "After all, he did make his money in trade. But he's done very, very well."

"I thought he was a carpenter," Luty said bluntly.

"He was. Started out workin' at his father-in-law's boatyard fifteen—or was it twenty?—years ago." Myrtle paused and her eyes narrowed thoughtfully. "Yes, that's right. Then he married Francis and took over the business when old Mr. Strutts died. The business should have gone to his son, Edmond Strutts, but he was already dead." She reached for a tea cake and popped it into her mouth. Chewing delicately, she cocked her head to one side. "Why are you so interested in Henry Albritton?"

Luty was ready for that question. "I'm thinking about buying into the boat business."

"You can't, the company isn't public." Myrtle reached for another cake. "And it's really a pity, too, as he's done well. He turned that one boatyard into seven."

"Seven!"

"Three in London, two in Liverpool, one in Southampton and one somewhere up in Scotland." Myrtle eyed the cake in her hand, made a face and then put it back. "Of course, he didn't do it alone. As soon as old Mr. Strutts was buried, Albritton took in a partner. A man named Sherwin August." Her eyes took on that greedy gleam Luty had seen many time before. It meant she had something really juicy to say. "But there's been some strange talk lately too. August has told several people he thinks Albritton may be ill." She gently tapped the side of her head. "You know, this kind of illness."

"You mean crazy?"

"I wouldn't put it as strongly as that," Myrtle replied. "But supposedly, Henry Albritton's become"—her voice dropped—"a radical."

"Hmm, well, I guess I won't be puttin' my money there," Luty mused. She thought this information interesting, but she wanted more. It would be a cold day in hell before she would let that stiff-necked butler of hers beat her to solving this crime. "So when did Mrs. Albritton die?"

"A few years back," Myrtle replied. "What's so odd is that Albritton's a handsome man for his age. Half the widows in London had their eye on him. You'd have thought he'd have married again."

"Some people don't much like bein' hitched," Luty declared bluntly. Her own marriage had been a relatively happy one, but she'd seen enough of life to know the misery of being tied to someone you didn't love. Luty knew half a dozen women who'd happily buried husbands and declared that nothing short of a bullet aimed at their heads would ever induce them to marry again. No reason a man couldn't feel the same way.

"I think he'd have liked to have married again," Myrtle protested. "I mean, it's only natural that he would."

"Nothin' natural about it at all . . ." Luty tried to interrupt.

But Myrtle wasn't listening. She kept right on talking. "But, of course, Lydia made sure no one got close enough to do any real damage to her position. She wasn't going to have anyone take her place as the mistress of the house."

"Lydia?" Luty prodded, pretending ignorance of the name.

"Lydia Franklin. She lives in the Albritton house. Once Frances died, she took over as mistress. Her husband was Warren Franklin. Quite a good family, the Franklins, but Warren was exceedingly unlucky. Lost every cent he ever made. He and Lydia lived in some awful little house south of the river. He left Lydia so destitute she had to move in with her sister when Warren died." Myrtle smiled coyly. "The gossip has it that Lydia set her sights on Henry the day they buried Frances." She giggled. "Gossip also has it that Henry can't stand the woman."

CHAPTER 7

Mrs. Jeffries stared curiously at the woman sitting at the next table. She frowned. The lady had her back turned and was swaddled in a heavy gray coat, a bright red scarf and an enormous hat. It was impossible to tell who she was. Yet there was something very familiar looking about her. Perhaps, Mrs. Jeffries thought, she really should have taken the time to glance at the woman's face when she'd noticed the lady coming behind her into the tearoom. But she pushed that notion aside. She had more important things to think about than whether or not someone who looked vaguely familiar was an acquaintance or not. Still, she thought, she mustn't get careless. She didn't want to take the chance that one of her neighbours might mention seeing her this morning. That wouldn't do at all. She didn't want the inspector to know who she was meeting for tea. Then again, she told herself, it was highly unlikely that any of the people from Upper Edmonton Gardens or thereabouts would have any idea of the identity of the young man she hoped to meet here.

She glanced up as she felt a cold draft coming from the door. She smiled in delight as she spotted the familiar face. Hanging on to his hat, Dr. Bosworth pushed the door closed against the heavy wind and started towards her, picking his way carefully through the crowded tables.

Her spirits soared. Her quarry had risen to the bait!

"Good day, Dr. Bosworth," she said gaily. "I'm delighted you could come. It's so very kind of you."

Bosworth pulled out a chair, accidentally bumped the elbow of the lady swathed in heavy coats at the next table, muttered an apology and sat down. "Not at all, Mrs. Jeffries. I was quite thrilled to get your note this morning."

Red-haired, tall and earnest, the doctor might be able to give Mrs. Jeffries some answers. She wasn't sure how much she should tell him, though. Bosworth was quite an honest young man and she certainly didn't want him to compromise his position by assisting her. Unless, of course, he wanted to.

The waiter appeared and Mrs. Jeffries slipped into her role as hostess. "You will have tea, sir?" she queried. At his nod, she told the young man to bring them a full tea complete with cakes and fancy biscuits. "I do so love these Lyons Tearooms, don't you?"

"I don't get a chance to frequent them all that much," Bosworth said politely. He cocked his head to one side and studied her for a moment, his eyes amused. "Mrs. Jeffries, you'll forgive me for getting right to the point, but I must return to the hospital soon. However, you'll be pleased to learn I did have time to nip in and examine Annie Shields."

"You examined her?" Mrs. Jeffries watched his face

carefully. Her note had mentioned the victim's name, but she hadn't dared hope Bosworth would take it upon himself to do precisely what she needed done without more prodding on her part.

He grinned broadly and his pale, serious face was immediately transformed. "I did. I had to do it on the sly too. Old Potter hung about for a long time."

"Oh dear, I do hope you won't get into any trouble," she said earnestly. "I know my note was rather vague, but you see . . ."

"Your note wasn't just vague, it was deliberately intriguing. You must have known the moment I realized it was one of the inspector's cases, my curiosity would be aroused."

Mrs. Jeffries decided to take the bull by the horns. This young doctor was far too intelligent to swallow the story she'd cooked up to lure him here. "I was counting on it. You see, doctor, you've been so helpful in the past. On that case last spring, your insights were so useful I was rather hoping you'd lend your expert opinion to this one as well."

"I'm not certain my opinion is all that expert," he said with an embarrassed smile. "All I did was identify the kind of weapon used in the murder." He paused as the waiter brought their tea.

"Don't be so modest, Dr. Bosworth," Mrs. Jeffries said as soon as they were alone. "Your identification of the gun used in that crime helped to solve it."

He picked up his tea and stared at her, his expression thoughtful. "Do you always take such an interest in the inspector's cases?"

"Actually . . ." She hesitated, not sure of exactly how much she should admit. He was, after all, a man. Like many of that sex, he might resent a woman using her mind. On the other hand, he might not. Constantly trying to dream up stories and excuses to pry information out of people without their knowing what she was up to was getting very wearing. Furthermore, an ally like Dr. Bosworth could come in handy on future cases. "Yes. I do," she admitted. "However, I make certain the inspector has no idea of my interest or my involvement."

"Good." He took a sip from his cup. "The world could use more people like you. You care. Even better, you manage to make sure your inspector keeps his pride. A rare quality, in either a man or a woman. How can I help you?"

"Thank you," she said modestly. She was enormously relieved that he was reacting so splendidly. But her instincts had told her she could trust him. "As you have examined the victim, is there anything you can tell me that might be useful?"

"By useful, I take it you want my opinion as to the murder weapon?"

"That and anything else you think important." She didn't wish to interrupt at this point by telling him that her methods of investigation deemed all information useful in some form or another. That could come later. "I realize you probably can't be specific about the weapon, but I would like your opinion nonetheless."

"My examination was very cursory. But I'm inclined to think she was killed with a hammer." He grinned as he saw her start in surprise. "That's right, Mrs. Jeffries. I'm fairly sure that poor woman was bashed on the head with a common hammer."

There was an audible gasp from the woman at the next table. Mrs. Jeffries leaned closer. "Perhaps we ought to keep our voices down," she said in a low voice. "Goodness, doctor, you are full of surprises. I'd no idea you'd be able to tell what it was that actually killed Annie Shields. Why do you think it was a hammer?"

Bosworth leaned forward too. "Naturally, I'm not one hundred percent certain. I could be wrong, but I don't think I am. I examined the victim's wounds very carefully. There were three separate blows."

Fascinated, Mrs. Jeffries asked, "Gracious. You can tell how many times she was hit just by looking?"

"Certainly," he said, his voice rising enthusiastically. "Each blow leaves some kind of wound mark. Naturally it would have been better had I been able to examine a bare skull, one without flesh and hair. But I could hardly soak the poor woman's head in acid and see what the skull would tell me. Even old Potter's bright enough to notice I'd been poking about if he saw a skull instead of a head."

There was a strangled, choking sound from next to them. Bosworth glanced at the woman, who was now sitting bolt upright and ramrod straight. He lowered his voice a fraction. "Mind you, I am guessing. But by carefully examining the wounds, I was able to come to some conclusions. You must realize, though, not every physician agrees with these methods. Some claim it's all nonsense."

"I think it's jolly clever of you, doctor." She beamed at him. Her attention was caught again by their neighbour. The woman now appeared to be leaning back, her ear turned towards them. Mrs. Jeffries still couldn't see her face; that wretched scarf was in her way. She couldn't be certain, of course. But it was almost as if the lady were trying to eavesdrop.

"Thank you, Mrs. Jeffries. As I was saying, there were three separate and distinct blows. Two of them left round, blunt-edged wounds. Admittedly, there are many objects that could hit a person and leave such an edge, but the third wound left a jagged edge. A very interesting edge that looked to me like the kind of wound the claw end of a hammer might make."

"So you think the killer struck twice with the blunt end of the hammer," she said slowly, trying to picture the action in her mind, "then turned the hammer around and struck a third blow with the sharp end?"

"That's correct," he said. "Either that, or he used two separate weapons."

"It hardly seems likely he'd have used two weapons." She frowned slightly. "Yet in order to use both ends of the hammer, the killer would either have to turn his hand completely over—"

"Or turn the hammer over," Bosworth finished calmly. "It's not quite as farfetched as it sounds, Mrs. Jeffries, once you think about it. First, imagine the killer. He hits his victim twice using the blunt end, the end most people would think likely to do the most damage. The victim falls. The killer kneels beside her and drops the hammer to check for signs of life. The victim perhaps moans or flutters an eyelid, even people on the doorstep of death can groan or twitch a bit. The killer panics. He grabs the hammer. Remember, he'd dropped it hastily, it could easily have shifted or rolled. For all we know, there might be blood on his hands and he can't get a decent grip on the weapon. But for some reason, the wrong end is up, and when he strikes the third and killing blow, it's the claw end not the blunt end that does the poor woman in."

Mrs. Jeffries was speechless. She gazed at him in admiration. "I'm amazed, doctor. Your analysis makes perfect sense."

The lady next to them leaned farther back. Alarmed,

Mrs. Jeffries watched her, certain that any second she was going to topple in Dr. Bosworth's lap. She nodded her head and the doctor quickly looked around. He moved his chair slightly and the woman hastily drew back into her own seat.

"Thank you," Bosworth whispered. "But it's not all that difficult, really. Anyone who sat down and actually thought about it could have come to the same conclusion. Assuming, of course, that I'm correct about the identity of the weapon."

"Dr. Bosworth, you're brilliant." Whether he was right or wrong wasn't really the point, though. Coming up with a sequence of events that was both plausible and possible was what impressed Mrs. Jeffries most.

"Thank you, again." He smiled modestly. "That's the only way I can account for the blows and, more importantly, for the difference in the kinds of wounds they made. I mean, can you think of another instrument that's blunt on one side and claw-edged on the other?"

She couldn't, but that didn't mean such an instrument didn't exist. "Not one which is easily obtainable and available to most people," she replied. "In murder, people generally use the kinds of weapons that are convenient, and let's be blunt, doctor—practically anyone can get their hands on a hammer." She noticed the woman leaning their way again. Really, how very rude.

Bosworth nodded, picked up his teacup and drained it. "Was there anything else you needed to know?"

"I'm not certain. Was there anything else about the body you think worth mentioning?"

"I can't really say," he replied, frowning. "Old Potter was hovering so close I only just got a good look at the wounds. I didn't have a chance to examine the rest of her."

"Oh dear, that's a pity."

He pushed back in his chair. The woman quickly leaned forward over her own table. Bosworth got up. "Yes, it is. Next time I'll try and slip in early of a morning."

"Next time?"

Bosworth grinned. "Our next case, Mrs. Jeffries. Only you'll have to be a bit quicker in contacting me. Here, let me give you this." He reached inside his pocket and drew out a card. "This is my address. Send someone round early the next time, and I should be able to slip into the mortuary before old Potter gets there. He doesn't like doing postmortems on an empty stomach, so he's never in before nine in the morning."

Stunned and grateful, she took the card. He was actually agreeing to help them! "Thank you so much, doctor. You've been so very, very kind. And I promise, on our next case we'll get word to you straightaway."

"Yes, well, let's just hope whatever bodies we have get sent to St. Thomas's. It would be a bit difficult even for me to be snooping around corpses at another mortuary or hospital. In case you haven't noticed, medics are dreadfully territorial about their patch. Now I must be off, but do let me know if there's anything else I can do to help on this one."

"Thank you so much," Mrs. Jeffries said again. "You really must come round for tea soon. I'll send you a note, shall I?"

"That would be lovely." He bowed to her, threw an amused glance at the nosy woman's back and left.

The woman rose as well. She turned slowly and faced the housekeeper.

Shocked, Mrs. Jeffries stared at the slender, blond-haired woman standing in front of her. "Lady Cannonberry," she exclaimed. "You're supposed to be in Devon. What are you doing here?"

"Actually, Mrs. Jeffries"—Lady Cannonberry gave her an innocent smile—"I followed you."

"Hello, hello," the inspector called out as he entered the front hall of Upper Edmonton Gardens. "Mrs. Jeffries, Betsy. I'm home." He waited for a moment, but no one answered his summons. That's most odd, he thought. There's generally one of the staff home at this time of the day. Shaking his head, he started towards the backstairs when suddenly he heard the front door open.

"Why, hello, Inspector," Mrs. Jeffries said. She hurried forward, taking off her hat and coat as she went. "This is certainly a nice surprise."

"I thought I'd pop home for a spot of lunch," he said.

"Lovely." She smiled. "Why don't you just have a seat in the dining room and I'll go get you something to eat."

"If you don't mind, I'll just nip down and get Fred. We could both use a ramble out in the gardens."

"That's a wonderful idea, sir." Mrs. Jeffries fervently hoped Wiggins hadn't taken it into his head to take the dog with him. "Lunch should be ready in just a few minutes."

She watched the inspector disappear down the backstairs, heard the sound of Fred's excited barking and heaved a sigh of relief. Really, she thought, today has been just full of surprises.

She dashed down the kitchen stairs and found Mrs. Goodge hurrying towards the larder. "It's a good thing the inspector weren't ten minutes earlier," she warned. "Otherwise he'd have caught me talkin' to one of my sources. The rag-and-bone man is a cousin to someone who works at Albritton's boatyard. He give me a right earful too."

"Excellent, Mrs. Goodge. Now let's hope you have something for the inspector's lunch."

"Not to worry, I'll heat up some soup and there's some sliced cold beef and fresh bread. That'll do him."

"Good." Mrs. Jeffries leaned closer to Mrs. Goodge. "You'll never guess who I ran into this morning. Lady Cannonberry. She's back from the country. She followed me to the tearoom and then managed to eavesdrop on my conversation with Dr. Bosworth."

"Followed you?" Mrs. Goodge frowned. "Why would Lady Cannonberry be following you and eavesdroppin'?"

"It's a long story and quite accidental, I'm sure. I'll tell you all about it when the others get back. They'll be here for tea, won't they?"

"Right. Luty and Hatchet will be round too."

Mrs. Jeffries went back upstairs and set the dining table. Her mind was working furiously.

The murder weapon was probably a hammer. That may or may not be important. But it was definitely something the inspector should know. But how to get that information to him without revealing her involvement?

Ten minutes later Witherspoon, looking very relaxed, came into the room and took his chair. "I say, this looks jolly good."

Mrs. Jeffries poured herself a cup of tea. "Well, sir, how has your investigation gone so far?" she asked calmly.

"Not as badly as I'd first feared, but not as well as I'd hoped." He shrugged and told her what he'd learned that day.

"I do fear," he said as he finished his narrative, "that

I've wasted an awful lot of time at the Albritton house. But really, I could hardly refuse to question the man's relations."

"Then you don't think one of them could have done it?"

"I don't think it's likely." He took a bite of roast beef. "Not only do the rest of the family have alibis of a sort, but there's no evidence that any of them even knew of Albritton's interest in Annie Shields. Albritton, of course, has an idea that people have been rifling through his desk. He claimed he'd started inquiries about finding a house in San Francisco for himself and Annie Shields, and that someone had gone through his correspondence, but he's no proof."

"Had he bought many flowers from the victim?"

The inspector stared at her. "I don't really know . . . why? I mean, what made you ask that?"

She laughed. "Come now, Inspector, that's the sort of question you'd ask yourself. I was merely thinking that if he'd been in the habit of buying flowers from the girl every day, and from what you said yesterday it sounded as though he had, then I'm sure all of his female relations would have noticed. A man bringing in fresh flowers every day soon becomes the talk of the whole household. Unless, of course, it had always been his habit to do so." She fervently hoped she was right. For all she knew, Henry Albritton could have brought flowers from Annie Shields by the basketful and then dumped them in the Thames to avoid his relatives getting suspicious. But she didn't want the inspector to give up so easily.

Witherspoon grew thoughtful. "You're right, you know. By his own admission he bought some from her every day. Of course the women would notice. I'm going back there this afternoon; perhaps I'll have another talk with Mr. Albritton."

"Have you spoken to Mrs. Shields's female friends at Covent Garden?"

"I've got police constables doing that this very afternoon and I believe I might go round there again myself tomorrow morning." He speared another piece of beef. "Of course, it would be most helpful if we knew what the murder weapon was. Although I'm not all that sure why it would be useful. The killer probably tossed whatever he used in the Thames."

Mrs. Jeffries sent up a silent prayer of thanks. The inspector had inadvertently given her the opening she needed. "You know, it's quite odd you should mention that. You'll never guess who I ran into this morning. Dr. Bosworth—you remember that bright young man who was so very helpful in the case of that American who was killed during the Jubilee?"

"Oh yes, I remember him. He also helped out in that servant girl's murder last year. Clever chap." Witherspoon's fork was halfway to his mouth. He set it back down on his plate and stared at her incredulously. "You don't mean to say that Bosworth has some ideas about this case?"

Mrs. Jeffries was ready for that question. "To be perfectly honest, yes. As a matter of fact, I suspect young Dr. Bosworth has become something of an admirer of yours."

"An admirer of mine? Gracious. Really." He beamed with pleasure.

"Don't be so modest, sir," she said. "Why shouldn't he admire you? You're brilliant at solving homicides. Why, everyone says so."

"Thank you, Mrs. Jeffries. It's good of you to say so."

"I must say I was rather surprised when I ran into Dr. Bosworth," Mrs. Jeffries continued chattily. "He invited me to have tea with him. I'm not altogether sure that he didn't plan to run into me all along."

"Goodness. Why would he do that?"

"Because, sir, I suspect Dr. Bosworth sneaks over to the mortuary and has a good long look at every one of the victims whenever he learns you're investigating the case." She hoped the good doctor wouldn't object to her stretching the truth this way, but she had to do something. "Naturally, he couldn't come right out and approach you with what he thought. Officially, it was Dr. Potter who had charge of the postmortem. From what I hear, medical men are dreadfully territorial about their domains, so poor Dr. Bosworth had to sneak his peek on the sly, so to speak. Yes, indeed. He's become an admirer. It seems to me that Dr. Bosworth just can't keep away from your corpses."

Witherspoon gulped and pushed his plate away.

"So he approached me with what he'd found out," she continued.

"I take it he had examined Annie Shields?"

"Yes, sir. As I said, I don't think he can keep away. He thinks the murder weapon was probably a hammer."

"How on earth could he determine that?" Witherspoon was enormously flattered to have the doctor's admiration. But of course, he really did have to know how Bosworth had reached his conclusions. The young chap was very bright, but it wouldn't do to accept anything he said at face value.

"That's just what I asked him," she replied. She went on to tell him about Bosworth's examination of the three head wounds, taking care not to be too colorful in her description. Though the inspector gamely fought to hide it, the truth was he had a dreadfully weak stomach.

"Very interesting," Witherspoon said as he reached for his tea. "But even if it's true, it won't be much use to us. Anyone can get their hands on a hammer."

Witherspoon was deep in thought as he waited in front of the Albritton house for Constable Barnes, who was rounding the corner and heading his way at a fast trot. "No need to exert yourself, Constable," he called.

"Thank you, sir," Barnes puffed between breaths. "I just got word from the lads, sir. Still no word on Emma Shields. She's probably with the Maxwells. Should we send a telegram to the local police in Leicester and Nottingham and have them do some checking?"

Witherspoon pondered this as he turned towards the front door. "Yes," he said slowly, reaching up and banging the brass knocker, "I think we must. I don't like the idea of that poor child being unaccounted for."

Nestor let them inside. "Mr. Albritton is in his study," he said. "This way, gentlemen."

Witherspoon and Barnes followed the butler down the hallway. They were still some distance away when they heard raised voices. "I believe we'll wait here until Mr. Albritton is free," the inspector said, waving at two chairs outside the study door.

The butler looked uncertain. Finally he said, "As you wish, sir."

As soon as the man had left, they each took a chair. The voices behind the door rose in volume. Barnes whipped out his notebook and flipped it open. The inspector leaned his ear closer to the oak door.

"You can't keep going on this way," they heard an unfamiliar voice shout. "The business isn't going to run itself. We've got orders on three boats held up because you can't be bothered to decide which supplier to use."

"I've told you," Henry Albritton replied, "we won't use Cantilever's because of the way they treat their workers. Heddleston's no good because of the transport schedules, so that only leaves Bickston's. I gave my clerk instructions to wire them yesterday. So don't tell me I can't run my business. I'm doing my duty."

"You're doing your duty, but nothing else. Don't you see, the delay on this decision is only the tip of the iceberg. You really must put your heart back into work, Henry. You must or we'll all be ruined."

"We'll be ruined," Albritton repeated, his voice rising. "Have you ever stopped to think of how many other people are already ruined? People who through no fault of their own have no decent employment, no decent place to live, no decent chance to educate their children or provide them with anything but the most meager of existences?"

"Oh, for God's sake," the voice shouted. "Are we back onto that nonsense again? I thought you'd finally come to your senses. We're hardly responsible for the plight of the poor."

"If we're not responsible, then who is?" Albritton yelled. "Besides, why should I care if we're ruined? Who have I got to leave my money to? An idiot nephew with a greedy wife and a mean-spirited sister-in-law on the hunt for a husband? Why should I care if we all go to hell in a handbasket!"

"Henry!"

There was a heavy thump and the sound of something crashing. Alarmed, Witherspoon and Barnes both leapt to their feet and flung open the door.

Henry Albritton was standing in front of an overturned chair, the other man was flattened against the study window, his eyes wide with alarm and his face pale.

"Er, we didn't mean to interrupt," the inspector began, "but . . ."

"It sounded like there was an altercation takin' place," Barnes supplied helpfully. "Are both you gentlemen all right?"

Henry Albritton flushed slightly. "My apologies. Inspector, Constable, Sherwin." He nodded to all of them in turn. "I quite forgot myself." He picked up the chair and sat it upright. "Clumsy of me. I knocked it over when I jumped to my feet. Poor Sherwin was quite alarmed."

"That's quite all right. You've been under a considerable strain lately." The man peeled himself away from the window. "I shouldn't have pressed you about business. My apologies, Henry." Turning towards the inspector, he extended his hand. "We mustn't let the police believe this sort of behaviour is common to us. Despite appearances, Albritton and August Boatbuilders generally have very sedate business discussions. My name's Sherwin August. I'm Henry's business partner."

Witherspoon took the proffered hand and introduced Constable Barnes. August was portly, of medium height with thick blond hair and muttonchop whiskers. Behind the smile in his bright blue eyes, he regarded the policemen cautiously.

"Why don't we all sit down?" Albritton said, once the amenities were finished. "Perhaps I should ring for tea?"

"I can't stop long, Henry," August replied. "I must get back to the office."

"Where are your offices located?" Witherspoon inquired. He was still rather puzzled over the argument he'd overheard. Gracious, it sounded as though Mr.

August thought Henry Albritton had become a radical socialist! But just as the thought entered his mind he pushed it to one side. Annie Shields's murder had nothing to do with Albritton's political ideas.

"We've three yards here in London," August said. "Our offices are at our largest one. On Castle Street, just near St. Paul's Pier."

"Sherwin," Albritton said softly, "I think perhaps you ought to tell these gentlemen where you were Sunday night."

The inspector was rather irritated. He'd have gotten round to asking the man himself, and he didn't much like having someone put their oar in, so to speak. Furthermore, they had no evidence that Sherwin August knew anything at all about Annie Shields.

"Where I was?" August was more puzzled than annoyed. "Why should the police wish to know that?"

"Because someone very dear to me was murdered," Albritton snapped. "And you've got as much motive as anyone for wanting to get rid of her."

Mrs. Goodge had a lovely tea laid when they all returned at five o'clock. Betsy had arrived home first, but instead of saying a word to Mrs. Jeffries or the cook, she'd dashed up to her room. Luty and Hatchet, quarreling with one another, arrived next, followed immediately by Wiggins. By the time Betsy came back to the kitchen carrying two brown paper parcels in her arms, Smythe had strolled in and taken his customary seat.

"What's that?" he asked, nodding at the parcels.

"Some old clothes," Betsy said airily. "I'm giving them to one of Annie's friends. She needs them worse than I do."

"Excuse me," Hatchet said stiffly. He glared at Luty

and then quickly looked at Mrs. Jeffries. "But before
any of us begin, I do think there's something we must
discuss. We must decide what to do about Emma."

"Oh dear." Mrs. Jeffries had hoped they could wait a
day or two before dealing with that. "Is the child being
troublesome?" she asked.

"Not at all," Hatchet replied. "She's a very sweet
little girl. It's just that she misses her mother. She's
very confused right now, very frightened. I do feel that
we must get her settled somewhere soon—"

"You mean afore you get so attached to her it'll break
yer heart to let her go," Luty interrupted.

The butler shot his mistress another fierce glare. "I'm
not getting attached to the child. But I could hardly let
the poor little thing cry all night, could I? She was
frightened. She was in a strange place with unfamiliar
people."

"Hatchet's been fussin' over Emma like a mama cat,"
Luty explained. "He spent most of the night rockin' her
in my old rockin' chair."

"Me! What about you? You were in and out of that
room so many times last night it's a wonder the poor
child got any sleep at all," Hatchet shot back. "Go
ahead, admit it, you're getting quite sentimental over
Emma yourself. You let her sit on your lap all through
breakfast."

"Really, Luty, Hatchet," Mrs. Jeffries interjected. "Do
you think we could get back to the point? I quite agree
with Hatchet. For the child's own good, we must get
her settled somewhere. Now, I do have an idea. But
before I tell it to you, I'd like to hear what you've all
learned."

"Can I have another slice of cake?" Wiggins asked,
pointing to the Madeira cake in front of Mrs. Goodge.

Mumbling about people's teeth rotting out of their heads, she cut him a second slice.

"Well, I didn't have much luck today," the cook announced as she slapped Wiggins's plate in front of him. "Albritton's not got any scandal to him, at least not that I've sussed out yet. Me sources told me he's rich as sin, but he made it all in trade. Seems like he's been havin' some trouble with his partner lately, though. Albritton's got some newfangled idea about how the workers ought to be treated, and Sherwin August—that's his business partner—is goin' round tellin' everyone that Albritton's gone off his head."

"You've learned quite a bit, Mrs. Goodge," Mrs. Jeffries said. "Before anyone else goes, why don't I tell you what I've found out." She told them about her meeting with Dr. Bosworth and about everything she'd learned from the inspector at lunchtime.

"The Struttses are lyin'," Wiggins said around a mouthful of cake. "I know 'cause the kitchen maid told me she found Mr. Strutts's coat hangin' on the banister. Said Gordon Strutts is real particular about his clothes and it were damp through and through, like he'd been out."

"Hmm. It was a particularly foggy night on Sunday as well," Hatchet put in. "Did she have any idea when Mr. Strutts was out?"

"She didn't know fer sure. She and the other kitchen maids had been out to church and then taken their sweet time comin' home. She didn't get in till almost eleven."

"A young kitchen maid out till eleven!" Mrs. Goodge was positively scandalized.

Wiggins grinned. "I don't think they was at church either. More likely they was out larkin' about with friends. Anyway, Abigail told me about Mr. Strutts's coat bein' so damp and she'd no reason to lie."

"How'd they get in the house that late at night," the cook asked.

"Seems they'd cooked up a scheme with one of the footmen to leave the back door unlatched. Guess they knew they was goin' to be gettin' in late."

"Shocking," Mrs. Goodge muttered. "Absolutely shocking."

Wiggins ignored her. "Abigail also told me something else. Mr. and Mrs. Strutts coulda known about Annie. Seems Mrs. Strutts listens at keyholes. Abigail saw her doin' it about two weeks ago, and one of the other maids told her that she'd seen Hortense Strutts do it lots of times."

"How does that mean that the Struttses could have known about Annie Shields?" Luty asked.

"What if Mr. Albritton had been talkin' about Annie to this solicitor fellow and Hortense overheard it?" Wiggins suggested.

"Do you think you can find out for certain if Hortense Strutts knew about Annie?" Mrs. Jeffries asked the footman. "It's very important." To establish that anyone in the house had killed Annie Shields, it was urgent to establish that they knew about her in the first place. If one of them had known, there was a good possibility the others had as well. People did tend to talk, especially in matters of self-interest. As far as Mrs. Jeffries could tell, everyone in the household had something to lose if Henry Albritton opened his house and his bank account to an illegitimate daughter.

"But Abigail doesn't know," Wiggins replied, frowning. "I already asked her."

"Then try askin' someone else," Betsy ordered impatiently. "Try askin' Hortense's maid. She'd probably have some idea." She wanted them to get on with it.

She was dying to see the look on Smythe's face when she told them what she'd learned.

"I guess I can try," he murmured, looking very dubious. Trying to get more information out of that household would mean that he had to see Abigail again. He didn't feel right leadin' the poor girl on. But blimey, what else could he do? He had to help solve this case. If one of the women come up with the right answer, the men'd never live it down.

"Do the best that you can," Mrs. Jeffries said. "If no one in the household knew of Annie's existence or her importance to Mr. Albritton, then I'm afraid we're all wasting our time on this particular course of inquiry."

"Someone knew of her existence," Smythe said softly. "You can count on it. Fact is, someone knew plenty about the poor lass." He gave them a cocky grin, leaned forward and waited till he had everyone's attention. "Someone had been following Annie Shields for over a week before she was murdered."

CHAPTER 8

"How do you know *that*?" Betsy demanded, glaring at the coachman. He gave her an insolent grin. Honestly, she thought, Smythe looked as smug as a cat that'd just stole the cream. She'd love to wipe that silly smirk off his face. She was itching to tell everyone what she'd found out today. Now she was going to have to sit through another one of his puffed-up, drawn-out speeches. Leave it to a ruddy man!

"The same ways as I get all my information," he replied with a nonchalant shrug. "I use me brains." It would be a cold day in the pits of hell before he'd ever let on he'd paid for everything he learned today. But what else could he do? Fair was fair. Betsy wasn't above battin' her eyelashes at some footman to find out what she needed to know. He'd seen her use her wiles a time or two when they was on the hunt. Besides, this wasn't just another one of the inspector's cases they was investigatin', this was a matter of pride. Male pride. "A man can learn a lot if 'e's clever enough."

Betsy's eyes narrowed, but she clamped her mouth shut. Mrs. Jeffries, watching the pair, was sure the maid was biting her tongue. "Then do tell us," she said calmly. "We've quite a bit more to get through this evening."

"Yeah, stop wastin' time and git on with it," Luty put in. "I've got me own story to tell, you know."

"Give the man a chance," Hatchet said defensively. He smiled at Smythe and Wiggins. "I suppose we must forgive the ladies their impatience. The fairer sex is so much more emotional than we."

"Now you're wastin' time," Luty charged.

The butler lifted his chin. "I'll have you know, madam, neither of us is 'wasting time,' as you persist in saying. If you were a man, you'd understand. One must tell what one has learned in a logical, rational and calm manner if it is to have any true meaning."

"You mean you're all too slow-witted to get out more than five words in a row without havin' to stop and think," Luty muttered darkly. She stroked her fur muff. The other women were just as irritated as she was by Hatchet's pompous speech. Mrs. Goodge snorted, Betsy sighed irritably, and Mrs. Jeffries rolled her eyes.

Smythe, perhaps sensing an outright mutiny from the ladies, quickly said, "All right, all right, I'll get on with it. I know Annie Shields was being followed 'cause I met a man, feller named Fairclough. He's a friend of Bill Calloway's."

"But you didn't find Calloway?" Betsy asked.

"Not yet," Smythe retorted easily. "But I will. As soon as we're finished 'ere."

"Yes, yes," Mrs. Jeffries said, "I'm sure you'll find Calloway very quickly. Now, what did this Fairclough person tell you?"

"First of all, 'e claimed that Calloway ain't been seen since Sunday night."

"It's only Tuesday," Mrs. Goodge muttered.

"I know what day it is, Mrs. Goodge," the coachman said in exasperation, "but that's not the point."

"Then what is the point?" Betsy demanded. "You've been rattlin' on for five minutes now and you haven't said anything interesting."

"Rattlin' on?" Smythe repeated incredulously. "I'll 'ave you know men do not rattle on. We leave that to the ladies."

An all-out argument erupted. Luty, Mrs. Goodge and Betsy were outraged. Hatchet and Wiggins, feeling, of course, that they must defend their gender, immediately jumped in on Smythe's side. Mrs. Jeffries let them shout at one another for a few moments and then she lifted her hand, balled it into a fist and banged the table so hard the teapot jumped. "I do believe we'll have to postpone the hot issue of which sex 'rattles' the most until another time," she said forcefully. "In case you've all forgotten, we've got a murder to solve. Time is wasting."

Muttering under her breath, Mrs. Goodge contented herself with giving the men one final good glare. Betsy flattened her mouth into a stubborn line and Luty fingered her muff as she stared at Hatchet's chest.

The men, chastened but not bowed, shut up as well.

Mrs. Jeffries turned to the coachman. "Would you please continue with your narrative."

"As I was sayin'," Smythe continued, giving Betsy one quick anxious glance, "Calloway ain't been seen since Sunday evenin', and that's not normal 'cause the bloke practically lives at the Sail and Anchor. Fairclough told me that Calloway had told 'im he was worried cause 'e'd seen someone sniffin' around Annie Shields."

"You make her sound like a dog," Betsy mumbled.

"I don't mean it like that," he explained. "I mean, Fairclough claimed Calloway saw someone following the girl and then 'e found out this same feller was askin' questions about her."

"When did this happen?" Mrs. Jeffries asked.

"Accordin' to Fairclough, Calloway noticed the man about a week ago. That'd be last Tuesday or Wednesday. Fairclough wasn't sure exactly which day it was. But Calloway were spittin' mad about it. Supposedly, he watched the man follow Annie home on Tuesday night and then again on Wednesday. On Thursday the man started askin' people around the neighbourhood questions about 'er."

"Calloway told Fairclough all this?" Mrs. Jeffries frowned. "Why?"

"They was good friends," Smythe explained, his big hands toying with the handle of his mug, "and also, Calloway wanted Fairclough to 'elp 'im. You see, Calloway went after the bloke."

"Went after him," Luty asked. "What fer?"

"To find out why he was so curious about Annie," Smythe replied. "That's why 'e told Fairclough what was goin' on; 'e needed 'im. They waited until Saturday night. Fairclough was to 'elp Calloway if they spotted him anywhere near Annie Shields. Well, they did spot 'im. 'E was followin' 'er 'ome from work. They took off after the bloke, but 'e saw 'em comin' and give 'em the slip. But Fairclough says while the fellow was runnin', he dropped one of them little white cards out of 'is pocket. 'Ad the man's name and address on it."

"What was the name?" Mrs. Jeffries asked excitedly. Finally they were getting somewhere on this case.

"Fairclough didn't know," Smythe admitted. " 'E can't

read and neither could Calloway. But Calloway was goin'
to take the card to another man down the tavern and get
'im to read it. Fairclough saw Calloway come in the tavern
on Sunday evenin', but he didn't 'ave no card with 'im.
Calloway just 'ad a pint of beer and took off."

"How unfortunate," Mrs. Jeffries said. "Do you know
where Calloway is now?"

Smythe nodded. "I'm goin' there right after we finish
up 'ere. I may not be back till late."

"That's not fair," Betsy protested. "I can't go back
out tonight and I've got plenty of things I need to find
out."

"Betsy, lass," Smythe said soothingly. He thought
perhaps he'd pushed her enough for one day. "It's too
dangerous for you to go runnin' about at night."

Mrs. Jeffries held up her hand. This was an old argument, one she'd just as soon not get into now. For once,
she had to agree with the coachman. She didn't relish the
idea of Betsy or any other pretty young girl being out by
herself. "Why don't you tell us what you've learned,"
she said, smiling sympathetically at the maid.

"All right," Betsy said grudgingly. "I tracked down
a woman that was workin' on the Strand with Annie
Shields the night she was murdered."

"Another flower seller?" Smythe asked softly.

Betsy turned and stared at him, her gaze meeting his
levelly. "A prostitute. Her name is Millie Groggins. I
found her in a pub over near Aldgate Pump."

Smythe's face hardened. He started to speak, but Luty
neatly interrupted him. "Good fer you, Betsy. What'd
she tell ya?"

"Millie told me that Annie was right nervous that
night," Betsy began.

"Did Millie say how she knew that?" Hatchet asked.

"Had Annie said anything that indicated she was apprehensive?"

Betsy shook her head. "No, but Millie says she could tell by the way Annie was actin' that somethin' was bothering her. Remember how bad the fog was that night? Well, Millie says it were really bad down on the Strand; 'course it would be with them bein' right by the river. You couldn't see more than a few feet in front of you."

"That's true," Mrs. Goodge murmured. "That was a terrible night. My rheumatism was actin' up somethin' awful."

"Anyway, Millie says it was awful quiet. Neither of them had much business," Betsy continued, blushing slightly. "But every once in a while, while they was out there, they'd hear footsteps. Millie says it were never anyone interested in what they was sellin'."

"Flowers and flesh," Luty interjected.

"But by then, Millie had noticed that every time they heard someone comin' close, Annie'd get all stiff like and cranin' her neck to try and see who it was. When they'd walk on, she'd sort of sag, like she was disappointed. Millie's sure she was waitin' for someone."

"Millie might be sure, but I think she's wrong," Smythe commented.

"What makes you so sure *she's* wrong?" Betsy demanded.

" 'Cause of what I just told ya," Smythe said patiently. "Calloway spotted someone followin' Annie. She wasn't stupid. She'd probably spotted the man as well. 'Course she'd be nervous, she was probably expectin' to see 'im poppin' out of the fog every time she 'eard someone comin'."

"If Annie had seen anyone following her and she was

worried about 'im," Betsy said stubbornly, "she'd have said something to Millie. Women out on their own like that look out for each other. As it was, she didn't. Besides, Millie is almost sure Annie was supposed to be meeting someone that night."

"Did Annie tell Millie that?" Hatchet asked.

"No, but Millie claims Annie never worked late," Betsy replied.

"But we know she worked the Strand before," Mrs. Jeffries said doubtfully.

"That she did, but accordin' to Millie, Annie always worked the streets *before* people went into the theatres and restaurants. She claimed the gentlemen were more apt to buy their ladies a nosegay or corsage early in the evening. Millie was right surprised to see her out workin' a half-dead street at almost ten o'clock at night. So I think that considerin' how Annie was actin', she was only workin' late that night because she was going to meet someone."

"Betsy, lass," Smythe cut in, "Annie probably was workin' late 'cause she needed the money."

"That shows how much you know." Betsy smiled triumphantly. "She wasn't short that night. If she had been, she wouldn't have loaned Millie Groggins money."

Luty cackled. "Sounds to me like you've proved yer point."

"I would hardly say she's actually proved anything," Hatchet retorted. "However, there is some rationale to Miss Betsy's deduction. Hardly precise, but rather logical."

"And Harry Grafton did tell Luty that Annie had on the opal ring. A ring she was supposed to show someone," Mrs. Jeffries said thoughtfully.

"It sounded more like Harry thought Annie was wearin'

it to show it off," Luty said doubtfully. "I didn't think he meant she was wearin' it 'cause she had to *show* it to somebody."

"But we don't know, do we?" Mrs. Jeffries smiled. "I'm not disputing your interpretation of what Harry told you, Luty. However, isn't it possible that Harry misinterpreted what Annie said that night in the pub?"

"It's possible, I suppose. Reckon we'll never know fer sure, though. Come to think of it, you might be right. From what we've heard of Annie Shields, she weren't no silly git. She don't sound like the type to wear a valuable ring out at night just to be impressin' someone."

"I think we ought to go on the assumption that Annie had that ring on for a specific reason," Mrs. Jeffries said. "The most logical reason, of course, is because she wanted to show it to Henry Albritton."

"But he was supposed to see the ring on Monday," Mrs. Goodge put in.

"True," Mrs. Jeffries agreed. "So that means the person she was going to show the ring to either wasn't Albritton or that Albritton had changed the time."

"Does he have an alibi for Sunday night?" Wiggins asked.

"According to what the inspector told me, his alibi is the same as everyone else's in his household. He was at home."

Mrs. Goodge made a face. "Sounds like a right miserable household, doesn't it? The whole lot of them at home together on a Sunday evenin' and no one saw or talked to anyone else."

"And Albritton had given the servants the evening off," Smythe said. "That makes you think, doesn't it?"

"Yes, indeed." Mrs. Jeffries smiled at Betsy. "You've done very well, dear."

"Any ideas on who done it?" Wiggins asked. He shot a quick look at Hatchet and Smythe.

"Not yet," the housekeeper replied confidently, "but I'm sure we'll continue making progress." She was nowhere near as self-assured as she sounded, but she wasn't about to admit it in front of the men.

Luty leaned forward. "Can I talk now?" As no one said anything, she plunged straight ahead. "I went to see Myrtle Buxton today."

"Who's she?" Wiggins asked.

"She's that friend of mine who lives across the road," Luty explained. "Remember, she was the one that give us all that dirt on that medium and the Hodges murder last fall. I asked her if'n she'd ever heard of Henry Albritton and she give me a real earful."

"Excellent, Luty," Mrs. Jeffries said. She hoped Luty had been discreet with her questions, but she could hardly ask her. Despite her colorful speech and seeming toughness, Luty Belle Crookshank was very sensitive.

"She told me that Albritton married his wife for money," Luty said.

"We already knew that, madam," Hatchet sneered.

"Yeah, but what you didn't know is that ever since his wife died, Albritton's sister-in-law has been eyein' him like he was a prize bull in a field of steers."

"Lydia Franklin," Mrs. Jeffries clarified. "Is she in love with him?"

"Don't know if she's in love with the feller," Luty said bluntly, "but she sure as shootin' does her best to keep anyone else out of the way. Myrtle told me that a year or so after Frances Albritton died, Henry started seein' another woman. Out of the blue, some really ugly gossip started about this woman and she cleared outta town like the devil himself was on her heels. Myrtle's purty sure it was Lydia who started the gossip and that there weren't no truth to it."

"That's very interesting," Mrs. Jeffries said slowly. "Does Myrtle remember the woman's name?"

"Oh, she recalled it just fine, but it ain't gonna help us none. Her name was Clara Hemmings. But she's gone. The woman was so humiliated she went all the way to India. Ain't been back since." Luty snorted. "Now, if'd been *me* someone was jawin' about, I wouldna been the one leavin' town. They would."

"What else did this Myrtle Buxton tell you?" Mrs. Goodge asked. Her tone was slightly petulant. But everyone pretended not to notice. Generally, it was the cook who had the richest sources of gossip in London. Understandably, she was a bit put out to hear that Luty had been tapping another, perhaps equally rich, vein.

"Not all that much. I didn't want to be gone too long," Luty admitted. "I just popped out fer a few minutes while Emma was havin' her nap. The only other thing Myrtle told me was that Lydia's husband left her poorer than a prospector with a empty mine. Franklin Warren sounds like he didn't have any more sense than a bank mule. Left Lydia flat busted broke when he finally died. She had to move in with her sister and rent out her house."

"What did this Mr. Franklin do for a livin'?" Wiggins asked, not because he particularly cared but because he wanted to contribute to the meeting too.

Luty frowned slightly. "I ain't rightly sure. But from the way Myrtle described him, I think he was a . . . well, what we'd call a travelling salesman back home. I ain't sure what you'd call it over here. But he travelled some and he sold as he went. You know the kind of stuff I mean, one month he'd be selling safes, the next month it'd be bicycles or ladies travellin' bags. Right before he died he was sellin' lawn tents, billiard tables and gout medicine."

"How very interesting," Hatchet said. "If you're quite finished, madam, I'd like to share what I have learned."

"When did you get out?" Luty asked sharply.

"Early this morning," he replied. "Naturally, I kept my inquiries short and to the point."

Luty snorted. "Yeah, so short you probably didn't learn nuthin'."

"On the contrary, madam." Hatchet gave her a smug smile. "I learned a great deal. To begin with, I can tell you that Mr. and Mrs. Gordon Strutts knew full well that Annie Shields might be Henry Albritton's daughter." He turned and beamed at Wiggins. "You were quite right in your supposition. Mrs. Strutts had overheard Mr. Albritton discussing the situation with Harlan Bladestone."

"Gracious, Hatchet, that is rather remarkable," Mrs. Jeffries commented. "How did you find out so very quickly?"

Hatchet's chest swelled with pride. "Like Smythe, I, too, have my sources."

"You got lucky," Luty muttered.

"I assure you, madam," he replied frostily, "luck had nothing to do with it. I got clever. Oh drat, what I meant to say was that in my usual calm, rational fashion, I ascertained the likeliest sources for the most efficient gathering of information and I pursued them. According to what I learned, both the Struttses were well aware of the possibility of Henry Albritton having a child, and more importantly, they were quite alarmed by the prospect."

"Alarmed?" Mrs. Jeffries asked curiously. "In what way?"

"They were alarmed enough to start following Albritton. Gordon Strutts has been keeping a close eye on Albritton's movements. His wife, Hortense, has kept an eye on Annie Shields."

"The veiled lady," Luty yelled. "Maybe Harvey Maxwell wasn't tellin' tales when he told me he'd seen someone hangin' around Emma."

"I fear it's far too early to make that assumption," Hatchet said, annoyed at his employer for trying to steal his thunder. "Hortense Strutts was watching Annie Shields, not Emma."

"Cor blimey, sounds like 'alf of London were watchin' the poor woman," Wiggins interjected. "Pity none of 'em was there to see who murdered her."

"One of 'em was there, all right," Smythe muttered. "Too bad it was the murderer."

Mrs. Jeffries tried to keep it all straight in her mind. Now there were several people who knew of the connection between Annie Shields and Henry Albritton. And at least two people who had been watching the victim on the sly! However, she didn't attempt to reach any conclusions yet. She'd wait till she'd gained the quiet of her own rooms to do her real thinking. And now she had so much to try to sort out!

"Seems to me the men have done their fair share of investigatin'," Smythe said with another one of his cocky grins. "And you ladies 'aven't done 'alf bad neither."

"What about Lady Cannonberry?" Betsy asked Mrs. Jeffries. Like the other women present, she was eager to change the subject. If the men got any more puffed up with pride, they'd have to knock a ruddy hole next to the door so it'd be big enough for 'em to walk through.

Mrs. Jeffries sighed. "I'm afraid we've a bit of a problem."

"Problem?" Mrs. Goodge asked. "With Lady Cannon-berry? What's all this about then?"

"Well, it's rather odd, really. Lady Cannonberry came back to London on Saturday evening." Mrs. Jeffries was suddenly determined not to discuss the subject of Lady Cannonberry in front of the men. First of all, she was irritated with the way they were all gloating, except for Wiggins, and that was only because he hadn't learned to gloat yet. Secondly, because she wasn't certain what she had to say was any of their business. It was women's business. Instantly, she made up her mind. "Actually, I ran into her today as I was leaving the tearoom. She sent everyone her regards."

"But I thought you said you 'ad a problem," Smythe protested.

"It's not really a problem," she replied airily, "I mere-ly meant we'll have to stay on our toes. Now that she's back, she does occasionally pop in to say hello to the inspector. We wouldn't want her suspecting we were all out nosing around, would we?"

Smythe gave her a suspicious look but said noth-ing.

"What should we do next?" Wiggins asked.

"Next!" Luty protested. "Nell's bells, boy, I still ain't finished with doin' my first job."

"Luty's right," Mrs. Jeffries said smoothly. "I think if we all continue digging, we're bound to come up with even more."

"I'm going to pop out for a bit," Betsy said, glancing at the clock. "It's important."

"Where are you goin'?" Smythe demanded.

Betsy ignored him, leapt to her feet and dashed for the coatrack. Slipping on her heavy cloak, she turned to Mrs. Jeffries and said, "I should be back in time to serve the inspector his dinner. There's just one little thing I want to do. It won't take long, I promise."

"Are you goin' to let her go, then?" Smythe asked Mrs. Jeffries. He looked outraged, incredulous.

"Of course I'm going to let her go," Mrs. Jeffries said calmly. "It may be dark, but it's still quite early. The streets should be safe enough. There are plenty of people about." She was leery of letting the girl go out, but really, it was only half-past five. Besides, she was rather annoyed at the way the men had learned so much more than the ladies. It didn't seem fair.

Over dinner, Mrs. Jeffries learned even more about the case from the inspector. "You were absolutely right about the flowers," he said as he leaned back in his chair. "The family and the servants had noticed he was bringing home huge bunches of them every day. Mrs. Franklin especially was most upset about it."

"How very clever of you," Mrs. Jeffries said.

"Really, Mrs. Jeffries," the inspector exclaimed, "you're the one who suggested it."

"Yes, but I'm sure you were the one who was intelligent enough to confirm it by talking to the servants and not the family." Under the table, she crossed her fingers that she was right.

He beamed. "Oh, you know my methods so well. I spoke with the housemaids, actually. Mrs. Franklin noticed the flowers the first day Albritton brought them home. Mrs. Strutts didn't notice for several days."

"Odd that Mrs. Franklin didn't mention them to Mrs. Strutts," Mrs. Jeffries said.

"Not really." The inspector reached for another peach turnover. "The ladies, so I was told by both the housemaid and the butler, don't have all that much to do with one another. As a matter of fact, they rarely ever speak. Mrs. Strutts seemed to feel that she should be the lady of the house, but as Mrs. Franklin had got there first, she was a tad resentful."

"I see." Mrs. Jeffries thought this very interesting. "How sad that they don't get on."

"It is, isn't it?" He eyed the last peach turnover on the plate as if trying to make up his mind. "And I found out that Mr. Albritton's business partner has an alibi for the night of the murder." He lunged for the turnover and slapped it onto his dessert plate. "Honestly, everyone seems to be accounted for. Despite what Mr. Albritton says about his relations and partner, I don't think any of them could have done it."

"Where was Mr. August?"

"He was working late at his office." The inspector smiled. "Of course, we'll be able to confirm it easily enough as well. Though Mr. August doesn't realize it. Luckily for us, there was a robbery at the warehouse next to the boatyard offices. The police were there taking a report from ten past nine until well after ten o'clock Sunday night."

"They questioned Mr. August?"

"Oh no, no. But Constable Barnes was going to check with them to see if they saw lights on and that sort of thing." He popped a bite into his mouth and chewed thoughtfully. "Gracious, one can't work in the dark. And according to the report, there were a number of police about. As a matter of fact, one of the constables was in the boatyard itself. The whole area was thoroughly searched. Good thing for Mr. August too. Otherwise, he'd be my prime suspect."

"Really." Mrs. Jeffries was all ears. "Why?"

"Because as far as I can tell, he was the only one who

had any idea who Annie Shields was, and furthermore, he was the only one who knew that Henry Albritton was planning on selling up and taking the girl and leaving. He admitted that today."

"Why the bleedin' 'ell should I tell you anythin' about Annie?" Bill Calloway sneered. He leaned back in the chair and glared at the huge black-haired stranger.

"I reckon talkin' to me would be a mite easier than spendin' the night 'elpin' the police with their inquiries," Smythe answered. He glanced around the small, filthy back room of the restaurant where he'd tracked his quarry. The walls were spotted with damp, the ceiling sagged, the floor beneath his feet felt slimy, as though it were coated with grease, and there was a faint stench of rotting fish in the air. Smythe was glad the only light in the room was from a stubby candle set in the middle of the table. God knew what there was lurkin' in the dark shadows of the corners. Smythe knew he didn't want to find out. Trackin' Calloway had cost him plenty, but that was all right. He had a feeling it was going to be worth it. "So what'll it be? Me or the coppers?"

He wanted to get this over with fast so he could get back to Upper Edmonton Gardens and make sure Betsy had gotten safely home. Ruddy women. Always worryin' a man half to death.

Calloway wiped one dirty hand over his pointed chin. His hazel eyes narrowed suspiciously. On his cheek there was a crooked, two-inch scar. A wispy brown mustache hid the top of his thin lips. If Smythe had met him on the street, he'd have described him as "shifty," not dangerous.

"Don't see no reason to talk to either of ya," Calloway sputtered. But his eyes were frightened.

"Don't waste me time. I'm twice yer size. Either you tell me what I want to know, or I'll drag ya down to that copper that's walkin' the beat on the corner," Smythe said lazily. "And they wants to get their 'ands on you. You'd make a right good suspect. You're the only person who 'ad a reason for killin' that poor woman."

"Look." Calloway's voice was desperate. "What's it got to do with you, then? Huh? Annie and me knew each other a long time. We was friends. Why would I want to kill 'er?"

"I 'eard she give you the boot." Smythe grinned. "The police 'eard it too. Lots of murders been done for that reason."

"You heard wrong," Calloway exploded. "Annie was stubborn and she sometimes got above herself, but she loved me."

"You're claimin' she didn't tell you to sod off?"

"She did." He obviously realized that lying would be pointless. Too many people had witnessed the incident. "But she didn't mean it."

"When was the last time you saw 'er?"

"Sunday evenin' before she went to work."

"Was she wearin' her opal ring?" Smythe asked, watching Calloway carefully. He was rewarded for his observations. Calloway flushed slightly.

"Yeah, so what? Sometimes she wore it."

"Did you see her that night?"

"I already told ya, the last time I saw her she was as alive as you or me."

"But you were angry at 'er, weren't you? You were mad 'cause she told you to sod off in front of the whole world."

"She might 'ave told me to sod off and maybe I didn't much like 'ow she did it, but I wouldn't hurt her."

"You followed her, didn't you? Followed her, killed her and stole her ring so it'd look like a robbery."

"No. Damn it, I loved her." Tears sprang into his eyes and Smythe found himself warming a little. "I loved her, I tell ya. I'da been good to her and to the kid. I offered to take her away and start a new life. But she said no. Said she had somethin' better planned than goin' off with me."

He was crying in earnest now. "She stood right in front of me and told me she never wanted to see me again. And after all I'd done for 'er."

"All you'd done fer 'er. You mean like findin' out who the bloke was that was followin' her?"

Calloway swiped his cheeks. "Who you been talkin' to? Did that little sod Fairclough sell me out?"

"You ought to pick yer friends more carefully. Fairclough's already told me you followed the man that was followin' Annie." Smythe leaned in closer, forcing Calloway to lean farther back against the wall. "Who was 'e?"

Calloway stared at him for a long moment and then shrugged. "If Fairclough's been shootin' off his gob, he musta told you I don't know."

"You found the bloke's card." Smythe pulled a handful of coins out of his pocket and tossed them next to the flickering candle. Intimidating and bullying people went against his nature. Even people like Calloway. "Listen, I don't have much time tonight. Tell me what you know about Annie and who it was that were followin' her that week and I'll pay ya."

Calloway looked at the coins and then up at Smythe. He hesitated a moment before he snatched them up. "Fair enough. Annie's dead. I reckon nuthin' I can say will 'urt 'er now."

"All right, talk."

"The bloke followin' Annie was a private inquiry agent. His name is Albert Caulkins."

"Where can I find 'im?" Smythe shoved his chair back and started to rise.

Calloway put his hand on his arm and stopped him. "Now, why do you want to be talkin' to Mr. Caulkins? He can't help ya."

"I want to find out who 'ired 'im." Smythe stared at the hand on his arm and then up at Calloway.

"You don't need to."

"Really." He wondered if he was going to have to pop Calloway one before he got out of here. He didn't much like being touched. Unless, of course, it was by someone like Betsy. Not that that happened all that much. Bloody hell, he was so worried about the girl he was letting his mind wander. "And why is that?"

"Caulkins can't talk right now. Seems he's had an accident. Someone busted his jaw."

Smythe pulled his arm away. He felt dirty. "I hope someone had the brains to ask 'im who 'e was workin' for before they took a swing at 'im."

"Oh, they did," Calloway said. "They did. But that information's gonna cost." His expression was a mixture of fear, greed and bravado.

Smythe didn't know whether to pity him or pound him.

Calloway obviously wasn't above using his fists to get what he wanted. He'd just admitted to breaking the man's face. On the other hand, Smythe could understand that. If someone had been hanging around Betsy, he wasn't sure he'd be above using his fists too.

But he hoped he wouldn't take such pleasure in it.

Sighing, Smythe reached into his jacket pocket and

pulled out a handful of pound notes. He was tired of playing guessing games. Tossing the bills onto the table, he said, "I want the name."

Calloway grabbed the money, stuffed it into the pocket of his filthy coat and then looked up. "Albert Caulkins was hired two weeks ago. The man who 'ired 'im was a bloke named Sherwin August."

CHAPTER 9

Mrs. Jeffries forced herself to sit down. If she continued pacing, she'd wear a hole in the floor. She cast another anxious glance at the clock, saw that it had gone nine and promised herself she wouldn't get genuinely worried until half past.

Surely Betsy would be back by then.

But what if she wasn't? Mrs. Jeffries would never forgive herself if some harm came to the girl. She should never have let her go out. This is what comes of letting pride dictate action, she thought.

If she'd insisted Betsy stay in this evening, she wouldn't be worrying herself to death now. Mrs. Jeffries sighed. But she'd honestly thought Betsy would be fine and she'd certainly expected to see her safely back home by now. Besides, she'd so wanted to learn more. Oh, be honest, Hepzibah, she told herself. The real reason she'd let Betsy go out this evening was because she'd wanted one of the women to bring in the clue that cracked the case. Childish, really. But sometimes one was childish.

Oh dear. She twisted her hands together and glanced at her cape hanging on the coatrack. Perhaps she should go looking for the girl. Then again, she'd no idea where Betsy had gone. She heard the back door open and she leapt to her feet. But the heavy steps stomping down the passage weren't Betsy's.

Smythe, his brows drawn together in a fearsome frown, charged into the warmth of the kitchen. He took one look at the housekeeper's anxious face and leaned against the doorjamb. "She's not back yet, is she?"

"No," Mrs. Jeffries admitted, "I'm afraid not."

For a moment he didn't say anything. He just stared straight ahead, his mouth grim and his jaw rigid. Finally he said, "Do you have any idea where she were goin' tonight? It's gettin' late, Mrs. Jeffries. Much too late for her to be out on the streets."

"I know, Smythe. She should have been back hours ago. This is all my fault. I shouldn't have let her leave after tea," Mrs. Jeffries said.

Again the back door opened, and this time Betsy's hurried footsteps could be heard running down the hall.

"Bloomin' Ada," Smythe exploded as soon as the girl popped into the kitchen. "Do you know what time it is?"

"It's only a little past nine," Betsy replied haughtily. She grinned at Mrs. Jeffries and started unbuttoning her coat.

"We were getting worried, Betsy," Mrs. Jeffries reprimanded her lightly. "I'd no idea you'd be out so late."

"Sorry, Mrs. Jeffries," Betsy replied, slinging the coat onto the rack. "I didn't mean to worry anyone, but it was worth it. You won't believe what I've found out."

"Why don't ya start with tellin' us where the bleedin' 'ell you've been," the coachman snapped, glaring at her as she sat down.

"Now, Smythe," Mrs. Jeffries soothed, "Betsy's home safe. That's what's important. Let her tell us what she's learned in her own good time. Should I get Mrs. Goodge and Wiggins?"

She wanted them here because she'd sensed today they were both feeling left out. Furthermore, this ridiculous rivalry had gone far enough. While she'd been pacing the floor and worrying about Betsy she'd realized one of the reasons she'd not gotten a clue about this case was because they'd all been so concerned with topping each other's information—and she considered herself equally guilty in this—that she hadn't done any proper thinking about the murder. It had to end. They had to work as a team.

"I'm going to get both of them right now," she announced as she headed for the stairs. "I've something to say that all of us should hear."

Leaving Betsy alone with the still-frowning coachman, she fairly flew up the stairs.

Betsy gave him a cheeky grin. "What are you looking so miserable about? What's wrong? Didn't you have much luck this evening?"

Smythe gave her a long, level stare. She didn't have a clue. Not a ruddy clue. When he'd walked into the kitchen and seen Mrs. Jeffries's anxious face, his heart had almost stopped. He'd been scared to death that something had happened to her. But by heavens, he wasn't going to let her know it.

"Nuthin's wrong," he said, forcing himself to smile. "I found out plenty. As soon as the rest of 'em gets down, I'll tell ya."

Mrs. Jeffries returned with Mrs. Goodge, a yawning Wiggins and Fred in tow. As soon as they'd all sat down and Fred had taken his usual spot beside the footman's chair, she started in on her speech.

For a good fifteen minutes she lectured. She didn't spare herself either, but took as much of the blame for their idiotic behaviour as she heaped on everybody else. By the time she was finished, they were all looking a bit sheepish.

Wiggins was the first to speak. "Thank goodness all this is over with, then," he said, reaching down to pat Fred on the head.

"We have been a bit silly," Mrs. Goodge agreed. "Reckon it's time to get on with getting this murder solved."

"Seems to me it was the men that started it," Betsy murmured softly. "But we did our share of stirrin' it up too."

"All right, then," Smythe agreed, "we've all been actin' like children. Startin' now, let's try and remember we're in this together. Betsy, why don't you go first?"

Surprised, she replied, "That's right kind of you. Actually, I will."

"Where did you go tonight?" Mrs. Jeffries asked.

"Covent Garden." Betsy put her elbows on the table and leaned closer. "I went to have another chat with Muriel. Once Smythe mentioned that someone had been followin' Annie, I realized there were some important things I needed to ask. First of all, Muriel agreed with what Smythe found out. Someone was following Annie and Annie knew it."

"For goodness' sakes," Mrs. Goodge exclaimed. "Why didn't the girl tell you that the first time you spoke to her?"

Betsy smiled. "Because I didn't ask. You've got to understand how a lot of those people are."

"What people?" Wiggins asked curiously.

"Poor people. Especially poor people from the East End. They don't much trust anyone. They can't. It takes a while before they'll open up even a little." Betsy gestured with her hands. "Most of them have never even seen a place like this, let alone lived in one. Muriel only answered the questions I asked when I talked to her that first time, and even that was like pulling teeth out of a tiger. Tonight I took some of my old clothes over to her and bought her a hot drink from one of them street costers. We got to chattin', you see, that's why I was gone so long. I knew it would take a while before she'd tell me much."

Wiggins looked puzzled. "You mean she was grateful like?"

"No, no." Betsy shook her head vehemently. "That's not what I mean at all. She weren't grateful. She's got 'er pride. Oh, it's hard to explain . . . it was sorta like, I told 'er a lot about myself, about my past and my family and watchin' my mother and sister die and about bein' so poor you didn't know where your next bite to eat was coming from. That made Muriel feel she could trust me. That she could tell me things and I wouldn't think less of her or use what she'd told me to take what little she's got away from her. I know it sounds downright peculiar . . . but in a way, I give her hope. I mean, she saw that I'd got out and made a better life for myself and maybe she can too. Oh . . . I'm not explainin' it very well."

"You're doin' just fine," Smythe said quickly.

"Yeah, I think I know what you mean now," Wiggins agreed. "It's like you convinced her you was a lot like 'er."

Betsy nodded. "Anyways, once she felt she didn't have to watch her back with me, she talked plenty. As I said, she knew Annie Shields was being followed. Annie had told her. But Muriel was pretty sure the person following her was a woman"—she looked at Smythe—"not a man. So I'm thinkin' there musta been two people keepin' their eye on her."

"Was Muriel absolutely certain it was a woman?" Mrs. Jeffries asked.

"Oh yes."

Mrs. Jeffries thought about that. "Perhaps it was Hortense Strutts. Did Muriel ever see this woman?"

Betsy nodded. "Last week. But she couldn't see her all that well, not enough to identify her. The woman was all covered up like, she had on a big hat with a veil and a heavy coat. Annie spotted her when they was loadin' their carts to go out that mornin'. She looked up, went right pale and said, 'She's back.' When Muriel asked her what she meant, Annie told her that she was bein' followed and she was gettin' right sick of it. Muriel told her she ought to have it out with the woman, but Annie wouldn't hear of it." Betsy paused and took a deep breath. "On Sunday, Muriel spotted the woman again. She pointed her out to Annie, but Annie wasn't in the least upset. Said she'd taken care of it. She was meetin' someone that night that was goin' to take care of it once and for all."

"So Annie Shields had arranged to meet someone the night she died," Mrs. Jeffries said thoughtfully.

"I'm sure of it," Betsy said slowly. "But Muriel told me she had the impression it wasn't somethin' Annie was lookin' forward to."

"What did she mean by that?" Mrs. Goodge asked.

"It was just an impression Muriel had," Betsy admitted. "So I don't much think we can consider it evidence, but Muriel said she had the strongest feelin' that Annie was bein' forced to meet whoever she was goin' to meet."

They fell silent as they digested Betsy's information. After a few moments Mrs. Jeffries glanced at Smythe and nodded for him to begin.

"I found Calloway," he began. He didn't tell them it had cost him an arm and a leg. "And he give me an earful." He told them every little detail of his meeting with Bill Calloway. "So you see," he finished, "Sherwin August had been keepin' an eye on the victim for two weeks. He knew everything about her."

"Including the fact that she was Henry Albritton's illegitimate daughter," Mrs. Goodge mumbled.

"Right."

"So that means that both the Struttses and Sherwin August knew who she was." Mrs. Jeffries frowned. "But only the Struttses knew that Albritton was planning on taking the girl and leaving the country. And we don't know *that* for certain. We're only guessing that Hortense Strutts did overhear Albritton's plans."

"I think it's pretty likely, though," Mrs. Goodge said thoughtfully. "I mean, if they knew who Annie was, then there's a good chance they knew what Albritton was plannin' on doin', right? Albritton had talked freely to his solicitor, and it was that conversation that we think Hortense was listening to. Besides, why would Hortense follow the girl unless she knew what was goin' on?"

"Huh?" Wiggins looked very confused.

"What Mrs. Goodge means," Mrs. Jeffries said smoothly, for she'd only just followed the cook's logic herself, "is that Annie Shields was a pretty young woman. If

Henry was merely infatuated with a flower girl, then there would have been no reason for Hortense Strutts to be alarmed. Infatuations with flower girls generally don't last very long, especially between middle-aged men and young widows. But the Struttses were upset enough to follow both Albritton and Annie. That means they must have realized that Henry's relationship with this young woman was not some temporary romantic infatuation. It was serious enough to threaten them into taking action." She reminded them of what the inspector had told her about Albritton's own suspicions concerning his relations.

"What about Lydia Franklin?" Betsy asked. "Wouldn't the Struttses have told her about Annie?"

"The inspector didn't think so," Mrs. Jeffries said. "According to what the Albritton servants told him, Mrs. Franklin and Mrs. Strutts didn't confide in one another. I think it highly unlikely the Struttses would have included Mrs. Franklin in any of their plans. Especially if those plans included getting rid of Annie permanently."

"But we don't know it was the Struttses," Smythe said.

"If it weren't them, then how come they lied to the inspector about their alibi that night?" Wiggins asked. "They claimed they hadn't gone out at all, but that maid told me that Gordon's coat was damp when she got home. Now, if Gordon was gone, seems to me that means Mrs. Strutts coulda been gone too."

"You're absolutely right, Wiggins," Mrs. Jeffries said hastily. "But so is Smythe. They may have both been out that night, but that doesn't mean they murdered anyone."

"Then 'ow come they lied?" Wiggins persisted.

Mrs. Jeffries shrugged. "Well, it's possible that Gordon Strutts was out doing something else, something he didn't wish the police to know about. He could have been gambling or seeing another woman . . ."

Mrs. Goodge choked on her tea. Wiggins, who was sitting next to her, immediately began pounding her on the back. "Are you all right, Mrs. Goodge?" he asked, thumping her hard between the shoulder blades.

"I'm fine," she sputtered, lunging forward in order to avoid another blow. "Leave off pounding me, boy. The tea just went down the wrong way."

Mrs. Jeffries gazed at her in concern. The cook's cheeks had gone bright red. "Mrs. Goodge, is everything all right?"

"All right . . . well, of course everything's all right. I just choked on my tea. Oh bother." Sighing, she made a face. "Well, if you must know, I've uh . . . learned a few things and well . . ."

"You've kept 'em to yourself 'cause you was afraid one of us men would get the jump on ya?" Smythe supplied helpfully.

Looking thoroughly chastened, she nodded wearily. "It was wrong of me, I know. But crimminey, you men were awfully arrogant. But that wasn't the only reason I didn't say anything." Her cheeks flamed again. "The information is a bit . . . it's not the sort of thing I'd want to talk about in front of Betsy or Wiggins."

Betsy gasped in outrage, Wiggins gaped at the cook, and Smythe laughed.

"I take it the information is of an intimate nature," Mrs. Jeffries guessed as she tried to keep a straight face.

"Gordon Strutts likes boys," Mrs. Goodge blurted. "He only married Hortense to keep up appearances. And she only married him to get away from her father." She dropped her gaze and studied the top of the table.

"Truth of the matter is, Gordon and Hortense can't stand each other. It's a marriage of convenience. Gordon was terrified his uncle would find out about his . . . er, habits and Hortense's old father was a real Tartar. She'd have married the devil himself to get away from him."

Betsy giggled. "Oh, Mrs. Goodge. You shoulda said something. Wiggins and I ain't babies. We both know about people like Gordon. And Hortense isn't the first woman to ever get married to get out of the house. Stop tryin' to protect us. Even Wiggins and I know about things like that."

"Well, you oughtn't to," the cook shot back. "You're both too young. You ought to have a better view of life and marriage. It's disgustin', that's what it is. Marriage of convenience, indeed!"

Mrs. Jeffries could see that Mrs. Goodge was quickly getting over her embarrassment. What had started as a delicate subject had soon become a matter for an informed opinion like her own.

"I think it's safe to assume, then," Mrs. Jeffries said, "that given Gordon's . . . uh . . . predilections, it's quite possible he was out on Sunday night visiting his, shall we say, friend." She heard Smythe mutter a word she hadn't ever heard before under his breath. She thought it best to ignore it. "That would explain his damp coat. In other words, he may have been gone from the house, but that doesn't mean he was out murdering anyone."

Mrs. Goodge nodded.

" 'Course," Smythe said casually, "even if Gordon was out with one of his 'friends' Sunday night, that still don't let the Struttses out as suspects."

"I know," Mrs. Jeffries said. "If Gordon was gone, then that means that Hortense has no alibi. Besides, there's something else about their story which convinces me he wasn't home reading on Sunday night. Remember, the inspector told me that Gordon had supposedly been reading a novel called *An Evil Spirit* that night."

"What about it?" Betsy asked.

"Gordon Strutts told the inspector it was 'amusing,' " Mrs. Jeffries said thoughtfully. "But the truth is, I've read that novel and there's nothing in the least amusing in it. It's a rather tragic tale. Gordon Strutts never read that book. He lied. And his wife lied too."

They discussed the case for another fifteen minutes. But nothing seemed to come to any of them regarding a solution. Finally Mrs. Jeffries said, "The inspector is going to speak to all the principals in this case again tomorrow. I've got to find a way to let him know everything we've learned. Perhaps by breakfast, something will have occurred to me."

"Have you come up with any ideas about gettin' Emma Shields out of Luty's house?" Smythe asked.

"Actually, I have." Mrs. Jeffries quickly told them what she'd decided to do. "However, I do think we ought to wait another day or two before taking any action. It could be dangerous for the child to go to the Albritton house until we figure out who the murderer is." They all agreed this was true.

"But Mr. Albritton does know about Emma?" Betsy asked. "He knows he's got a granddaughter?"

Mrs. Jeffries shook her head. "No. The inspector hasn't told him."

"But Albritton's Emma's grandfather," Mrs. Goodge insisted. "He's a right to know about the girl."

"We don't know that for a fact, Mrs. Goodge," Mrs. Jeffries said calmly. "Furthermore, until we find out who the murderer is, I'm not sure it is safe for Mr. Albritton to know of her existence. Annie Shields was probably murdered because someone suspected she was Henry's daughter. I don't think that person would take kindly to knowing there was now a granddaughter in the picture."

"But surely the killer knows about Emma already?" Smythe put in. "Cor blimey, 'alf of bleedin' London was watchin' the woman before she was killed. They was bound to know about Emma. And you can bet your last farthing that that inquiry agent, Caulkins, told Sherwin August."

"Yes," Mrs. Jeffries agreed. "And I find that most interesting."

"Have you got some idea who the killer is, then?" Betsy asked eagerly.

"It's far too early for that," she replied. She refused to speculate further, no matter how hard they pressed. "Come on now, it's getting very late."

"And what about Lady Cannonberry?" Wiggins said grumpily. "You still haven't told us about her."

Mrs. Jeffries hesitated. "It's a rather delicate situation," she began.

"I thought we agreed there'd be no more secrets," Smythe interjected.

She thought about that for a moment. "You're right." She took a deep breath. She wasn't really violating Lady Cannonberry's confidence. The woman had only asked her not to mention anything to the inspector. Furthermore, perhaps a male point of view might be helpful here. "Lady Cannonberry came up from Devon on Saturday. She came home early so she could participate in the march in Trafalgar Square on Sunday."

As one, they all gaped at her. For the first time that Mrs. Jeffries could remember, the entire household was speechless with shock.

Wiggins found his voice first. "Lady Cannonberry come up to riot?"

"No, of course not," Mrs. Jeffries hastily explained. "She came up to what she thought was going to be a peaceful demonstration. Lady Cannonberry is a woman of conscience. Remember her father was a vicar. He helped in the battle to end slavery in those places in the British Empire where that evil institution was established. He was a friend of Wilberforce."

"But what's the Metropolitan Radical Federation got to do with endin' slavery?" Smythe asked incredulously.

"My point is that Lady Cannonberry has followed in her father's footsteps," Mrs. Jeffries clarified. "Mind you, while her husband was alive she did try to avoid doing anything that would embarrass him. But, of course, he's dead now. So she can do what she likes."

"Wilberforce? Slavery? I still don't see what that's got to do with marchin' in Trafalgar Square?" Mrs. Goodge mumbled. "I'm confused. A widow of a peer riotin'?"

"Slavery has nothing to do with why Lady Cannonberry came to London. She came because she's opposed to oppression and injustice." Mrs. Jeffries folded her arms over her chest. "The march in the square wasn't supposed to be a riot," she continued, trying her best to hang on to her patience. "If you'll recall, a number of groups were represented."

"Bunch of Irish, anarchists and socialists," the cook muttered darkly, "and all of them plottin' to overthrow our way of life."

Mrs. Jeffries would have dearly loved to debate the issue of their way of life, but right now she didn't have time. "Nonsense," she said firmly. "Many of those people were motivated by the noblest of reasons. There is a great deal of injustice and downright misery in our way of life. But that's not the point."

Wiggins yawned. "What is the point, then?"

"The point is, Lady Cannonberry saw the inspector that day. Her conscience is bothering her."

"Why should her conscience be kickin' up a fuss?" Betsy said bluntly. "Seems to me she were only there to try and do something to make this world a better place."

"Her conscience should be kickin' up a fuss," Smythe interjected before Mrs. Jeffries could open her mouth, "because she and the inspector have a . . . a . . . well, they likes each other. So she shouldn't be trottin' off to do things 'e wouldn't approve of."

"Wouldn't approve of!" Betsy yelped. "What's it to him? Lady Cannonberry isn't his dog."

"But he wouldn't be pleased to know she'd been in Trafalgar Square," Wiggins gasped. "Why, the inspector could have actually arrested her! Oh, he wouldn't have liked that at all. It'd be ever so awkward 'aving her round to tea if the inspector 'ad carted 'er off to jail."

"Bother on whether or not the inspector approves," Mrs. Goodge snapped. "Lady Cannonberry can do what she likes. She doesn't have to answer to any man."

Surprised, Mrs. Jeffries stared at Mrs. Goodge. The fact that she'd just neatly turned her back on her own opinion was obviously not going to bother the cook. Female independence was altogether a much more important issue than a mere trifle like overthrowing governments. However, Mrs. Jeffries didn't want any more dissension in the group. At least not until after this case was solved.

"Please, everyone," she commanded. "Calm yourselves. Lady Cannonberry's dilemma will have to wait

for a few days. In case you've forgotten, we've a murder
to finish."

"Exactly what is her dilemma?" Wiggins asked curiously.

"I've told you. She wants to know whether or not she
should tell the inspector." Mrs. Jeffries didn't add that
Lady Cannonberry now suspected exactly what she and
the household were up to as well. That, too, could wait
until after this case was resolved.

Betsy and Mrs. Goodge both snorted.

The next morning Inspector Witherspoon dawdled over
his breakfast so long, he was almost late for his appointment with Harlan Bladestone. He hurried down the street,
his breath coming in short painful gasps. Constable
Barnes was right on his heels.

Of course, Witherspoon thought, it wasn't really his
fault. He dashed up the steps and yanked open the door
to the building where Bladestone had his office. Mrs.
Jeffries and he had had the most interesting conversation
over toast and eggs.

Witherspoon nodded to the porter and hurried on past.
Gracious, now he had all sorts of useful avenues of
inquiry to explore. Sometimes it was so good to talk
out one's thoughts. Why, he'd dozens of different things
to think about. He hoped the solicitor wouldn't beat
about the bush all day. Considering what he needed to
do today, he really must get cracking.

"Hurry, Constable," he called over his shoulder to
Barnes as he raced down the hall towards Bladestone's
office. "We're running a bit late."

A few moments later found them sitting in front of
Bladestone's desk. The solicitor was frowning.

"You mean you still haven't found the child?"

Witherspoon shook his head. "No, I'm afraid not. We've sent word to the local police in both Leicester and Nottingham. We're hoping they might be able to help us find Florrie Maxwell."

"Then you're certain Emma is still with her?"

"We think it's likely," the inspector replied. "We've checked the local orphanages and foundling hospitals. No little girls of Emma's age have turned up there, so we're fairly certain she's still with Mrs. Maxwell."

Barnes coughed slightly. "I wouldn't worry about her safety, sir. By all accounts, Mrs. Maxwell was right fond of the girl. Even if she isn't with her, I'm sure she wouldn't have turned Emma out onto the streets or given her to someone she didn't trust."

Bladestone looked worried. "I should never have kept her existence a secret. If I'd acted on my natural instincts instead of searching for proof about Annie's parentage, Annie would still be alive and both she and her daughter would be safely living with Henry."

This was the opening the inspector had been hoping for. "Mr. Bladestone. Why didn't you tell Mr. Albritton about Emma?"

"Because I wasn't sure," Bladestone said in disgust. "It's this damned legal training of mine. I needed proof. For the past year I've known Annie was probably Henry's daughter, but I delayed and did nothing."

"You realize," Witherspoon said softly, "that we must tell Mr. Albritton about Emma. If there is a chance she's his granddaughter, he has a right to know about her."

"Don't we have to find her first?"

"We will," the inspector assured him. "Could you tell me exactly what Mr. Albritton was planning to do once he found his daughter?"

"But I've already told you. He was going to take Annie to America."

"Yes, but what was he going to do about his business interests?"

"Sell everything." Bladestone's eyes narrowed. "Inspector, I do believe I've mentioned that before."

"Yes, of course you have." Witherspoon smiled sheepishly. "What I meant to ask was, did Mr. August know of Albritton's intent?"

Bladestone didn't answer for a moment. "I'm not sure," he finally said. "But I suspect he did. I do know that Henry didn't tell him. For that matter, Henry didn't tell anyone but me."

"Then what leads you to believe that Mr. August was aware of Mr. Albritton's intent?" Witherspoon was very proud of that question.

Bladestone hesitated. "Look, Inspector. You'll forgive me, but well, this is damned difficult. You see, August came to see me a while back. I told him that I couldn't help him, that I was Henry's legal adviser, but that didn't seem to make any difference to the man. Before I could stop him, he was insisting that Henry was losing his mind and for the sake of the company I had to help do something about it." Bladestone waved his hands angrily. "I asked him to leave, of course. Henry may have become interested in peculiar politics, perhaps picked up some ideas that none of us approve of, but that hardly means he's insane."

"I don't see how that means August knew what Mr. Albritton's plans concerning Mrs. Shields were," Witherspoon said slowly.

"It doesn't—not directly, that is," Bladestone agreed. "But naturally, August's attitude was no secret to Henry. Henry told me he thought Sherwin was spying on him.

Going through his papers, his desk, that sort of thing."

Witherspoon tried to hide his disappointment. "If there was trouble between the two of them, isn't it possible that Mr. Albritton only imagined this?"

Bladestone smiled. "Absolutely not. Henry's the most methodical man I know. He writes everything down. If so much as an inkwell has been shifted even one inch on his desk, he'd spot it. If he thinks someone was going through his papers, then take my word for it, someone was."

"What would happen to Mr. August's half of the business if Albritton had sold out?"

"Mr. August doesn't own half the business," Bladestone replied. "He's not a full partner."

"Really? But I most definitely had the impression . . ."

"No doubt Sherwin meant for you to get the wrong impression," Bladestone said tartly. "But believe me, he owns less than twenty-five percent of the overall company. He originally owned half, bought in when Henry's father-in-law died. But August is a terrible spender. He and his wife both love money. Over the years he's sold some of his interest in the company back to Henry. In the event of Henry selling to someone else, I suspect August would have lost his position. He'd still own his twenty-five percent, mind you. But Sellinger's would put their own people in to run the boatyards."

"Sellinger's, you mean the shipbuilders?" Witherspoon was most surprised to hear this. Sellinger's was one of the biggest shipbuilders in the world.

"Yes, they've approached Henry several times wanting to buy him out," Bladestone said. "The last approach was a month ago. Henry refused. Then, after he saw Annie, he began to reconsider."

"Did Mr. August know this?" Barnes asked.

"Yes. He knew Henry had refused the offer," Bladestone replied. "But I'm sure he'd heard the gossip that
Henry was thinking of changing his mind. It's impossible to keep that sort of thing quiet."

The inspector thought about this. Gracious. This case
was getting terribly complicated. He calmed himself and
cast his mind back to his breakfast conversation with
Mrs. Jeffries.

"Furthermore," the solicitor continued, "I think that
there is a good possibility that in addition to Sherwin
August, everyone in the Albritton household knew that
Henry had decided to make a major change in his
circumstances. A change which would affect all their
lives."

"Where does Mr. Albritton keep his papers?" Barnes
asked.

"In his study at home."

"Not in his office?" The inspector was surprised. "In
that case, it could hardly have been Mr. August going
through Albritton's desk."

"I beg to differ, Inspector," Bladestone said. "August
has very free access to Henry's home."

Witherspoon wondered what that meant. He could
hardly imagine Sherwin August sneaking through a window of Albritton's house. "You mean he was in and out
frequently. But surely, Mr. Albritton would have been
there while Mr. August was there?" Egads, this was
getting confusing.

Bladestone leaned forward. "Sherwin's very clever.
He could have waited till Henry had stepped out of
his study and then had a good snoop. But whether it
was August or not, I don't know, I'm merely saying
it's possible. Because someone had gone through that
desk. Someone had seen that correspondence. And in

that correspondence, Henry had made it clear he was looking for a suitable house for himself and his daughter. He'd also written a letter to Sellinger's telling them he was willing to open negotiations."

The inspector suddenly thought of another question. "If Mr. Albritton had moved to San Francisco, what would have happened to his relatives? Would they have stayed on at this home?"

"Hardly. Henry felt he had a duty to all of them, but he fully realized he didn't need to support them in quite the style they're living in now." Bladestone sighed. "You've got to understand, Inspector. Henry's done a great deal of thinking about his life. Why should his relatives live in a grand house with servants to do their bidding when so many others in this world have nothing?"

"Had Mr. Bladestone made provisions for his relations?"

"They were all going to be taken care of," Bladestone said. "The Struttses were to be given the leasehold on one of Henry's properties in Islington. Henry felt it only fair to provide them with a place to live. But he wasn't going to continue giving them an allowance. Gordon has a small income from his father and Henry thought it would do the young man good to get out and make his own way in the world. Mrs. Franklin was going to be given a small allowance and sent back to her own home. They wouldn't have been destitute or left wanting, but they wouldn't be living in luxury either."

"I see," the inspector murmured. "And when did he make these provisions? When did he tell you?"

"A few days after he first met Annie Shields. He asked me to come by and we went into his study. Mrs. Franklin and the Struttses were all there. They didn't come in, of course. But they suspected Henry was up to something.

He was terribly excited. Happy. He felt he had something to live for. Someone to care about and love."

"Why didn't you tell him about Emma at that time?" Barnes asked.

Bladestone looked down at his desk. "Because I still wasn't certain Annie was Henry's daughter. The circumstances were right and she did look enough like Dora to be her twin sister, but there was still the chance that she'd no connection to Henry whatsoever."

"Yet you were the one that made sure Henry saw the girl?"

"Yes. I deliberately steered him down Regent Street that morning two weeks ago. I knew Annie would be in front of the arcade." Bladestone smiled wistfully. "I told Henry I wanted to stop and buy some flowers for my wife. You should have seen his face when Annie turned around. He gaped at her. Stared at her like an awestruck boy. For the first time in weeks Henry was happy." He sobered suddenly. "A few days after that Henry asked to come round. That's when he made the provisions for his relations. It's also when he changed his will."

CHAPTER 10

"You're sure that the constable couldn't have made a mistake?" Witherspoon asked Barnes as they waited in Sherwin August's office. "They're absolutely positive there were no lights on here Sunday night?"

Barnes, who was keeping an eye on the door while they waited for August, nodded. "Not only didn't the constable see any lights, but he knows there was no one here 'cause he come up and pounded on the bloomin' door. No one answered."

Witherspoon took a deep breath. "Right then, we'll see what Mr. August has to say for himself."

"If he ever comes back," Barnes muttered, his expression suspicious. "You don't think he's made a run for it, do you?"

"No, no, Constable," the inspector said, with more confidence than he felt. "I'm certain he's just out in the yard checking on a shipment. The clerk will find him. Besides, he's no idea we know his alibi is false. Have the constables we sent round to the Albritton house reported back yet?"

"I spoke to PC Lund when you was in talking to the chief." Barnes whipped out his notebook and glanced at the open door of Sherwin August's office to make sure they weren't being overheard. "Lund's a good man, knows how to get the servants to feel at ease enough to speak freely, if you know what I mean."

"I certainly do, Constable," Witherspoon agreed. He was so glad he'd thought to send someone round to question the Albritton servants again. After his chat with Mrs. Jeffries this morning, he'd had a whole different perspective on the case. "What was he able to learn?"

"Well, he got a kitchen maid talking and she's fairly certain that Mr. Gordon Strutts had gone out that night. His coat was damp when the girl come in." Barnes squinted at the paper. "Oh yes, and the girl also admitted the kitchen door had been left unlocked. The maids had arranged with one of the footmen to keep it open so they could come in when they liked."

"That means anyone could have come in and out as they pleased," Witherspoon murmured.

"Yes, sir. It also means they coulda done it without bein' seen." Barnes glanced up, his face full of admiration. "You was right about that, too, sir. Lund says that door opens onto a passageway that leads to the Albrittons' back garden and that connects to the churchyard at the end of the road. Whoever was comin' and goin' that night didn't even have to walk down the street. They coulda nipped in through St. John's."

Witherspoon smiled modestly. Double-checking the physical entries to either a household of suspects or the scene of a crime was one of his prime rules. He was so glad Mrs. Jeffries had reminded him of that this morning. "Routine, Constable. Simply routine. Did Mr. Albritton give permission for us to search his house and grounds?"

"Yes, sir. Lund said they was still lookin' when he left. Mind you, the Struttses put up a fuss and so did that Mrs. Franklin, but Mr. Albritton soon quieted 'em down. But as of midmorning, they hadn't found either a hammer or a set of bloody clothes."

"And they may not, Constable," Witherspoon admitted honestly. "I really have been remiss in my duty. What was I thinking? I should have had that house and the grounds searched immediately."

"Don't be too hard on yourself, sir," Barnes said sympathetically. "We'd no idea how complicated this case was goin' to get, did we?"

"Indeed, not," Witherspoon agreed emphatically. "Did Lund have any luck in confirming Mrs. Franklin's alibi?"

"Oh, he did, sir. Said the vicar were a bit nasty about it, seein' as we'd already asked him about Mrs. Franklin before." Barnes chuckled. "He seems to think highly of the lady, sir. But he confirmed she were at evensong service and that he'd spoken to her afterwards for a few minutes. The earliest she coulda got home was half past eight. So that let's her out, sir. Mrs. Franklin couldn't of gotten from the Albritton house all the way over to the Strand and murdered Annie Shields by ten o'clock." He broke off at the sound of rapidly approaching footsteps coming down the hall.

"I'm so sorry to keep you waiting, Inspector," August said briskly as he came into the office. "Do forgive me. What can I do for you?"

"You can clarify a rather odd problem for us, sir."

"Certainly. I'm always happy to cooperate with the police." He gave them a wary smile. "Though I must say, I've no idea how I can be of help. I'd never even heard of this Annie Shields person until Henry mentioned her."

"Mr. August, you told us you were working late on Sunday night, is that correct?" Witherspoon watched him carefully.

August looked faintly puzzled. "Yes, it is." He sat down behind his desk and clasped his hands together in front of him. "My wife was visiting friends that evening and I thought I'd come in and get some work done rather than stay home alone. We're a bit behind these days. Henry hasn't been himself lately and he's . . . well, neglected a few, rather important matters. I thought I'd come in and clear them up."

"Are you sure you're not mistaken?" Barnes asked softly.

"I'm positive. Sunday night I was right here in this office." He began to drum his fingers on the desktop.

"Mr. August," the inspector said, "I'm afraid that's not true. We know perfectly well you weren't here. There was a robbery right next door. The police were there from nine until half past eleven. A good number of police, I might add." Witherspoon waited for August to realize the importance of his statement. He didn't need to wait long. August's jaw dropped in surprise.

"First of all," the inspector continued, "if you had been here, you'd have mentioned the commotion to us when we first questioned you. There was a good deal of noise and excitement here that night. If you'd been here, you couldn't possibly have missed it. Secondly, the constables investigating that robbery are certain this office was empty. There were no lights on. Unless you were working in the dark, sir, you weren't here."

August went pale. "I don't know what you're talking about," he sputtered. "I tell you I was here. I must have had the shades drawn."

"The constables pounded on the door," Barnes added. "No one answered."

"Then I was out in the boatyard," August said, his voice starting to shake. "That's right, I'd gone out to the yard to check that we'd received a rather large shipment of lumber. The lumber's stored in the back. That's why I didn't see or hear your men."

"The boatyard was searched," Witherspoon said softly. "One of the constables thought one of thieves might be hiding there. Come now, Mr. August. Why don't you tell us the truth? Where were you on Sunday night?"

"Where is everyone this morning?" Mrs. Goodge said irritably.

"They're all out digging for more information," Mrs. Jeffries replied calmly. "Smythe's questioning the hansom drivers over on the Edgeware Road. Betsy's going to have a go at some of the local tradespeople in the area and Wiggins is . . ." She paused. She'd no idea where Wiggins had gone.

"Wiggins is where?"

"I just realized I've no idea," she admitted. "But I'm sure he's doing something useful."

"I reckon." Mrs. Goodge plopped down at the table and stared at Mrs. Jeffries. "I've been doin' some thinkin' about this case. And I think maybe I've figured somethin' out."

"How very clever of you." Mrs. Jeffries wished she'd been able to come up with some reasonable ideas. But so far, she'd drawn a blank.

"I reckon that Calloway fellow is innocent."

"How did you come to that conclusion?" Mrs. Jeffries asked curiously. To her way of thinking, at this point, no one could be eliminated as a suspect.

" 'Cause of the way Annie Shields was killed," Mrs. Goodge replied. "Calloway wouldn't of left her lyin' in the middle of the street. Unless he were stupid, of course. Which I don't think he is. He knew that considerin' what had happened between him and Annie, he'd be the prime suspect. Now, maybe it would take the police a bit of time to suss it out, but accordin' to what Betsy found out, half of Covent Garden heard Annie tellin' Calloway to leave her alone. The police would be bound to find out about it sooner or later. If he were goin' to do her in, he'da hidden the body better, at least long enough to buy him some time to get out of town. But she were discovered not long after she was killed, laying flat out on the road for anyone to stumble over."

"That's true," Mrs. Jeffries said thoughtfully. "And I did put a flea in the inspector's ear this morning. I'm sure he's already got men over at Covent Garden questioning people again."

"Besides," Mrs. Goodge said quickly, "if Calloway was goin' to kill her, in the heat of passion, so to speak, he'd a done it the day she told him to leave her alone. He wouldn't have waited till Sunday night. He'da done it while he was still angry, not after he'd had a chance to cool down some. And he seemed to genuinely love the woman. He were angry at her, yet he still cared enough about her to try and protect her. After all, he's the one that chased down that inquiry agent that were watchin' her." She shook her head. "If he cared enough about her to do that, he didn't kill her. It don't seem right, you know what I mean?"

Mrs. Jeffries thought about it for a few minutes. Actually, the cook's theory did make a lot of sense. "All right, let's suppose that Calloway is innocent. That leaves us with the Struttses, Lydia Franklin, Sherwin August or Henry Albritton."

"I'd knock Albritton out of the runnin' too," Mrs. Goodge said. "As far as we can see, he'd got no reason to kill her."

"Fair enough. Unless, of course, Albritton's not telling the whole truth about what happened twenty years ago. We've only his word that Annie Shields was his daughter."

"What about the solicitor?" Mrs. Goodge pointed out. "He'd have no reason to lie and he's convinced Annie was Albritton's."

"True." Mrs. Jeffries sighed heavily. She wasn't making head or tails of this case. "I'm not thinking clearly."

"Let's go over it again." Mrs. Goodge gave her an encouraging smile. "We'll take our time and put our heads together and see what we come up with. First of all, let's look at the Strutts. They had plenty of motive. If Albritton took his daughter and left the country, their nice life would be gone. More importantly, they wouldn't be the heirs, would they?"

"That's right," Mrs. Jeffries agreed. "So even if they didn't know what Henry Albritton's plans were concerning Annie Shields, they'd still have a motive."

"And we're pretty sure they did know about Annie— Hortense listens at keyholes."

"What about Lydia Franklin?" Mrs. Jeffries murmured. "What did she have to lose? She probably wouldn't have been Henry Albritton's heir in any case."

"I reckon she's out of the runnin' too," Mrs. Goodge said. "We've no evidence she even knew who Annie was. The Struttses wouldn't tell her. Albritton didn't confide in her and I can't see Harlan Bladestone telling her anything either. In other words, she's the only one who didn't know about Annie Shields."

"But she saw the flowers coming into the house every day," Mrs. Jeffries countered. "Surely she'd realize something had changed in Mr. Albritton's life. A man doesn't start buying bushels of flowers every day for no reason."

Mrs. Goodge dismissed this with a wave of her hand. "She'd probably be more worried that he'd met a woman he was romantically interested in, not a long-lost daughter."

That made sense too. Mrs. Jeffries wished she knew what the inspector had learned this morning. There were times when she would dearly love to be a fly on the wall.

"All right," August said slowly. "I'll admit I wasn't here that night."

"Where were you, sir?" Witherspoon asked.

"I went for a long walk." August closed his eyes.

"In the fog, sir?" Barnes asked.

"Yes, it was foggy."

"Mr. August, did you walk on Southampton Street?" the inspector suggested. "That's less than a half mile from here."

"What makes you say that?" August had gone completely white now and his hands were shaking. "I uh . . . I'm not sure where I walked. Like you said, it was foggy."

"Mr. August," Barnes said softly, "why don't you just tell us the truth? You were walkin' on Southampton

Street, weren't you?" He gave the inspector a quick glance and went on. "And you had a hammer with you, didn't you?"

"No, no," August moaned, his voice shaking with fear.

Witherspoon would have stopped his constable, but he was too surprised to say a word.

"But of course you did, sir. And you came across a nice little flower seller," Barnes continued relentlessly. "A sweet young woman, she was, sir. But her very existence could ruin you, couldn't it?" His voice rose. "So you raised the hammer and you bashed her head in, didn't you, sir?" he shouted. "Didn't you, Mr. August?"

"No, no. That's not the way it happened at all," August screamed. "She was already dead when I got there. I swear, as God is my witness. She was already dead."

Wiggins stared in horror at the bundle Fred deposited at his feet. "Good dog," he said, kneeling down and patting the animal on the head. "Good dog."

Fred wagged his tail and began sniffing the blood-stained white material. Wiggins's stomach turned over, but he forced himself to move. Reaching down, he shoved Fred's nose out of the way and scooped up the tightly rolled garments.

From directly ahead, he could hear the sound of policemen searching the Albritton garden. Trying to avoid touching the bloodstains, he picked up the bundle and crouched lower behind the headstone where he was hiding. Fred wagged his tail again and started to woof softly as they heard the constables stomping around just ahead of them.

"Quiet, boy," Wiggins said sharply. "I've got to think."

He looked around for a way out. He had to get these bloodstained clothes back to Upper Edmonton Gardens. But he couldn't sneak out this way, there were police everywhere. He turned his head towards the church and chewed on his lip. The vicar was still in the sanctuary, so he couldn't nip out that way.

But he had to get back. He and Fred had found the clue that would solve this case. Bloodstained clothes didn't walk all by themselves into a churchyard. They didn't roll themselves under a bush. Whoever had murdered Annie Shields had hidden these clothes, and once he got 'em back to Mrs. Jeffries, they'd have this case solved.

He couldn't help but feel a surge of pride. Mrs. Jeffries had been right when she'd lectured them on actin' like a team. He didn't like all the arguing and fighting that had been going on lately. But he was ever so glad he'd gotten it into his head to nip round here with Fred and see if he couldn't find something. Wasn't he lucky Fred had been sniffing round those bushes and found them.

The back door of the church flew open and Wiggins crouched lower. "Down, boy," he whispered to Fred. He watched the vicar bang the door shut and then hurry off round the other side of the church. He waited till he'd disappeared before he stood up. "Come on, boy. This is our chance. Let's make a run for it."

"Why didn't you arrest him, sir?" Barnes asked. He raised his hand at a passing hansom and waved it to a stop.

"Because he sounded as though he were telling the truth," the inspector replied. He nimbly stepped into the hansom. Barnes gave the address to the driver and they were off.

"But he had Annie Shields's ring," Barnes said, as soon as he'd settled back against the seat. "And he admitted he knew who she was and that Albritton was planning on selling out the company and taking the girl to America. August would have lost everything. He had motive and opportunity."

"He also admitted to hiring that private inquiry agent, Caulkins," Witherspoon said, "and that's precisely why I didn't arrest him." Actually, the inspector wasn't sure why he hadn't arrested Sherwin August. But, as his housekeeper always said, he must listen to his "inner voice" and that voice was telling him that August was not a murderer.

"Furthermore," the inspector continued, "August showed us the money he was going to use that night. He still had the cash in his office. Now, that proves he wasn't going to kill her. He wouldn't have bothered to go to his bank and get that much money if he was going to cosh the girl over the head and steal her ring. It was obvious to me he was going to do exactly as he said. He was going to buy her off."

"Why should she take money from August when she could have it all if she was Albritton's daughter?"

"But she didn't know she was Albritton's daughter," Witherspoon said smugly. "Albritton hadn't told her yet. He was waiting to see the ring."

Barnes shook his head. "I still don't trust him. Any man who'd take a ring off a dead woman's finger is capable of the worst. Uh, Inspector, I hope you don't mind me takin' off after August the way I did . . ."

"Not to worry, Constable," Witherspoon said quickly. "I was a bit surprised, but your method did get results. As to why August took the ring, he explained why he felt he had to."

Barnes snorted derisively. "He didn't want Albritton to know for sure that Annie was his daughter. Even though he saw the poor woman lyin' there dead in the street, he was still worried about his precious position."

"Indeed, it doesn't speak well of his character." The inspector sighed. "Of course, once Albritton saw the ring, he'd know for certain Annie Shields was his own flesh and blood. Which would make Emma Shields his granddaughter, thus starting August's problems up all over again."

"Right. Albritton would just take his granddaughter and leave for America. Leaving Sherwin August with nothin' but twenty-five percent of a company bein' sold to someone else. Disgustin'. He'd get money for his share, but I reckon he didn't think he'd get enough."

"Sherwin August is a rather nasty person," Witherspoon commented. "But that doesn't make him a murderer. Gracious, if everyone who was a nasty person was a murderer as well, there wouldn't be enough prisons in the whole country to hold them all."

"You must put these back exactly where you found them," Mrs. Jeffries told Wiggins.

"Put 'em back," he said, clearly disappointed. "But I only just found 'em. Besides, it's right hard to get in and out of that place. There's police everywhere."

"Wiggins." Mrs. Jeffries gave him a warm smile. "You've done excellent work. You are a born detective. It was very clever of you to think to search the churchyard. However, this is evidence. We really must let the police find it for themselves."

"But what if they don't?" Mrs. Goodge said.

"We'll just have to make sure they do," Mrs. Jeffries replied. She took the bloodstained shirt and trousers and rolled them back into a tight bundle. Handing them to Wiggins, she instructed, "Take these back to the church-yard and leave them lying in plain sight."

"But what if the police still don't see 'em?" he asked worriedly.

"They will. Because you'll draw their attention to their presence. You'd better leave Fred here, though," she said. She thought for a moment. "Once you get there, find a small stone. You've quite a good throwing arm, Wiggins. Do you think you could hit a police-man?"

"You want me to throw a pebble at a copper?" Wiggins yelped in surprise.

"Precisely." Mrs. Jeffries gave him an innocent smile. "That's exactly what I want you to do."

"Mr. Albritton," the inspector said softly. "Do you recognize this ring?" He handed him the opal ring he'd gotten from Sherwin August.

Albritton stared at it for a long moment. His eyes filled with tears and he slowly shook his head. "I gave this to Dora twenty years ago. See, you can see the flaw. Where did you get it?"

"From your partner, Sherwin August. He took it off Annie's Shields's finger on Sunday night."

Albritton drew a deep, long breath. He swayed and stumbled. Barnes leapt forward, grabbed his arm and hustled him towards the settee. "You'd better sit down, sir. You're not lookin' well at all."

"Mr. Albritton," the inspector said quickly, "are you all right?"

Albritton seemed dazed. He shook himself. "Sherwin murdered my daughter?" he mumbled. "But why? Why would he hurt her?"

"He didn't murder her, sir. At least I don't think so." The inspector watched Albritton carefully as he spoke. He didn't want the poor man getting too distraught. Gracious, chap looked like he was getting ready to peg out. White as a sheet, eyes as big as saucers. "You see, Mr. August knew Annie was your daughter. He'd hired a private inquiry agent to look into the matter. He'd arranged to meet her on Sunday night. He was going to try to pay her off; give her money to leave town. But he claims she was already dead when he found her."

"He's lying," Albritton said bitterly. "The bastard is lying."

"I don't think so," Witherspoon replied. "August showed us the cash he'd withdrawn from his bank. Furthermore, his story has the ring of truth to it. He admitted searching your desk and he admitted he knew you were going to sell out your company and leave the country."

"But why did he take the ring?"

The inspector cleared his throat. Oh dear, this was going to be very difficult. Especially as they'd no idea where on earth Emma Shields might be. "Mr. Albritton," he said softly, his voice sympathetic, "Sherwin August took the ring because he wanted no absolute proof that Annie Shields was your daughter. You see, sir, Annie had a child. A daughter."

Albritton went utterly still for a moment. When he looked up, the expression in his eyes filled Witherspoon with pity. Wariness, fear and hope stared at him out of the face of a ravaged man. A man who couldn't take much more.

"A daughter," he whispered, as though he were afraid to believe it. "My Annie had a child. I've got a grand-daughter. For God's sake, why didn't you tell me? Where is she? When can I see her? Oh, dear God, please don't tell me that she's dead too."

"No, sir, she's fine." The inspector hesitated. Spotting Mrs. Franklin hovering in the open doorway, he said brightly, "Mrs. Franklin, would you mind getting us some tea. Mr. Albritton has had quite a shock."

An hour later the inspector left the new grandfather pacing in his study. "I do hope," he said to Barnes as they followed Nestor up to the Struttses' sitting room, "that we find Emma Shields quickly. That man is going to have a nervous collapse if he doesn't see his grandchild soon."

"We'll find the girl, sir," Barnes said confidently. "The lads haven't turned up anything on the grounds yet, sir. They've searched the shed and the garden, but they found nothing out of the ordinary. Just the usual gardening tools and a bicycle. They're searching the house now."

As before, the Struttses were sitting on the settee, waiting. The inspector didn't waste time with amenities. "Mr. Strutts, we've reason to believe you were not in this house on Sunday evening. Would you like to amend your earlier statement?"

"I don't know what you're talking about," Gordon Strutts said peevishly. But his voice lacked conviction.

"You were out, sir," Barnes said. "Unless'n, of course, someone else was wearin' your coat."

"That's absurd." Hortense Strutts sneered. "Gordon was right here. Reading. We've already told you that and you can't prove otherwise."

"I think we can," the inspector said calmly. "Once we start looking."

"You may look all over London," Hortense snapped. "But it won't do you any good."

"I think it will." Witherspoon steeled himself to be ruthless. Much as he disliked the subject, the gossip he'd gotten Mrs. Jeffries grudgingly to repeat this morning echoed in his mind. "And I'm quite sure that neither of you would want Mr. Albritton to learn about the kind of people we'll be forced to question." He kept his gaze on Gordon Strutts. "Young men."

Gordon gasped.

"Young men who are paid for certain services," Barnes added.

"How dare you?" Hortense whispered furiously. Her eyes narrowed dangerously as she rose to her feet. "How dare you imply such disgusting things about my husband?"

"I assure you, madam," the inspector said, "we're implying nothing. However, if you persist in your original story, we'll be forced to question—"

"No. You'll not question anyone," Gordon said. He grabbed his wife's hand and pulled her back to the settee. "Sit down, Hortense. For once, I'll handle this."

"Don't be ridiculous—"

"Shut up," he snapped. "I'll not let George get dragged into this mess."

"Oh, you'd protect your precious George, would you?" Hortense glared at her husband with loathing. "Well then, I'll leave you to it." She turned to the policemen, her eyes blazing with contempt. "I'd like to amend my earlier statement. Gordon wasn't here that night. He was gone from eight o'clock until almost eleven. I was alone."

Witherspoon, who was trying terribly hard to keep from looking shocked, nodded.

Gordon laughed harshly. "You're a fool," he jeered at his wife. "Why don't you tell them the rest? Why don't you tell them the truth? I'm not the only one who was gone that night," he said maliciously. "And unlike you, I can prove I wasn't over on Southampton Street committing murder. I was with someone."

"Someone who would die before they'd ever publicly admit you'd been with them." Her temper flared. "Do you really think that the son of a peer of the realm is going to tell them the truth to save your sorry skin?"

"Er." Witherspoon looked helplessly at Barnes, who shrugged. "Excuse me," he tried to say. But the Struttses were now going at it like cats and dogs.

"You fat cow." Gordon gave his wife a hard shove. She toppled to the side and slipped off the settee onto the floor.

"Don't touch me, you sickening ponce," she screamed as she bounced onto the carpet.

Appalled, Witherspoon leapt towards the hapless woman, who was now tangled up in her own heavy skirts. "Please, Mr. Strutts," he commanded. "Calm yourself. We can't have this sort of behaviour. I won't stand for it."

He reached down to offer Mrs. Strutts his hand, but she pushed it away. Her round face was red with rage, her eyes filled with loathing as she glared pure hatred at her husband. "He killed her," she said. "No matter what he says, no matter who he claims he was with, he murdered that poor woman. I can always go home to my father. But if Uncle Henry had taken that bastard daughter of his and left the country, Gordon would be out on his ear. He can't work. He's too stupid to do even the simplest thing. He's not got enough money to live on and none of his little friends would lift a finger to help him if he didn't pay them. That's what he does, you know. He pays them."

"Shut up, you stupid fool! How would you like it if I told them what I found in your room when I got home that night," Gordon yelled. "You were still wearing your coat and hat when I walked in. Where the hell had you been? Out taking a lovely walk in the fog? And you were the one that had been following Annie Shields. You were the one who was going out to meet her that night. Not me."

"You bloody liar," Hortense screamed. "You know very well I never saw her. I told you."

"Could you please calm yourselves?" the inspector shouted.

Still glaring at one another, they both shut up. Hortense rose stiffly to her feet and stumbled towards the chair. As soon as she'd sat down, Witherspoon tried again. "Now, why don't we start from the beginning? Apparently, both of you would like to amend your earlier statements."

There was a commotion from downstairs. "Should I go and see what that is, sir?" Barnes asked.

Witherspoon started to nod, took another look at the Struttses and said, "No, why don't we all go downstairs? There's no reason we can't discuss this calmly in the drawing room."

He wanted everything out in the open. This case was getting far too muddled and complex. Suddenly no one had an alibi, half of London seemed to have been on Southampton Street the night Annie was murdered, and he was getting a dreadful headache.

Barnes nodded and motioned for Hortense Strutts to go ahead of him. No doubt the constable felt there might be a good deal less chance of further bloodshed if he placed himself between husband and wife.

Witherspoon came behind Gordon Strutts. They trooped towards the stairs.

Below, two uniformed constables, one of them holding a bundle tucked under one arm, were trying to get Lydia Franklin or Nestor to go and get Inspector Witherspoon.

"You can wait a few moments," Lydia Franklin said sharply. "Nestor doesn't work for the Metropolitan Police. He works for this household and I'll not have him neglecting his duties running up and down the stairs for the police."

"Please, ma'am," the younger of the two policemen pleaded. "It's very important. If you'll just tell us where he is, we'll go find him ourselves."

"I'm not having your muddy feet all over the carpets," she retorted. "You can just wait outside."

"Lydia," Albritton called. "What's going on here?"

She gave him a stiff smile. "Henry, why aren't you resting? There's nothing at all going on. I was merely trying to get these gentlemen—"

"I know what you were trying to do," Albritton said. Witherspoon saw him glance up as he heard the noise from above. Puzzled, he stared at the spectacle of four people, their faces grim as death, marching single file down the stairs.

"Inspector?" Albritton queried. "What on earth—"

"Inspector Witherspoon," the constable with the bundle interrupted. "We think you'd better take a look at this." He thrust the bundle into the inspector's hand.

Witherspoon, recognizing the heavy red stains on the material, felt his stomach tighten. But he knew his duty. He unrolled the top garment and held it up.

"Looks like a man's shirt," Barnes said, stepping forward and examining it closely. "And this is blood, or I'm not an English copper."

"Yes, I'm afraid you're right," Witherspoon muttered. He handed Barnes the shirt and unrolled the dark brown material still in his hand. It was a pair of trousers. Holding them up, he couldn't see any bloodstains, but as the trousers were a dark colour, he realized they'd need to be examined in strong light before they'd reveal much.

"Probably what the killer was wearin' that night," Barnes said.

"Probably," Witherspoon agreed. "Where did you find these?" he asked, turning to the two constables.

"Well . . ." The younger policeman looked at the older one, who nodded encouragingly. "Go on, tell it like it happened," he ordered.

"We found them in St. John's churchyard," the younger one continued.

"On whose authority did you search the churchyard?" Witherspoon suddenly had visions of nasty defense lawyers and equally nasty Judges' Rules.

"We wasn't tryin' to search the churchyard," the young policeman explained. "But you see, I was standing on this side, searching Mr. Albritton's garden, when I felt something sharp sting me neck. Someone had thrown a pebble at me. When I looked up, I saw a lad disappearing through the headstones. Well, you can't have boys throwin' stones at policemen and gettin' away with it, can you?"

"Er, no. I suppose not."

"So I nipped after him. When I got into the churchyard, I practically stumbled over these." He jerked his chin towards the bloodstained clothes.

"I see." Witherspoon frowned. "Well, thank you, Constables, you were absolutely correct in bringing this to my attention. I think it may be very important evidence. These garments could well be what the killer wore that night."

The two constables took their leave.

As soon as they were gone, Albritton said, "Let's go into the drawing room. Maybe one of us will be able to recognize the garments."

"That won't be necessary," Lydia Franklin said bluntly. "I know who those clothes belong to." She smiled maliciously toward the Struttses. "They're Gordon's."

CHAPTER 11

"I almost got caught," Wiggins exclaimed. "Cor, I didn't think that copper could run so fast! Lucky for me, he didn't grab that bicycle he and the other copper'd been larkin' about on and take out on it. He'da caught me for sure."

"What're you complainin' about?" Betsy grumbled. "At least you've had a bit of excitement in your day. I talked to every ruddy shopkeeper on the Edgeware Road and all I learned was that Hortense Strutts is fond of chocolates and Lydia Franklin's got thin blood. Oh yes, and Gordon Strutts's got asthma."

Wiggins made a face. "Thin blood? Are you 'aving me on? 'Ow'd a shopkeeper know anything about someone's blood."

"Thin blood means you feels the cold," Mrs. Goodge said impatiently.

Betsy giggled. "Lydia Franklin wore her coat in church during the whole service last Sunday evenin'. The butcher's wife was sittin' behind her the whole time. Said she didn't so much as unbutton the collar. Some people. Rich as sin but that don't keep 'em from sufferin' like the rest of us. Even poor old Gordon don't get to enjoy himself much, the least little bit of exertion and he's wheezin' like a teakettle." She glanced at the coachman. "Did you learn anything interestin'?"

"No. Between the riots and the fog, the streets was empty." Smythe grinned. "No one picked up any fares near the Albritton house. I'm goin' out in a few minutes, though. One of the Albritton footman goes into the local pub for his pint as soon as they finish up after lunch. This is their half day. 'E might know somethin'. Seems to me like the only one that's 'ad a brush with excitement 'ere is our Wiggins."

"Now, now," Mrs. Jeffries said soothingly. "You should all be very proud of yourselves. We're finally getting somewhere on this case. Once those clothes are identified, I'm sure an arrest will follow." Even as she said the words something tugged at the back of her mind.

"Who do you think it'll be?" Mrs. Goodge asked eagerly. "My money is on that Hortense Strutts. From what I heard about her old father, she'd do anything to keep from livin' with him again."

"What does Annie Shields's murder have to do with Hortense Strutts livin' with her father?" Wiggins asked curiously. "Ain't married ladies supposed to live with their husbands?"

"Of course they are," the cook said. "But if Mr. Albritton had taken his daughter and gone off to some heathen land to start a new life, the Struttses might not have stayed together."

The footman looked stunned. "You mean they'da"— he lowered his voice—"divorced?"

"I don't think they'd of gone that far," Mrs. Goodge replied. "But from the gossip I heard the last couple of days, they probably wouldn't have bothered to live together. Gordon Strutts probably would have moved into some den of sin in Chelsea with one of his 'friends,' so poor old Hortense wouldn't have had much choice. She'da had to move back in with her family."

"My money's on Gordon," Smythe said. "He's the only one of the lot who we knows was actually out of the house on Sunday night." He shoved his chair back and got up. "I'd best push off, then, and see what this footman knows."

Smythe disappeared down the hall. Mrs. Jeffries said, "I was rather hoping the inspector would pop in for luncheon. But as it's past two, I don't think he will." Her head jerked towards the window over the sink as she heard a hansom pull up outside. She got up, hurried over and peeked outside. "I told a lie," she called to the others. "The inspector has come home."

They leapt into action. Wiggins called for Fred, Mrs. Goodge dashed towards the larder, and Betsy hurried upstairs to set the dining table. Mrs. Jeffries was right on her heels.

She made it to the front hall, smoothed her hair out of her face and smiled serenely as the door opened and Inspector Witherspoon stepped inside. "Good afternoon, Mrs. Jeffries."

"Good day, sir. What a delightful surprise. I'm so glad you were able to come home for lunch. Mrs. Goodge has a lovely cheese-and-onion tart ready."

"Thank you, Mrs. Jeffries." The inspector handed her his hat and coat. "But all I really want is a cup of tea and some of those remarkable headache powders of yours. Would that be too much trouble?"

"Of course not, sir," she said. "I'm so sorry you're not feeling well. Is the case going badly?"

"Oh no, it's actually going quite well. We've arrested Gordon Strutts."

"Mr. Strutts?"

"Naturally, he started to deny everything. Then he shut up tighter than a bank vault and refused to say another word until his solicitor arrived. But we've quite good evidence against him."

"I'm sure you do, sir."

"But it's still been a most distressing day. I left Constable Barnes in charge and thought I'd nip home and get something for this headache. You won't believe the way people behave. Why, it's positively shocking. The Struttses at each other's throat. Mrs. Franklin refusing to say anything to anyone and Mr. Albritton practically having to be locked in his study to keep from murdering his nephew."

"Poor inspector. You have had a most trying time." Mrs. Jeffries gestured towards the drawing room. "Why don't you go and sit down, sir? I'll get you some tea and those headache powders."

Betsy, who'd been hovering by the dining-room door, popped out, nodded at Mrs. Jeffries and hurried towards the backstairs. Mrs. Jeffries, knowing full well that the maid was already putting a tea tray together, hurried up to her own rooms for the headache powder.

Now that an arrest had been made, it would be safe to get Emma to her grandfather. They didn't have a moment to lose. The plan she'd come up with yesterday had to go into effect. Immediately.

If they were going to get Emma Shields into Henry Albritton's house without anyone finding out where she'd been and what *they'd* been up to, they had to act fast.

A few minutes later Betsy appeared with the tea tray. "I've brought you some sandwiches, sir," she said to the inspector as she set the tray down. "Mrs. Goodge was afraid them headache powders might upset your digestion if you took them on an empty stomach."

"How very thoughtful of her," Witherspoon said. Gracious, he was such a lucky man. "Do tell her I said thank you. I'm sure the sandwiches will be delicious." He reached for a sandwich and eagerly took a bite. "I say, these *are* good."

"You were telling me about your terrible day, sir," Mrs. Jeffries prompted.

"Oh yes." The inspector told her everything. From his interview with Henry Albritton to the discovery of the bloodstained clothes. Before he knew it, he felt much better. His headache was gone, his stomach was full, and he could think far more clearly.

"I say, that was quite nice," he said as he wiped the last of the sandwich crumbs from his mouth. "I hadn't realized I was so hungry." He pulled out his pocket watch. "Egads, look at the time. I must get back. Strutts will have had time to talk to his solicitor by now, and we're still searching for the murder weapon."

"Now, you will make sure she don't get scared," Luty instructed Betsy. "She don't like loud noises and she don't like goin' to bed without a story. You be sure and tell Henry Albritton that." She blinked back tears as she lifted the child into Betsy's waiting arms.

"I'll make sure," Betsy promised. Behind Luty, she could see Hatchet fighting his own tears. She shifted Emma onto her hip and tried to give them both a reassuring smile. Emma giggled, threw her arms around Betsy's neck and hugged her tight.

"Emma will be just fine," Mrs. Jeffries said quickly. "You'll see. Her grandfather will be good to her."

"He'd better," Hatchet said darkly. "Or he'll answer to me."

"And to me," Luty muttered.

That both Hatchet and Luty were miserable was obvious. Mrs. Jeffries was utterly heartsick. These two had grown very attached to the child. Watching Emma cuddle and giggle with Betsy showed what a loving, sweet-natured child she was. Who wouldn't grow to love her? But she had to go. It was only right that she go to her grandfather. And it was best she go quickly. Before they all ended up in tears.

"I'd best get started, then," Betsy said.

"Do you remember what to say?" Mrs. Jeffries asked.

"I'm to tell the inspector that a young police constable brought the girl here, thinkin' he was still here havin' lunch," Betsy said, repeating the plan they'd all agreed upon. "And then I'm to say that the child started fussin' and the constable got flustered. I offered to take her to the inspector myself."

"Excellent. Now, you'd better hurry. I'm not sure how long the inspector is going to be at the Albritton house."

It was another five minutes before Betsy got out the door and into a hansom cab. Luty and Hatchet kept delaying her with last-minute instructions and last-minute hugs for Emma.

"She'll be just fine," Mrs. Jeffries said reassuringly as they all trooped back into the kitchen. "Just fine. Come on now, why don't we all have a cup of tea and cheer up."

Ten minutes later their spirits were a little better. Mrs.

Jeffries had filled Luty and Hatchet in on everything she'd learned from Witherspoon at lunch.

"That sure is somethin'." Luty shook her head. "But I ain't so sure it is Gordon Strutts."

"But they were his clothes I found," Wiggins pointed out.

"But money's a pretty powerful motive," Luty pointed out. "And seems to me that the person who really had the most to lose was Sherwin August. He's admitted he was fixin' to meet the girl. How do we know she was dead when he took that ring?"

"Took what ring?" Smythe asked as he came into the kitchen.

"Annie Shields's opal," Mrs. Goodge replied. "There's been an arrest."

"And *I* found the clue that did it." Wiggins jabbed himself in the chest as he spoke.

"Good work, boy." Smythe pulled out his chair and sat down. "Cor, it's gettin' bad outside. Another fog's rollin' in. So they've arrested her, have they?"

There was a stunned silence.

Her? Mrs. Jeffries felt her insides grow cold. "What do you mean, Smythe?"

Smythe stared at their faces. "Lydia Franklin. The footman I spoke to, he saw her Sunday night. He was in the churchyard with a . . . well . . ."

"This is not time for delicacy, Smythe," Mrs. Jeffries said. Dear God, she prayed silently. Please let the inspector still be there when Betsy and Emma arrive at the Albritton household. She knew what Smythe was going to say. That odd note in the back of her mind had turned into a full symphony now.

"He and a girl were takin' advantage of Albritton

givin' 'em the evenin' off," Smythe said slowly. "They was bein' intimate, you might say. That's why neither of 'em would tell the police what they'd seen. They didn't want to lose their positions. But about ten-thirty, Lydia Franklin come flyin' into that churchyard on a bicycle. She was wearin' men's clothes and a flat cap."

"Is the footman absolutely certain it was Lydia Franklin?" Mrs. Jeffries asked anxiously. "The fog was terrible that night, how could they tell who it was?"

"They're sure. She come right close to where they was hidin'. And they was scared she'd recognize them too. So when she ducked behind a tree to change, they snuck off."

"Nell's bells," Luty yelled. "Betsy and Emma are on their way to the Albritton house now."

"Don't worry, Luty," Mrs. Jeffries said hastily. "The inspector and Mr. Albritton are both there. But I do think it would be a good idea . . ."

Smythe and Hatchet had already gotten to their feet and were racing towards the back door.

"Hey, wait for me," Wiggins yelled, charging after them.

Betsy stepped down and lifted Emma out of the cab. She paid the driver and turned to the front door. Taking the child's hand, she shivered. The day had changed.

The sun was gone and a mean, yellow-gray fog was settling over the city like a grim, ugly blanket.

Emma whimpered and Betsy bent down and picked her up. The child was dead on her feet. "Tired, lovey," she cooed as she studied the Albritton house. "Well, we'll soon have you cuddled down in a nice warm bed." She laughed and started up the pavement towards the front steps. "If your grandfather lets you out of his sight, that is."

Betsy's footsteps faltered as she came up the steps. She shifted Emma onto her hip so she could free a hand to bang the door knocker. This is odd, she thought, the place looked deserted. Empty.

Inside her head, her old instincts, the ones that had kept her alive on the mean streets of the East End, suddenly urged her to take the child and run away. But the door opened and Betsy told herself she was just being silly.

A tall, blond woman stood in front of her. "Yes," she asked coldly, "what do you want?"

"I'd like to see Inspector Witherspoon," Betsy began. "I work for him, you see."

The woman didn't say anything for a moment. "And who is that?" she asked, nodding at Emma.

"This is Mr. Albritton's granddaughter," Betsy replied. "And she's very tired."

"Please come in." The woman opened the door wider. "I'm Lydia Franklin. Henry's sister-in-law."

Betsy stepped inside. Again, she felt the urge to run. Something was wrong. "Uh, is the inspector here?"

The house was utterly silent.

"Wait here," Lydia Franklin ordered, her gaze never leaving the child in Betsy's arms. "I'll get him." She turned and went down the hall.

For some reason, Betsy had the urge to follow. Tightening her grip on the now sleeping child, she tiptoed after her.

Lydia Franklin disappeared inside a room at the far end of the long hallway. Betsy, holding her breath and praying Emma wouldn't wake up, peered through the crack between the door.

She could only see one side of the room, but it was the side that counted. Lydia Franklin was standing by a massive mahogany sideboard. She closed the top drawer and Betsy saw a flash of silver. Then she turned, and what she held in her right hand made Betsy's blood run cold.

Lydia Franklin had a carving knife.

The biggest ruddy knife Betsy had ever seen.

Betsy tightened her grip on Emma, turned and ran, not caring that her pounding footsteps made enough racket to wake the dead. She wanted people to hear her.

From behind her, she heard footsteps.

"I don't want to hurt you," Lydia called. "It's the girl I want. Drop her on the floor and I won't kill you."

"Sod off," Betsy yelled. She dashed past the drawing room and flew round the staircase into the foyer. For a split second she hesitated. Then, spotting the fog through the window, she charged for the front door. Thank God, she'd had a head start. She'd taken the woman by surprise and bought herself a few precious seconds to escape. No doubt the silly bitch had thought she'd drop the child and save her own skin. Well, she had another think coming.

Luck was with Betsy, for Lydia hadn't closed the door properly. She yanked at the handle and jerked it open. She flew out and down the stone steps into the now thick fog. Emma whimpered. Betsy could hear the woman close behind her. Frantically, she looked up and down the street. No one. Nothing but thick fog.

She turned to her left. Towards the churchyard. She had to hide, to lose this lunatic woman in the mist until she could find help.

"Come back, you stupid girl!"

Betsy ran on. Emma woke and started to whimper

again. "Hush," Betsy gasped as she kicked open the iron gate and charged through into the churchyard. Her feet pounding over the uneven ground, Betsy rounded the corner and almost slammed into a tree. She skirted it at the last second and then stumbled on a low headstone. She almost went flying, but managed to right herself and retain her grip on Emma at the last moment.

"Just leave me the girl and I won't hurt you," Lydia screamed again.

Betsy stopped. It sounded like she'd put some distance between herself and the lunatic. She didn't know what the ruddy 'ell was wrong with Lydia Franklin, and right now she didn't much care. She had to get help. She had to get that crazy woman as far away from Emma as she could.

"Mmm . . ." Emma struggled to be put down.

"No," Betsy whispered sharply. Quietly, barely daring to breathe, she edged towards the other side of the church building. Fingers of fog moved and shifted, obscuring shapes and sound. One second, Betsy could see clearly ahead; the next, the gray mist descended and she'd have to creep at a snail's pace, picking her way over graves and grass.

Harsh laughter sliced through the eerie silence. Betsy froze. The woman was close. Too close.

She glanced down at the child in her arms and knew she was running out of time. The fog wouldn't hide them long. The mist drifted and Betsy could make out more headstones ahead of her.

"Where are you?" Lydia called out in the singsong voice of a child.

Chills raced down Betsy's spine and fear turned her insides to jelly. The woman was mad as a loon. And she had a knife.

Betsy ran for the headstones. Emma whimpered.

"I can find you . . ."

Suddenly a figure leapt out of the fog, the knife raised high and slashing madly at the air. Betsy skidded to a halt, screamed and jerked the other way.

She ran like a demon was after her. Emma was howling her head off, Betsy was dodging headstones and trying not to fall. She could hear horrible laughter and pounding steps right behind her. She ran straight for a pocket of thick fog, hoping against hope she'd find the gate of the churchyard directly ahead. She slammed into a low stone wall. From far away she heard voices.

"Help," Betsy screamed. Emma howled. Betsy had to act fast. She dumped the child over the wall and turned to face her pursuer. She had no idea where she was. She had no idea what she'd do when that crazy woman burst through the fog.

"Run," she whispered to the terrified child.

Emma stared at her, confusion and fear on her little face.

"Run," Betsy ordered again.

Lydia Franklin came running straight at her, the knife held high. She screamed when she spotted Betsy standing with her back to the wall and charged straight for her.

"Run," Betsy yelled at the child. Emma ran just as Lydia Franklin leapt out.

But Betsy hadn't survived on the London streets without knowing how to take care of herself. As the woman came at her her hand shot up and she grabbed Lydia's wrist. She could hear Emma screaming. But the girl had started to flee; the screams were moving away from the struggling women.

"Run, run, run," Betsy kept yelling as she grappled

with the the madwoman intent on killing her. They fell backwards. Betsy's shoulder slammed against the wall and she lost her footing.

Lydia jerked her hand free of Betsy's grip and shoved her hard, forcing her onto the ground. She raised her hand to strike. The knife flashed. Betsy closed her eyes, praying quickly that Emma had made it to safety. Suddenly Lydia screeched in rage as she was yanked back and tossed to the ground.

The knife went flying as Smythe's booted foot kicked it hard to one side.

"Good God, Betsy. Are you all right? Did she hurt you?" Smythe asked, his voice frantic. He dropped beside her and quickly began running his hands over her arms, searching for wounds.

"I'm . . . fine," Betsy panted. She heard Lydia howling like a banshee as she struggled with two police constables who were dragging her away. "Emma, oh God. Where's Emma?"

"Now, now, she's fine. We found her as we come into the churchyard," Smythe said, tenderly helping Betsy to her feet. "She's being taken to her grandfather."

Betsy, who'd never been so glad to see anyone, threw her arms around Smythe's neck, collapsed against his chest and promptly burst into tears.

Hours later Betsy and the rest of them were gathered round the table at Upper Edmonton Gardens. Smythe, who couldn't seem to move more than a foot away from Betsy, kept shooting her anxious glances. "Are you sure you're all right?" he prodded. "'Adn't you better lay down and 'ave a rest?"

"I'm fine," she retorted. "Thanks to you, Emma and I are both in one piece."

"I don't think I'll ever forgive myself for this fiasco," Mrs. Jeffries said. "It's all my fault."

"Leave off, Mrs. J," Smythe said soothingly. "Stop blamin' yerself. You didn't know it was Lydia Franklin and you didn't know the house was empty when you sent Betsy and the child over there."

"But that's just it," Mrs. Jeffries moaned. "I should have known! All the clues were there. If I'd been thinking clearly, I'd have realized the killer was Lydia and not Gordon."

"Come on now, Hepzibah," Luty said bluntly. "You couldn't have possibly figured that out. There was no way to know until Smythe come in and told us about that footman."

"True, madam," Hatchet agreed. "Your powers of deduction are truly remarkable, but in this case, you didn't have all the facts until after Miss Betsy had left the house."

Mrs. Jeffries knew they were trying to comfort her. But they were wrong. Had she been thinking clearly, none of this would have happened and Betsy wouldn't have had that horrible experience. "We didn't need all the facts," she said firmly. "The whole problem was that I kept looking at the case the wrong way."

"Wrong way?" Wiggins muttered. "What does that mean?"

"It means," Mrs. Jeffries explained, "I fell into the trap of accepting everything at face value, including the reason for the murder itself. We all assumed that Annie Shields was killed because of who she was— namely, Henry Albritton's daughter. But if I'd been thinking clearly, I'd have realized there was another motive in this case. A motive Luty discovered almost immediately."

"I discovered?" Luty said in surprise. "Uh, would you mind refreshin' my memory?"

Mrs. Jeffries laughed. "Remember what Myrtle Buxton told you about Lydia Franklin. According to her, Lydia Franklin was so distraught over the idea that Henry Albritton might be seriously interested in another woman that she started some vicious gossip about that poor lady. The woman was so humiliated, she left the country."

"So you're sayin' Mrs. Franklin was insanely jealous," Wiggins asked curiously.

"In a sense, yes," Mrs. Jeffries replied. "But I don't think she was jealous of him so much as she didn't want to lose what he provided. Lydia Franklin had spent a good part of her life being poor and humiliated. I think she'd determined from the moment she came to live at the Albritton house that she was never going back."

"She killed Annie Shields because she didn't want to be poor again?" Wiggins asked, his tone incredulous.

"Precisely. Let's look at the facts. One, Henry Albritton had had some very real changes in his attitude about wealth and privilege. I'm sure that frightened her. Two, she was living in that great house on sufferance, and three, she was the only one who didn't positively know that Annie was Albritton's daughter."

"Then why would she kill her?" Betsy asked.

"She was afraid Henry was in love with the girl," Mrs. Jeffries said thoughtfully. "Remember, the only information she had to go on was that he was suddenly happy and he was suddenly very interested in flowers. Now it's one thing to live in a house with a niece and nephew. It's quite another to think a new young wife would let you stay on as mistress."

"I wonder how she found out about Annie?" Hatchet mused. "If the Struttses or Sherwin August didn't tell her, how could she know that Annie even existed."

"I think I've got that sussed out," Smythe said. "I reckon the first time old 'Enry walked in with a big bouquet of roses, she got suspicious he was seein' another woman. She followed 'im."

Luty shook her head. "Well, I still don't see how we coulda known it was her. Not until today. I mean, Nell's bells, the woman had an alibi. Who'da thought she'd hop on a bicycle and run all over town on the foggiest night of the year to murder someone."

"But that's precisely what we should have realized," Mrs. Jeffries said earnestly. "The clues were all there, but I didn't interpret them correctly. Lydia's husband sold bicycles at one point and there was a bicycle available to her. I should have realized that she could easily ride one. It's not so very difficult. Secondly, she kept her coat buttoned in church at evensong service. Betsy told us that today."

"What's that got to do with anythin'?" Mrs. Goodge asked. "Sometimes I don't take off my coat in church."

"True, but I'll bet you unbuttoned the collar. Lydia didn't dare. She couldn't risk anyone seeing that she was dressed in Gordon's clothes."

"Hello, hello," the inspector's voice called from down the kitchen hall.

"What's he doin' using the back entrance?" Mrs. Goodge asked in a shocked whisper.

"Good evening, everyone," he said as he came into the kitchen. "How are you feeling, Betsy?" he asked, hurrying towards the girl. "I must tell you, I was so shocked at what happened to you today. Thank goodness Wiggins had the good sense to get those constables."

"I'm feelin' fine, sir." Betsy gave Smythe a quick, adoring smile. "Smythe saved my life. If he hadn't come and pulled that madwoman off of me, I'da been done for."

"What's going to happen to Lydia Franklin?" Mrs. Jeffries asked quickly.

"Huh? Oh, she'll be charged with murder," Witherspoon replied. "She's admitted killing Annie Shields. Do you know, I think she's quite mad. She stood right there in front of Henry Albritton and accused him of ruining *her* life. Claimed it was all his fault she'd had to kill his daughter. Said if he'd left well enough alone, they could have all continued living happily together." He shuddered. Happy was the last word he would use to describe the Albritton household. "Apparently, she was under the impression that Albritton was romantically interested in Mrs. Shields. She'd been following him, you see. On the night of the murder, Mrs. Franklin admitted she'd followed Hortense Strutts. Mrs. Strutts had sent the girl a note, asking her to meet her. But Hortense Strutts got frightened in the fog, couldn't find Annie's flower stand and came home. Obviously, Lydia Franklin was made of sterner stuff." He sighed in disgust. "She found poor Annie, used a hammer she'd taken from the garden shed, killed her and then tossed the hammer in the river. Then she got on a bicycle and went home as though nothing had happened. Horrible."

"Well, at least you've got your murderer safely behind bars," Mrs. Jeffries said cheerfully.

"Yes, indeed." Witherspoon frowned. "But I must say, I can't seem to find any constable who'll admit to bringing Emma over here and leaving her. I'm rather annoyed about that. Poor Betsy was almost murdered because she tried to do a good deed."

"Yes, well, luckily Betsy's just fine," Mrs. Jeffries said. "And all's well that ends well."

"But it could have ended very badly for Betsy," the inspector persisted. "Still, I don't think I'll ever solve the mystery of the missing constable. I'm sure whoever it was that brought the child here must have heard what had happened and realized they'd made a grave mistake."

"True, sir," Mrs. Jeffries prompted. "So perhaps it's best to get on with other things."

Witherspoon yawned. "Oh, dear. Excuse me, but I'm dreadfully tired. I think I'll go right on up to bed."

He said his good-nights to Luty and Hatchet, patted Betsy sympathetically on the shoulder and told her to spend the next day resting and left.

Mrs. Jeffries let out a long sigh of relief when he was gone.

"You know what I don't understand," Mrs. Goodge said. "Who was sendin' Annie money every week?"

"I think I know," Betsy said quickly. "I think it was Harlan Bladestone."

"I do too," Mrs. Jeffries agreed. "I think Bladestone knew deep in his heart exactly who Annie was the first time he saw her, but being a solicitor, he needed proof."

"That's how I figure it too," Betsy added. "He couldn't bring himself to tell Albritton, but he knew Annie's husband had just died and that she'd be needin' money. So he sent 'er some every week. Not enough to make her feel bad or anythin'. Just enough so's she'd be sure and take it without feelin' beholdin' to 'im."

"Reckon no one wants to feel obligated to someone else," Smythe said, his expression enigmatic.

Betsy gave him a soft, very private smile. "Oh, I'm not so sure about that, Smythe. There's some people I don't mind bein' beholdin' to at all."

*   *   *

A few days later Luty, Hatchet and the household were having their very own celebration. The case was closed and the murderer brought to justice.

"I wonder how Emma's gettin' on?" Luty said wistfully.

"She's doin' fine," Betsy said. "Mr. Albritton invited me over yesterday so he could thank me for keepin' her safe from Mrs. Franklin. You ought to see them together. He loves her so much. He's fixin' to leave soon, though. He's goin' through with his plan to move to San Francisco. But guess what? He's takin' Hortense Strutts with him to help out. Well, he told me he didn't really have much choice. Gordon Strutts has left and moved in with his 'friend' and he didn't feel right leavin' Hortense on her own."

Mrs. Goodge snorted. "I don't wonder that Hortense is leavin'. Her husband takin' off and livin' with another man! Why, it'll be the talk of London. Poor Hortense wouldn't be able to hold her head up."

"What's goin' to 'appen to Sherwin August?" Smythe asked.

" 'E's retirin'," Betsy replied. "Takin' his wife and movin' to the country."

"Well, this case has indeed been an odd one," Mrs. Jeffries said.

Fred woofed softly.

Wiggins turned to the dog. "Be quiet, Fred . . . good gracious, it's Lady Cannonberry."

"I'm so sorry," Lady Cannonberry said softly. "I did knock on the back door but no one answered. The door was open, so I just came in."

"Of course, ma'am," Smythe said quickly, getting to his feet.

"Please." She held up her hand. "Do sit down. I didn't mean to intrude. Actually, I came round because I saw Mrs. Crookshank's carriage." She looked at an empty chair. "Do you mind if I sit down?"

"Where are our manners?" Mrs. Jeffries said hastily. "Please, Lady Cannonberry, do have a seat."

Still shocked, the others watched her sit down.

Lady Cannonberry took a deep breath. "I know my barging in like this must seem odd," she began. "But I had to ask you something."

"If it's about your participating in that march in Trafalgar Square," Mrs. Jeffries said, "I was planning on coming round and talking to you about it this afternoon."

"Oh no, it wasn't that," Lady Cannonberry said quickly. "But your opinion on that issue would be most welcome."

"Lady Cannonberry," Luty began.

"Do please call me Ruth," she interrupted, giving them all a big smile. "I wish all of you would call me Ruth. I've always thought 'Lady Cannonberry' sounded rather silly."

"Uh, Ruth." Luty frowned. She'd forgotten what she was going to say.

"Would you care for some tea?" Mrs. Jeffries asked politely. Mrs. Goodge and Hatchet both looked as though they'd gone into shock, Wiggins and Betsy were staring at the woman with puzzled frowns, and Smythe was trying not to grin.

"I'd love some, thank you." Ruth took another deep breath. "I'm sure you're all wondering why I've come."

"Yes, madam." Hatchet finally found his voice. "We are."

"I . . . oh dear, there's no way to say this except to just say it." She took another breath. "The truth is, I overheard Mrs. Jeffries talking to that young doctor about the inspector's case. Well, that got me to thinking and I well . . . I know you all help him. Don't worry," she said hastily. "I won't say a word. But you see, that got me to thinking."

"Thinking about what?" Mrs. Jeffries prompted.

"You see, I've got this friend and she's in a great deal of trouble. Do you think you could possibly help her?"